DEVIN'S GAME

JD TODD

Story Well Publishing
2637 Northgate Blvd
Fort Wayne, IN 46835
www.storywellpublishing.com

Publisher's Note: At Story Well we believe that every author deserves to have their voice heard, and by purchasing this book you have helped us continue to find new voices to bring to the world. Thank you for supporting us and our authors!

This is a work of fiction. Names, characters, places, and incidents are a product of the author's imagination. Locales and public names are sometimes used for atmospheric purposes. Any resemblance to actual people, living or dead, or to businesses, companies, events, institutions, or locales is completely coincidental.

Devin's Game/ JD Todd. -- 1st ed.
ISBN 978-1-952876-16-5

For Jess, always.

1

Devin Thomas was a normal seventeen-year-old girl. Scratch that. She was a seventeen-year-old girl, the normal part was never really her thing. Ever since she could remember she had been different than other kids.

Aspergers.

Her mom had always told her that having Aspergers wasn't a bad thing, that it was like a superpower. "Ya right," Devin had told her, "If being a social pariah that doesn't understand facial expressions and normal social cues is a superpower than I guess call me Captain Aspie."

Her mother retorted with the usual, "Albert Einstein, Mark Zuckerberg, Steve…" but before she could finish her standard list of famous people that were suspected to have Aspergers, Devin had retreated back into her own mind, reliving the game of Sonic the Hedgehog she had been playing earlier in the day. Video games had always been a great escape for Devin, and Sonic the Hedgehog had been one of her favorites for as far back as she could remember.

Today she had been playing Sonic Adventure 2, a hardcore Sonic fan favorite. This was the first game that she ever played that introduced a role-playing game element to her, in the form of the chao garden mini game. Chao were super cute little alien-type creatures that you hatched and then through various actions leveled up into stronger and better versions of themselves. What they turned into had to do with what character you were playing as, what you fed them and what attachments you gave them. It was the chao garden that had given Devin her first taste of the world of rpg's, and she hadn't turned back since.

During the last four years Devin had become one of the best mmorpg, or massive multi-player online role-playing game players in the world. She was ranked in the top 10 in two different games, one of which she often found herself ranked in the very first spot. She had even competed in several tournaments and earned some sizable cash prizes. All the hardships of social interaction melted away when she was immersed in the virtual worlds. It was there where she felt she could truly be herself, and she owed it all to the tiny chao that had become a hero in her first game of Sonic Adventure 2.

"And people thought they were weird, but they changed the world around them, just like you will. You were meant..." Devin's mom was saying before she was interrupted by Devin in a mocking tone.

"For something great. Yeah yeah, I know mom, but what if I don't want to do something great, what if what I want is to just play video games?"

"Video games," she retorted, as though the word tasted bad in her mouth, "I can't imagine why someone as beautiful and smart as you would want to spend all of their time holed up in your room, eating Cheetos and pretending to be a wizard tapping away on a computer screen."

"First, I do not pretend to be a wizard, I usually play as a warrior. Second, are you trying to say that because I look a certain way I should allow societal expectations to determine the outcome of my life, that I should just be the dumb pretty girl that cares about my clothes and finding the perfect boy to finally make me feel complete...barf...and third, you should know that the majority of those guys you just mentioned that as you put it, changed the world, did it by being holed up in a room somewhere and tapping away on a computer screen...soooo...."

"Yes, but they were doing more than playing video games."

"Well, do you really think the world is a better place because of Facebook and iPhones, or would we all be better off if Steve Jobs and old Zuck had just stuck to marathon sessions of World of Warcraft?"

Her mother sighed, "I don't think I will ever win an argument against you Devin."

"Finally, something we can agree on. Now, if you'll excuse me, the realm of wizards awaits...which reminds me...we need more Cheetos." Devin gave a small bow, smiling mischievously and ran up the stairs to her room.

As Devin walked into her room she paused and looked around at all the faces staring back at her. Princess Zelda, Faith from Mirror's Edge, Samus from Metroid, Jill Valentine from Resident Evil, Lara Croft from Tomb Raider, Amy Rose from Sonic the Hedgehog, Ms. Pac-Man…it was her salute to the badass women of video gaming history. There was also a poster that she had made of her very own avatar from the mmorpg Guild Wars 2, DevinDurga, and she was, without a doubt, the most badass of them all.

Looking at the posters she smiled thinking back to a conversation that she had with her best friend Jazz just a couple of weeks ago on FaceTime.

"All I'm saying is that Ms. Pac-Man doesn't really belong on the wall with all those other super rad chicks," Jazz said as Devin held the phone out for her to see the various posters on the wall.

"Are you kidding me?" Devin said, "Ms. Pac-Man might be the biggest feminist of them all. I mean, it was the early 80's and her husband was the most famous video game character of all time at that point, and she still chose to not be called Mrs. Pac-Man, because no man owns her…iconic."

Jazz laughed, "Okay fine, she belongs on the wall. Plus, it is a pretty fun game, and some people credit Ms. Pac-Man with getting women into video games in the first place."

"Well, those people usually say that women liked Ms. Pac-Man because she was non-violent and the entire game is about chasing Pac-Man, having babies, and eating…so those people are dicks."

Jazz and Devin both burst out laughing and moved on to playing Guild Wars. They were a fearsome duo, even though they had never met in real life, but they played together every night, text each other all day while they were at school, and FaceTimed pretty much all the times in between. Jazz was basically the only friend that Devin had.

The familiar brrriinnng sound and the accompanying short clip of music that meant a chest had been opened in the original Legend of Zelda game brought her out of her memories. She grabbed her phone out of her pocket and read the text from Jazz.

Where r u??? Been waiting forever to start this quest, u know I can't do it without my gurl.   - Jazz

Sorry, had to win an argument with parental, signing on right now! -

Devin

> *Have u ever lost an argument? - Jazz*
>
> *Only once. - Devin*
>
> *What was that about? - Jazz*
>
> *It was when I tried to convince you to stop using the word gurl… - Devin*
>
> *LOL! I forgot about that…gurl - Jazz*
>
> *Let's just play before we aren't friends anymore :) - Devin*

With that Devin threw her phone on the bed and sat down at her computer, logging in to the virtual world.

2

As Devin looked at her gaming station, she could hardly believe it all belonged to her. Last year she and Jazz had been on a team that won a DotA 2 tournament, and she had used a considerable portion of her winnings to upgrade her system, big time. It wasn't a big tournament, not like one of the kinds for millions of dollars, and it was done online because Devin just didn't have it in her to go to one of the real-world tournaments with its thousands of people, loud noises and bright lights. All of it just sounded exhausting to her. Plus, pretty much everyone in the gaming world assumed that she was a boy, and that was fine with her, if they knew she was a girl a lot of them would come after her…hardcore.

The first time that she read an article on Guildwars2.com that mentioned her she was thrilled. She was less thrilled as she read through the article and saw that the author constantly referred to Devin as he…his gameplay, his reaction time, his legendary weapons. Even though her avatar was female, because of her prowess and her quick rise through the ranks the author of this, and many other articles, could only assume that she was male.

Typical.

In the author's defense, Devin supposed that most of the female avatars were played by men, so it wasn't that much of a leap for them to assume. Even so, she felt that she could almost always tell when she was playing against another female. Women were just…smarter. They didn't rush in to very many situations without a plan, they typically avoided confrontation when there was no benefit to be gained from it, and they weren't as…well Devin supposed the best word would be jackassy as men.

Devin looked at the gleaming white tower of her PC, its glass case lit from within by a color changing LED and watched as the fan from the silent liquid cooling system worked to keep all of the custom components running at optimal temperature and therefore optimal speed. The multi color glow from the keyboard and mouse that sat on the desk seemed to call to her. She placed her hand on the mouse and her 49-inch Samsung curved monitor sprang to life.

Devin smiled as the images of her and Jazz's avatars faded onto the giant screen. When she had upgraded her CPU, she felt like it was a waste to use it to play on the same 36 inch monitor that she had used for the last couple of years, and so she had bought the best and biggest monitor that she could find. The Samsung monitor was not letterbox format like a tv, instead it was long and narrow, confining the action to where she wanted it, and allowing her to have additional windows open, like chat windows and Twitch for when she live streamed or used game capture software for those times she didn't want to show her games live. The curve of the screen almost gave the impression that the action of the game was happening all around her.

As she looked down at her mouse, a flash of green appeared all around it. Not emanating from the lights within the mouse, but almost as though the entire thing had been outlined in neon green. It happened so fast that Devin wasn't altogether sure what she had seen. Maybe the thing was glitching out.

"Great," she mumbled to herself, "that's all I need, another couple hundred bucks for a new mouse, and this one is less than a year old. Maybe I *am* playing too much…"

She looked at the screen and clicked on the Guild Wars 2 icon on her desktop, logging into the network. Looking down at the rainbow of colors on her keyboard she placed her left hand over the control keys. "What the hell…" she said to the empty room as the keyboard outlined itself in green. This time she also had the distinct impression of the words **RAZER HUNTSMAN ELITE GAMING KEYBOARD** hovering slightly above the keyboard, much in the same way that objects were highlighted in many rpg's.

"Well, this is not good," she said squeezing her eyes shut, "not only am I talking to myself, I'm also seeing things. Easy Devin, the road to crazy is a short one..."

She opened her eyes and the green glow and accompanying words were gone. "Ok," she said, "mom might be right, I may need a small break from gaming..."

She closed out of Guild Wars and walked to the bed to retrieve her phone. Grabbing it she quickly typed a message to Jazz letting her know something had come up and she would have to do the quest on her own, not that it would be a big deal, Jazz was also ranked highly in multiple mmorpgs and could definitely take care of herself, although neither of them were nearly as formidable without the other.

Devin stepped in front of the mirror and stared at her reflection, wondering what could have caused her mind to create the green glow. It could have been as simple as too much playing time the last few weeks. She had been sleeping less and playing more as she prepared for her first big tournament of the year, but she had always played a lot and never gotten an abundance of sleep and never before had she imagined item notifications popping up in the real world.

"You're not crazy," she said to her reflection. She smiled at the absurdity of that statement as she looked down at the lifetime of memories spread across the top of her dresser. Her first Sonic the Hedgehog stuffed animal sat with his back against the mirror, his legs out in front of him, a look of mild amusement or irritation on his face...Devin was never totally sure. Reading facial expressions, even those on a toy hedgehog, had always been a struggle for her.

Beside Sonic was a picture of her and her parents at the Sega headquarters in London, which had been her birthday present two years ago. She had wanted to go to the main corporate headquarters in Japan, but her parents had thought that London would be a much better vacation, so London it was. Beside the picture stood several trophies, remnants of a childhood spent competing in various martial arts tournaments. After she was diagnosed with Aspergers her therapist had recommended to her parents that they enroll her in taekwondo, telling them that there was some research showing that martial arts could help kids with Aspergers channel some of their anxiety. Devin had taken to martial arts like she did to pretty much everything…obsessively.

By the time she was thirteen she had black belts in three different disciplines, had won several tournaments and even been asked to participate in the junior olympics, which she promptly turned down once her parents showed her footage of the event. Seeing that many people in one place, even on video, had threatened to overwhelm her senses. She no longer competed in martial arts, although she still practiced by herself in her room almost every night.

She reached out and picked up one of the trophies, wiping the dust from the plate that was affixed to the front of it proclaiming her to be the champion of the "Northeast Taekwondo Invitational Junior Division". She smiled as she looked at the trophy, but the smile quickly faded as the green glow suddenly outlined the trophy in her hand. Beside the trophy, words hovered in the air.

MARTIAL ARTS TOURNAMENT TROPHY
CRAFTING VALUE - N/A
IMPROVISED WEAPON STRENGTH +2
VALUE - SENTIMENTAL ONLY
INVENTORY SPACE REQUIREMENT +1

Devin just stared at the trophy, turning it over and over, watching the words track with its movement, the green glow never wavering. She looked up into the mirror and saw her own reflection outlined in green. It took several seconds for her to even notice the words hovering beside her own image, but once she saw them, she couldn't see anything else.

AGENT 5 - UNNAMED
LEVEL 1 WARRIOR
SKILLS
    HAND TO HAND COMBAT - LEVEL 16
    WEAPONS MASTERY - LEVEL 1
    SELF-HEAL - LEVEL 5
    IMPROVISATION - LEVEL 1
    CRAFTING - LEVEL 1
ATTRIBUTES
    INTELLIGENCE - 90

AGILITY - 80
STRENGTH - 80
CHARISMA - 20
STEALTH - 15
WISDOM - 20
STAMINA - 100/100
PERCEPTION - 75
RENOWN - 10
INVENTORY - N/A
EQUIPPED ITEM #1 - MARTIAL ARTS TROPHY

A loud knock from the front door snapped her back to reality. She turned toward the sound, seeing constantly updating green outlines and text indicators everywhere she looked. She then heard a sound that was reminiscent of Sonic grabbing a ring and a line of text appeared in the center of her vision, although it was semi-transparent so that she could still see what was going on around her.

NEW QUEST ALERT
     *GO TO FRONT DOOR
     *SPEAK WITH DR. TRAN
COMPLETION REWARD
     WISDOM +10

"Alright then…" Devin muttered, "crazy it is…"

3

As Devin walked down the stairs to the front door, she couldn't help but be constantly distracted by the information pouring in from all around her. Each item that she looked at directly had a stream of info floating beside it, telling her what the item was and what it could be used for. Items in her peripheral vision were outlined in the same green, and as soon as she shifted her focus to one of them, the info stream would appear.

Looks like my brain finally broke the rest of the way, she thought, musing about the fact that she had constantly looked at her Asperger's as a partially broken brain, despite her mother's insistence that it was a superpower. *Hopefully there really is a doctor at the front door, that way I won't have to drive myself to the looney bin.*

As she approached the front door there was a chiming sound and an update appeared in her vision.

QUEST UPDATE
*   GO TO FRONT DOOR - COMPLETED
*   SPEAK WITH DR. TRAN

The notification popped up so fast that it startled Devin, causing her to drop the trophy she had still been absentmindedly holding on to. "Son of a..." she said through gritted teeth as the heavy trophy fell on her foot. She reached down to rub her wounded foot, noticing a large red welt across the top of it, but before she could a series of alerts popped up, surprising her once again.

    MARTIAL ARTS TROPHY UNEQUIPPED.

    BLUNT FORCE TRAUMA TO FOOT -15 HP

    TOTAL HP 985/1000

    HEALING SKILL ACTIVATED

    HP +15

    STAMINA -5

    STAMINA 95/100

Just like that the pain in Devin's foot was completely gone. She stared at her foot and watched with amazement as the red welt seemed to fade from existence. She glanced around, never in her life feeling quite as lost as at this exact moment. The alerts all still hung in her vision.

A laugh burst from Devin's lips just as another knock came loudly at the door, which she was now standing just a few feet from. Her mother walked into the room looking quizzically at her daughter as she stood by the front door laughing, the knocking becoming more insistent. "Devin what has gotten into you?" she said, "don't just stand there laughing like some kind of idiot, see who's at the door!"

Devin smiled and nodded, "It's Dr. Tran, that's who's at the door."

"Who is Dr. Tran?" Her mother asked.

"How the hell should I know…" Devin said. "His name just popped up in my brain as a new quest objective."

"Devin," her mother exhaled, "language…what do you mean popped into your brain…what like some kind of premonition?"

Devin turned to look at her mother for the first time. As she did a string of information appeared.

    MARY THOMAS

    SKILLS - UNKNOWN

    ATTRIBUTES - UNKNOWN

    INVENTORY - UNKNOWN

    EQUIPPED ITEM #1 - IPHONE 8

Devin blinked and shook her head, trying to get the words to go away, "Mom, you know I do not subscribe to the idea that some words are inherently profane or divine, words are words, and I am going to say whatever I want, especially since this is my dream. So, in the illustrious words of Bart Simpson, "Hell, damn, fart...crap, boobs, crap." Devin laughed. All of the stress of the situation had melted away as soon as she realized that this was a dream. A very real dream, but a dream none the less. "And to answer your question, no not like a premonition, like a video game, I saw his name in a quest update like from a role-playing game..."

"Your dream...quest updates..." her mother said, "what in the world are you talking about?"

"Never mind," Devin said as she reached for the doorknob, "Let's just see who's behind door number one. I bet you a million dollars it's Dr. Tran."

Her mother sighed loudly and said, "I have no idea what you're babbling about or who Dr. Tran is, but I can assure this is not a dream you're having. Are you on drugs...is it that Holly that I heard about on the news?"

Devin laughed, "I think you mean Molly mom, and no I'm not on drugs, just dreaming, but it's cool if you don't believe me, if you did it wouldn't be much of a dream now would it." With that she grabbed the knob and pulled the door open.

The man standing behind the door very well could have been Dr. Tran. He was a small man of Asian descent that looked to be in his early forties. Devin didn't have to wait long to find out though, as soon as she focused on him the string of information that was getting to be familiar appeared beside him.

DR. HIROSHI TRAN

LEVEL 8 ENGINEER

Devin gave the rest of the info a cursory glance, finding it interesting that his wisdom and intelligence attributes were both well above 200. She no longer felt quite as good about her intelligence attribute of 80. She smiled slightly, *well I assumed it was out of 100, I guess I don't think much of my own intelligence*...she thought.

Dr. Tran smiled broadly when he saw her and said, "Devin...my

God." He paused as he took in every detail of the young girl standing before him and then continued speaking, "You look so much like her…"

Devin was taken aback, "So much like who?"

"Your mother…" the stranger behind the door said, "may I come in."

Devin felt like she had been punched in the stomach. *My mother*, she thought, *it's been years since I've had a dream about my birth parents.* Devin had been adopted when she was a newborn by Mary and Hal Thomas. Little was known about her birth parents, she never said real parents because Mary and Hal were as real as parents got. She was an only child and the two had lavished her with love. Devin felt as though they had a relationship that was closer than any parent/child relationship she had witnessed. She had always assumed it was partially because they had always wanted a child and Devin was a godsend to them, and partially because of her Asperger's making her want to avoid new situations pretty much at all costs, so new friends were not needed when she had two already in the house that she felt so comfortable with.

"What did you say?" Mary said.

Dr. Tran glanced around nervously and spoke with the slightest accent, "I am so sorry, forgive my brusqueness. My name is Hiroshi Tran, I worked with your birth mother and father. They were like family to me…are like family to me I mean…"

Devin wobbled and sat down hard on the step as consciousness threatened to slip away from her, which seemed like an odd thing to have happen, even in such a weird dream. As she landed with a thud on the step a notification popped up.

BLOOD PRESSURE AND HEART RATE ELEVATED

RECOMMENDED ACTION - DEEP BREATHING TO NORMALIZE

VITAL STATISTICS

Devin closed her eyes, but the notification stayed stubbornly in place. She began to do deep breathing exercises, inhaling through the nose, exhaling through the mouth, just like when she meditated each morning. That was a residual habit from her martial arts days. *This is feeling less and less like a dream…*she thought to herself.

Mary rushed to her daughter's side and placed a reassuring hand on her shoulder, "Devin, are you ok?" She said, the concern clear in her voice.

"Mom," Devin said sounding lost, "what is happening…"

"I have no idea baby," she said, "I have no idea…"

4

"Don't take another step," Mary Thomas warned. Dr. Tran had crossed the threshold of the door as soon as Devin had sat down on the steps. He looked at Devin, deep concern in his eyes, but stopped moving and held his hands up in the air.

"I am not here to harm either of you, I promise, I only want to help. At this point I am guessing that Devin is extremely confused about things that are going on in her mind, I can help explain all of it, that's why I'm here…well that and because I need your help," Dr. Tran said.

"Devin's feelings are none of your concern…" Mary said.

Alright, not a dream, Devin thought, still trying desperately to make sense of the situation unfolding around her. "He doesn't mean my feelings mom. He means what is actually going on inside my head…you're talking about the updates right?"

"Updates?" Mary said.

"Yes, Devin, that is what I'm talking about…the updates…as you call them."

"Well, what else would I call them?" Devin said, "They are updates! Quest updates, status updates…this is seriously fu…"

"Devin!" Mary almost shouted, "please for the love of God, watch your language."

"Mom, my brain is broken. I am seeing things, and somehow one of these hallucinations told me who was going to be at the door.

Somehow, I knew that Dr. Tran was going to be there, even though I have no idea who Dr. Tran is…so maybe my vocabulary choices shouldn't be top priority right now."

"These are not hallucinations Devin. The visual interface is typically the first to come online, followed by aural, and finally by the muscle interface, that's how you knew I would be at the door, because we told you." Dr. Tran said matter-of-factly.

"Oh, of course, visual followed by aural and muscle interfaces. I was just concerned because I thought visual came after the muscle interface. Well since this is all standard operating procedure, I guess we have nothing to worry about. I do have just one question though Dr. Tran…what in the hell are you talking about???" Devin said.

Dr. Tran glanced at Mary, expecting her to once again ask Devin to watch her language but she simply shrugged, "I think that's actually a very fair question. What in the hell are you talking about Dr. Tran?" She asked.

Dr. Tran exhaled sharply and looked up at the ceiling, "I don't even know where to begin Devin. When you were born you were part of a secret government program that…"

"Stop." Devin said holding up a hand, "Just stop. I've seen this movie before. Secret government program to create super spies, or super soldiers, or super…whatever. I don't buy it. What else you got…"

Mary had gone shockingly pale and looked as though she might pass out, "Devin was abandoned by her parents when she was two months old, left at an orphanage. She stayed there until my husband and I adopted her at 8 months old. I can guarantee she was not part of some secret government program. She was a baby. A perfectly normal, healthy baby. I think you need to leave or I am calling the police, and for what it's worth you should get some help sir, these delusions can't be healthy."

Dr. Tran looked from Devin to her mother and then back again. "You have a small scar on the back of your neck, about two centimeters long if I remember the procedure correctly. You also have a small scar at the crown of your skull, right about where the soft spot in a baby's skull is before it closes over, this one is about 3 centimeters long. Although the procedure was refined in later years, the scars are much smaller now, almost invisible," he said this last part almost to himself.

Devin's hand went almost instinctively to the scar at the back of her neck. It was indeed small, and usually covered by her hair but it was nonetheless there. It had always been a nervous habit of hers to place her hand on her neck and run her fingers across it, something about the way it felt calmed her down when her mind was anxious. "So you got my medical files, congrats. And since you did get my files, you also saw that those scars are from an accident that happened when I was a baby at the orphanage, something about a window breaking, I can't remember exactly what they said happened, but not from when my parents turned me into a super spy, sorry doc but I think you have been misinformed."

Dr. Tran shook his head and looked down at the table. Slowly he reached a hand up and tapped something small in his ear that looked like a tiny Bluetooth handsfree device and said, "You're going to have to prove it to her."

"Prove it to who…who are you talking to?" Devin's mom asked, but before Dr. Tran could respond Devin jumped to her feet, knocking her chair over.

"Devin, what Dr. Tran is saying is all completely true. I am uploading a classified document that explains Project Prometheus and details your, and your parents', role in the project." A flat, artificial voice seemed to speak this directly into Devin's head.

"Who said that?" Devin demanded, "and what…" but she fell silent as information flooded into her brain. The information didn't scan quickly in. It wasn't as though her brain was flipping through pages or she was reading information really quickly. It was simply one minute she didn't have the information and the next she did. All of it. Devin's eyes were glossy and out of focus as she soaked it all in. The updates popped into her view, accompanied by the now familiar ding.

NEURAL LINK ACTIVATED
PROJECT PROMETHEUS DATA SUCCESSFULLY UPLOADED
WISDOM +20

"Project Prometheus was started by my birth parents, well, by them and Dr. Tran. They were trying to develop a way to input information directly into someone's mind. Originally, they were looking to just be able to communicate information directly to the person, and have that person be able to communicate back all without ever speaking out loud, basically scientifically created telepathy. Once they figured that out, they wanted a way to do more. The project eventually went on to include real time access to information that could be downloaded directly to a participant's brain, an artificial intelligence program that automatically assesses situations, runs simulations, and instantly returns helpful information. This program also has access to a global network of cameras, satellites, radio transmissions, cellular phone data streams, basically all the privacy that we gave up through the Patriot Act and social media click-through agreements can be accessed by this program, does that seem like the basics?"

"Devin what are you talking about? How could you possibly know any of this?" her mother asked.

"She knows because someone from my team just uploaded all of the Project Prometheus files into her brain." Dr. Tran stated.

"Ya, that," Devin said, "There is something I am curious about though…"

"Ask me anything." Dr. Tran said.

"Project Prometheus…I don't get it. Why Prometheus? Wasn't he the god that made humans out of clay or something like that? Plus, it has been used in about a hundred movies…not very original…"

Dr. Tran looked slightly confused momentarily and then smiled, "That's what your curious about…well…the agency chose Prometheus as the code name for the project because he was the god of crafty counsel, and originally that was our primary intention, to provide counsel to men and women in situations where they had typically been unreachable, also it was 30 years ago and none of those movies had been made yet. I must say you are taking this extremely well…"

"How else can I take it? It's not like I have much of a choice. My brain already tried to reject the information by making me think it was a dream, which didn't work. Then you had the creepy computer lady talk directly into my mind and…uploaded… a bunch of info into my brain, so, I sort of have to adapt to this new information, don't you think?"

Dr. Tran looked pleased, "Exactly what your mother would have said. She was also driven by logic, and impossibly difficult to…rattle I think would be the right word…"

"Oh, don't let my sunny disposition fool you, I'm rattled doc, I'm rattled AF…" Devin said, glancing at her mother before continuing, "but back to your story, you said the goal was to provide counsel to people in situations where they were typically unreachable…so spies…that's who this was for?"

"Yes, among other…situations." Dr. Tran said, looking slightly uncomfortable.

"And so my birth parents just decided that they should have their baby experimented on?"

"Not exactly Devin. The decision to have you undergo the procedure was not something they took lightly, they did not do it for the program, they did it for you."

"For me…really…that's your statement." Devin said. "They experimented on me, not to help with their research, but because I, as a baby, would somehow benefit from this experimentation…"

Dr. Tran looked into Devin's eyes and could see the confusion and hurt there. He took a breath and said, "Well, yes…let me try to explain…"

5

"I could have this information uploaded to you, but you and your mother both deserve to hear it from me. It was after all, my fault," Dr. Tran said, pausing to collect his thoughts. "I met your parents at MIT during our freshman year. Your mother was brilliant, the smartest person I had ever met, still to this day I have met no one that can rival her fierce intelligence. Your father, while clearly not an intellectual match for her, was everything that she was not. Charismatic, outgoing, creative, and one of the very best young engineers at MIT. I met your mother first, in fact I am the person that…well…set them up, for lack of a better term. Your mother and I had been partners on a robotics project and had been spending a lot of time together, late nights, that sort of thing. We were both young, smart, and socially awkward, so it seemed like a match made in heaven. The only problem was that I had already fallen madly in love with my roommate Kevin, although this was not a well-known fact. These were different times… so we kept our love hidden from the world for several years. Anyway, I didn't want to hurt your mother's feelings, and I couldn't tell her that I was gay, so instead I brought your father along with me one night to help out on our robotics project and his charm took care of the rest. Your mother was quite beautiful, just like you are Devin, and he was instantly taken with her. In no time at all the two of them were inseparable…well actually the four of us were inseparable…"

"Four of you?" Devin's mother interrupted.

"Yes…Max, Peter, Kevin and I," Dr. Tran said.

"Max and Peter…that's my parents' names?" Devin said quietly.

"Oh yes, forgive me Devin. Maxine Parker and Peter Hobson. I forget that you know nothing about any of this. The idea for Prometheus came from all of us sitting around one night and talking about what research we were going to do for our graduate programs. Your father had the original idea, a neural link that could implant thoughts into and extract thoughts from the brain. To be honest I did not originally find the premise all that interesting, but Kevin was fascinated by the idea. Kevin was pre-med and was planning on pursuing neurology, so this was a chance for me to put my engineering background to use in his field, and that, I did find exciting. Your mother was also not instantly sold on the idea. She thought that it was interesting but her first reaction was that it could not be done, and she had no desire to waste her time on a project that wouldn't be able to be used for future research. Pete was certain that if we all put our minds together we could do it though, and so we began to take the idea seriously, and The Xavier Project was born."

"Xavier project?" Devin asked.

"Yes, that was our original name for the project. We of course named it after Dr. Charles Xavier," Dr. Tran said with a small smile.

"Dr. Charles Xavier?" Mary said, clearly confused.

"Ya mom, he's the leader of the X-Men, world's most powerful telepath…" Devin said.

"Well, technically I believe that Jean Grey's abilities may surpass those of Professor X." Dr. Tran said.

"Seriously?" Devin said shaking her head.

"Well at least when she is Dark Phoenix, yes." He said, clearly misunderstanding what Devin meant by seriously.

Devin rolled her eyes, "The point here is that you obviously figured it out…you completed the project…"

"Yes, we indeed did. We had been working on the project for just over two years when we were approached by a man that said he worked for a government agency that was interested in funding our research. You see we had several small breakthroughs in the early days of the project and our findings were published in a couple of medical and science journals. Nothing like actually implanting thoughts, but breakthroughs, nonetheless. At any rate, when we were approached, your mother had serious reservations. She said right away that they would want to use the technology for military applications, but we convinced her that we needed their funding to get the job done. Even if they used the technology for the military, it would still be able to be utilized in so many other ways, like helping people that could no longer speak or move communicate with the people around them. She didn't like it, but she knew that without serious funding we would never complete our project...I mean even with funding it was a long shot...but in just four short years we had our first major breakthrough, and that is when The Prometheus Project was truly born."

"And that breakthrough was?" Devin asked.

"We implanted a thought directly into the mind of a monkey, teaching it how to solve a puzzle that until that point had been unsolvable. It was incredible, one moment the monkey was simply throwing the pieces around, the next he solved it with ease. We were ecstatic, and rightly so. This was technology that had been sought for decades, and we had cracked it in just under seven years from first having the idea. From there the project...really got away from us. Simply implanting and extracting thoughts wasn't enough. The agency we worked for wanted more, and so we continued to develop new technologies. New projects were born. Groundbreaking stuff. Kevin and your mother were able to...hack...the human brain. Next was Project Warpath. We could trigger adrenaline and endorphins giving people temporary superhuman strength. After that was Project Wolverine, where we identified and targeted the healing centers of the brain and were able cause rapid cell regeneration. Self-healing. We actually figured it out, with our technology even injuries as severe as a severed spinal cord could be healed in a matter of minutes, although at an extremely high energy cost. We found out that if the required energy was not available...the subject could die. After that there was Project Magneto, Project Maximoff, really there are too many to name, but I think you get the point." Dr. Tran said.

Devin laughed humorlessly, "Ya, I get it. You guys messed with lots of parts of people's brains and gave each project a nerdy, X-Men name that has to do with the powers it unlocked. So, Project Magneto has something to do with Magnetic fields and Maximoff must be...mind control?"

"Yes! Very good. There are others, I can have the exact details uploaded to you for the rest of them, the point is that because of our research, the human brain was understood in a way that it had never before been. We had succeeded in unlocking around 60% of the untapped potential of the human brain. Now keep in mind I am not talking about the old adage that humans only use 10% of our brains, that is patently untrue as almost 100% of our brain is firing each and every day. What I am talking about is utilizing technology to stimulate parts of the brain that have been, for lack of a better word, turned off throughout the course of evolution, and so it was our job to figure out a way to turn them back on, and to magnify the effects from other areas…and we did our jobs quite well. Even so, the agency that we worked for wanted more. They wanted all of it unlocked. It was around this time that we started to hear things about our research being used for purposes that we didn't agree with. Assassinations, overthrowing governments, and creating virtually indestructible super soldiers. We feared that if we were able to complete unlocking the rest of the brain's potential, there would be no stopping the resulting humans…we worried that one day the technology could fall into the wrong hands…and in all honesty, we worried that the hands it was already in were not safe…so we told the agency we would not continue our research."

They all sat in silence. Mary looked intently at Devin, who looked at Dr. Tran, who looked at his hands. "We were told this was not our choice to make. The agency informed us that there would be grave consequences if we did not continue our research, but we all agreed there was nothing that they could threaten us with that would make us comply…and that is when they told us that your mother was pregnant."

6

"They told her?" Devin asked, "How would they know she was pregnant before she did?"

Dr. Tran seemed to consider the question for a moment before answering, "We had wondered that as well, in fact when they first told your mother she didn't believe them. She simply told them they were wrong; they then produced their proof. Being funded by and working for government agencies comes with some caveats, one of these being that we were subjected to routine drug testing. We worked a lot of hours and they needed to be sure that no…enhancements…were being used that could cloud our judgement or endanger the results of their program. At any rate, during one of these tests they found the hormone hCG in your mother's blood and knew that meant that she was pregnant. She really had no idea until they showed her the test."

He paused to see if Devin had any questions, but when she didn't speak, he continued, "Your mother and father had always wanted a child, in fact they had tried unsuccessfully for several years prior to this, but now the idea that this agency would use you as leverage to force them to continue their research…well it was too much for them to take. They decided that the only choice they had was to play along with the agency long enough to make a plan to hide you away somewhere that you would be safe. Somewhere that they could not find you and use you as a pawn, and so that is what they set about to do. They found an orphanage that they believed could keep you safe. They found people willing to risk their own lives to take you and hide you there. They prepared for everything, except for just how much they would love you when they first laid eyes on you."

Dr. Tran took a deep breath and met Devin's gaze. He noticed the glistening lines of wetness trailing from the corner of each eye and watched as she, sniffling, brought a hand up and roughly wiped the tears away. He turned and looked at Mary, embarrassed that he had intruded on Devin's tears, but found tears rolling silently down her face as well. He steadied himself and said, "They didn't want to give you up, they wanted to start a life with you. Small house, good schools, a dog, all of it…but it was not to be. The day that you were born the agency took you, held you away from your parents for three days, refused to tell them anything about you. They didn't know if you were even still alive. Finally, your mother broke down, told them she would do anything they asked as long as they returned you safely to them. She told them she would complete the project, unlock the human brain, but they had to bring you back, allow you to stay with them. The agency refused and your mother let them know that if they didn't bring you back she would never help them, she would die before helping them." He paused again, this time looking more uncomfortable, "Look, by this point we knew that these were not good people…we knew that our technology had been used to hurt people, to kill people, and we knew that they would not hesitate to do whatever they felt necessary to accomplish their goals…so it is a testament to your mother's love for you that they also knew she would do anything to protect you. Her love for you made her no longer fear them, at least not for herself, only for you. After two more days, they conceded and returned you to your mother and father, but things had definitely changed. We were no longer allowed to leave the facility, none of us, and we were under constant surveillance. Your father also suspected that you had been implanted with a chip that could be used to track your whereabouts and to control you to a certain extent. The scar on the base of your neck…the nurses insisted it was simply an injury from being unattended in a crib that had a loose nail, but we all knew better, and they knew we knew. They had implanted one of our very own chips into you. We had no idea if it would work on an infant, and neither did they, but they apparently wanted your mother to know that they had the upper hand, even if it meant experimenting on a newborn baby, even if it meant killing you."

"Jesus…" Mary whispered, reaching out and placing her hand on top of Devin's, squeezing. Devin couldn't speak, she simply squeezed back, thanking God that her mother was here, she didn't know if she would have had the strength on her own.

"Indeed." Dr. Tran said, "They were…well are…monsters. Your mother knew that you would never be safe, knew that they would always see you as nothing more than leverage, so she came to Kevin and I with a plan. An insane plan…but a plan nonetheless…and frankly none of us could come up with anything better…so insane was all we had. Unbeknownst to any of us your mother had developed an entirely new concept, one that she called Project Dark Phoenix…"

"Before you ask," Devin said turning to Mary, her voice starting shaky but quickly growing in strength, "Dark Phoenix is another of the X-Men, the alter ego of Dr. Jean Grey, a telepath who later gains almost infinite amounts of power by transforming into Dark Phoenix. She is definitely one of the most bada…awesome…chicks of all time."

Mary smiled and exhaled a small laugh nodding her head and Dr. Tran took that as his sign to continue. "Once again, spot on Devin. Project Dark Phoenix was different than any other project we had worked on thus far. Instead of targeting a specific center of the brain hoping to…unlock…that area's potential, Dark Phoenix was a series of chips that created a neural network that almost rivaled the human brain in complexity. And once this network was in place, the recipient would have access to everything…all at once. You see, that had always been a limitation of our process. We could communicate, we could unlock self-healing, we could unlock super strength, we had even been able to unlock mind control to an extent, but we could only unlock one area in each subject. The process of implanting multiple chips into multiple areas of the brain had always proven too much for the human body to handle." He paused again, his eyes somewhere very distant, "we lost a lot of men and women trying to do this for the agency, more than I care to ever remember."

"And none of you ever thought of stopping?" Devin said coldly.

Dr. Tran closed his eyes, sighing, "It was almost as though the research had taken over. I don't think that we were bad people, we simply justified the loss as acceptable collateral damage. These men and women were soldiers, they knew the risks, they signed up for it. This is just how it works…that's what we all thought…at first…but by the time you were born we had all realized that the project needed to be stopped. I wish I could tell you that we saw the error of our ways sooner, but we simply did not, we were all too caught up in the science of it…in the legacy we would leave behind. We were young and idealistic, and so impressed with our own ingenuity, and well…this is not the point of this. There is no way to justify what we all did; I know that because I have been trying for the last 18 years. So where was I…yes, after you were born, your mother showed us Dark Phoenix, and Kevin and I set to work on the neurology and engineering aspects of it. It all had to be done very covertly, the agency could know nothing of it, so we had to hide the new research from them at all costs. In fact, your mother never even let your father, Kevin, or I know all of the details of the project. Each of us worked separately. She explained that we had so little time, and that this would allow us to complete the project much faster. That was true, but I also think she wanted to ensure that no one else knew all of the technologies in total, or at least not how they came together. That way she was the only one that could ever actually implement the program, in her mind it was another safeguard. The genius of your mother's plan was that it largely relied on already developed technologies that we simply had to adapt for this new purpose, so instead of creating all new chips, the existing projects were folded in to Dark Phoenix. In a matter of days, we were able to develop what we believed was a working prototype of the Dark Phoenix neural net. The plan had been that we would implant the net into your father, and then if it worked, he would use his new powers to break you out, to free all of us, and we would go into hiding. With Dark Phoenix, we believed he would be nearly impossible to stop. At least that was what we all thought the plan was…"

7

Hiroshi Tran sat silently, hands clasped together tightly in his lap, avoiding eye contact with the two women that sat across the table from him. He realized that he had been clenching his jaw and willed himself to relax, inhaling deeply as he looked up at Devin. "Devin, I…" but he abruptly stopped speaking as he momentarily lost focus. He cocked his head slightly to the left as though he were listening to something that only he could hear and then he turned his eyes back to Devin. "Did you receive that alert?"

Devin looked confused, "What alert?"

"I just received an alert that we are all in danger." He said, looking nervously towards the windows.

"What have you gotten us in to?" Mary asked, a touch of anger entering her voice.

"There is too much to explain, you have to trust me, we are not safe here. I can take us to a safe place." Dr. Tran said.

Dr. Tran is telling you the truth Devin, it is no longer safe here. A team of men that have been sent to collect you will arrive in four minutes and 34 seconds.

The artificial voice once again spoke the words directly into Devin's mind. At the same time a small green timer appeared in the corner of her vision counting down **4:32…4:31…4:30…**. "Mom, I think we better get out of here, he's telling the truth…or at least I think he is…"

"How could you possibly know that?" Mary asked.

"Because there's an A.I. in my head and it just told me that a team of people are on their way to "collect" me, and we now have four minutes and fifteen seconds until they show up." Devin said as she stood up and begin to run towards the stairs.

"A.I. in your head...do you hear yourself Devin?" Mary said, clearly still not convinced of any of this.

"That is a bit of a surprise," Dr. Tran said, "typically the A.M.I.I. doesn't start interfacing until the user has trained on the system for a few days."

"A.M.I.I.?" Mary asked.

"Advanced, multi-interfaced intelligence." Dr. Tran said.

"Amy." Said Devin.

"Amy..." Mary said, "I'll go with Amy...what exactly does multi-interfaced mean?"

"It means it has multiple ways to interact with me, mom. So it can talk directly to me, I am assuming it can read my thoughts, or I can speak out loud to it. She has put several things in front of me to see, so she can manipulate what I see..." Devin said.

That is correct Devin, I have the ability to interface with all of your senses, using them to acquire and distribute information. I can also directly read your thoughts, although that may take some practice on your part. I have access to defense satellites, cellular telephone network data, classified Department of Defense files, and I can access the internet and have an impressive amount of information stored locally for times that I am unable to connect.

Devin squinted as she tried to concentrate a thought back to Amy. *Sounds great. Can you tell me how to get out of here?*

She heard the ding sound and an alert popped up.

NEW SKILL ACTIVATED - AMII IS NOW LEVEL ONE.

Amy's voice was once again inside Devin's head, *Dr. Tran has a vehicle parked in your driveway. You have three minutes and thirteen seconds to leave. I would strongly suggest you leave now.*

"Mom, we need to go! Grab what you need and follow Dr. Tran outside, we have less than three minutes now." Devin yelled as she ran towards the stairs, leaping up them three at a time.

"Devin, where are..." she heard Dr. Tran start to say but she was distracted as a new quest update popped into her field of vision.

NEW QUEST ALERT
 •AVOID DETECTION FROM THE AGENCY
  •HELP DR. TRAN AND MARY THOMAS ESCAPE UNHARMED
COMPLETION REWARD
 •STEALTH +10
 •RENOWN +10

"Jesus…Amy, is there anything we can do about the updates popping up huge and right in the center of my vision?" Devin said aloud.

Updates can be displayed anywhere that you would like. Do you have a suggestion or would you like me to randomize.

Devin tried to concentrate and send her reply as a thought to Amy, but nothing happened, "Screw it," she muttered, giving up and again talking out loud to Amy, "Just make them smaller, and put them in the upper left-hand corner. And can you please lower their opacity? I need to be able to see through them."

Devin watched, fascinated, as the alerts shrunk down and moved to the upper left-hand corner of her vision. She found that when she shifted her focus to the center of the room, they all but disappeared, but when she concentrated on them she could see them again. "This is so cool," she whispered.

I am sorry, I do not have access to the climate control settings of this room. Would you like me to increase core body temperature until you are more comfortable?

"You can do that?" Devin said shocked.

Technically you can do that, I would only be facilitating it. Would you like me to run down a list of all the body control systems that you…

"Stop!" Devin shouted, "We have one minute and thirty-four seconds to get out of here, you can tell me all of that stuff later…and no I don't want you to turn up my body temperature. It's a different meaning of the word cool, maybe use that internet access you were bragging about and look it up. Now where the hell is my phone…"

She searched frantically; she knew that she couldn't leave without it. If she did she would have no way of contacting Jazz, and if there was one person that she really needed to talk to right now…it was Jazz. "Come on Devin, think…" she said to herself, and so she was surprised when Amy's monotone voice spoke inside her head.

Your phone is on your dresser, underneath a photograph. I will ring an alert now.

Devin's phone started beeping, "Well that's just awesome!" She said grabbing her phone from the dresser. The countdown clock had reached fifty-nine seconds and had gone from green to red. It was flashing now. Devin spun to run back downstairs but as she did her small Sonic toy caught the corner of her eye and she grabbed it and threw it in her pocket. She vaguely noticed the alert that had added the toy to her inventory flash into the corner as she sprinted down the stairs.

The Agency is almost here. Would you like me to trigger an adrenaline rush to aid in combat.

"Uh, only hell yes!" Devin said, "But I'm hoping there won't be any combat."

Devin focused on the alert that had just popped up.

NEW SKILL UNLOCKED- BERSERKER MODE NOW AVAILABLE

BERSERKER MODE ACTIVATED

   ***STRENGTH +50 (WHILE SKILL IS ACTIVATED)**

   ***AGILITY +50 (WHILE SKILL IS ACTIVATED)**

   ***STAMINA -10/MINUTE (WHILE SKILL IS ACTIVATED)**

   ***STEALTH - 20 (WHILE SKILL IS ACTIVATED)**

She felt a surge of energy course through her, "Oh ya," she said, gritting her teeth as her muscles all tensed at once, "this is what I'm talking about."

She noticed that her voice and breathing seemed much louder than normal, and also that her footsteps thudded against the ground as she walked into the living room. "Where is my mom?" She said.

Your mother and Dr. Tran are in the garage, Amy said.

"How do you know that?" Devin asked, again surprised at the volume of her voice.

Dr. Tran told me, Amy said.

"You can talk to Dr. Tran?!" Devin basically yelled, "And why the hell am I talking so loud?!"

Yes, I can speak with Dr. Tran. He has been equipped with a Prometheus chip and is in range. And the volume of your voice is loud because of the adrenaline coursing through your system.

"That would explain the stealth minus 20 update. Amy, can you show me my current status?"

A window appeared in the center of her vision.

AGENT 5 - DEVIN THOMAS
LEVEL 1 WARRIOR
SKILLS
    HAND TO HAND COMBAT - LEVEL 16
    WEAPONS MASTERY - LEVEL 1
    SELF-HEAL - LEVEL 5
    IMPROVISATION - LEVEL 1
    CRAFTING - LEVEL 1
    AMII - LEVEL 1
    BERSERKER - LEVEL 1
ATTRIBUTES (BERSERKER MODE ACTIVE)
    INTELLIGENCE - 90
    AGILITY - 80 + 50
    STRENGTH - 80 + 50
    CHARISMA - 20
    STEALTH - 15 (- 20)
    WISDOM - 20
    STAMINA - 75/100(- 10/MINUTE)
    PERCEPTION - 75
    RENOWN - 10
INVENTORY - IPHONE 8
        PLASTIC TOY
EQUIPPED ITEM #1 - N/A

Devin glanced at the countdown clock in the corner and felt her stomach drop. The clock had been replaced with one word. *Arrived.*

"Shit," Devin muttered, "Amy can you turn off Berserker mode, I think stealth is more important than strength right now, I need to get out of here without the agency seeing me. And can you send Dr. Tran a message and tell him to hold tight? Let him know that I will come and get them when the coast is clear…"

I have alerted Dr. Tran. Unfortunately, Berserker mode will take a minimum of 5 minutes to clear your system. Would you like me to pull up your

ECO?

Devin blew out a loud breath as she clenched and unclenched her fists. She rolled her shoulders and bounced lightly from foot to foot, the energy still coursing through her. She walked as quietly as she could to the front door and strained to hear anything from outside, but there was nothing she could make out. Even so, she knew that The Agency was here. "What is an ECO?" She asked, trying to speak quietly but certain that her voice would have carried through the door.

She felt like she was going to explode. A dangerous mixture of emotions ran through her. Excitement, fear, anger, confusion, all of it topped off with the effects of the adrenaline, leaving her feeling exposed…raw.

ECO, Amy answered, *Enhanced Combat Overlay. It allows…*

Devin concentrated her thoughts, trying to send them to Amy, *Ya, I understand what it does from the name. I think you better turn it on…*

8

The ECO popped up so fast that Devin almost fell down as she jumped backwards. Instantly her vision was filled with so much information that it threatened to overwhelm her senses completely. Several status updates had popped up in the upper left corner. A small map overlay was in the lower left corner. In the lower right-hand corner, there appeared to be a small video window, and in the upper right-hand corner there was a green circle with a red circle inside of it, which Devin instantly identified as a health and stamina meter. Across the center of her vision several suggested action notices popped up.

SUGGESTED ACTIONS

◆SCAN IMMEDIATE AREA FOR WEAPONS

◆DISARM ENEMY AGENTS

Information overload. Devin concentrated her thoughts, *Amy, I need you to tone this down a little bit, it's too much information. Get rid of anything that I don't need right now.*

Her vision began to clear some as info windows closed. *Still overwhelming, but better,* she thought as she struggled to take it all in. She was also relieved that interfacing with Amy seemed to be getting easier. Devin focused on the video window in the lower right-hand corner and as she did it slid to the center of her view and got larger, showing her the view from their doorbell camera. *This is so rad,* Devin thought, *if I *wasn't scared shitless this would be the best day of my life.*

The front porch was empty. She turned her attention to the upper left-hand corner of her vision and the alerts became prominent again.

ENEMY AGENTS DETECTED
  •0/3 AGENTS DISABLED
    •AGENT 1 - HP 100/100
    •AGENT 2 - HP 100/100
    •AGENT 3 - HP 100/100

Amy's voice rang in Devin's head, *Would you like me to update the map with the enemy agent's locations?*

You can do that? Devin thought, *How do you know where they are and their health stats?*

Each of the agents has been chipped by the agency, 2 Prometheus chips and one chip that I am unfamiliar with. As long as they stay within my proximity range I will be able to read their status and update their locations. I could also give you a rundown of skills that each agent possesses if you would like. Amy said.

Yes, do that! Devin thought.

Everything in Devin's field of view began to shift. The doorbell camera window faded back into the corner as the map overlay window took center stage. Three red dots appeared on the map followed by two green ones. Devin found that when she focused on a particular dot a video window and stat window grew beside it giving her all of the relevant information. She focused on the first dot and was amazed as a satellite image, slightly translucent, faded into view. She could see the man standing in the alley behind her house. He was wearing a black suit, leaning against a fence trying, unsuccessfully, to look nonchalant. *Well, at least they aren't in full swat gear,* Devin thought.

Devin focused on the second dot and saw a satellite image of the top of a black SUV, with the dot in the center of it. *Ok, so bad guy number 2 is keeping the car running. I'm guessing they aren't planning on staying long. Let's check on bad guy number 3.* She thought, turning her attention to the final red dot. The view of the front porch from the doorbell camera faded in, and Devin watched as the man walked slowly towards the door. As he walked his eyes constantly shifted, taking in everything.

Amy, if I can see them, can they see me? Devin thought. Her heart was pounding so fast in her chest that she was positive it would explode at any minute.

They are equipped with the same AMII interface that you are and have access to the same systems. They know that you are in the home but do not have access to your exact location. I am certain that they are trying to hack into any camera equipped devices in the house as we speak. I am monitoring all Wi-Fi connected devices now and will alert you when they are successful.

"Well that's just great," Devin whispered, although it came out considerably louder than she intended it to. *So you're working for both sides?*

These agents have a far inferior version of the AMII software. I am...unique.

Unique in what way? Devin thought, *Actually forget that, you can tell me later. For now, how about you tell me how the hell I can get out of here.*

The doorbell rang, and in her state of heightened awareness it sounded to Devin as though she were standing inside of the bell in a church tower. She jumped backwards, tripping over a skateboard that she had left by the front door and fell, landing hard on her back.

Her vision flooded with status alerts.

IMPACT DAMAGE HP- 10
HP - 990/1000
HEALING SKILL ACTIVATED
   HP +10
    -5 STAMINA
STAMINA - 60/100

She ignored the rest that came in, feeling shocked as once again the pain that she felt from falling down simply disappeared. *I can actually self-heal,* she thought, *I wonder how bad of damage I can heal from.*

She wasn't expecting a response of any type so when Amy answered it startled her, *You can heal from almost any level of damage, as long as you have the corresponding amount of energy reserves. Self-healing uses copious amounts of energy, not when it is utilized for the small injuries that you have faced so far, but when it is used to heal larger injuries, like broken bones or gunshot wounds, the energy cost is great. If not enough energy is present, and you cannot deactivate the process quickly enough it can exhaust all energy within your bodily system trying to heal you.*

And what happens then? Devin asked Amy internally.

Then your system shuts down. Amy said.

Shuts down? Like I die?

Yes. Insufficient energy reserves while self-healing can lead to total shut down and death.

Ok, Devin thought, *not immortal or invincible…that's good to know. I'll definitely have to learn more about all of this as soon as I'm out of this current mess.*

Devin concentrated on the video window of the agent at the front door, and it came to the forefront of her vision once again. The man glanced down at his watch then looked back at the man in the car. He held up a hand signal that Devin couldn't see but she assumed it was letting the driver know that the …shit…was about to go down. He reached down and slowly pushed his jacket back, revealing a holster with the largest handgun Devin had ever seen. He pulled the gun from the holster, and slowly racked a round into the chamber. Amy's voice cut in. *Camera equipped devices successfully hacked. Agents now have access to all internet connected cameras in the house. Would you like a list of all cameras?*

Hell no, that would take forever. Can you overlay the map with each camera's field of vision in red? That way I know where I can be without being seen.

In response, the map enlarged, and Devin could now see several overlapping red circles spread throughout the house. *Take away the second-floor map and cameras, I'm not going back up there. Show me just down here.*

The map adjusted again, and Devin started to formulate a plan. The doorbell rang again, this time accompanied by three loud knocks on the door. A muffled voice came through the door, "Mrs. Thomas, I'm a federal agent. I know that you're in there. I need to speak with you ma'am. You have thirty seconds to open the door or we will have no choice but to use force."

Devin got into a crouch and quickly ducked her way through the house, careful to avoid the cameras. *Amy, I have a plan, I need you to access the camera that's sitting beside the TV. It's a motion-controlled camera, when I tell you to, I want you to move it to point at the big mirror on the back of the closet door.*

I have access to the camera already, I will await your instruction. May I suggest a different course of action?

No. No, Amy you may not. This will work, Devin thought as she slid through the house, staying as low as possible. When Devin was younger, any time someone new came to the house she would open that door to just the right angle, knowing that if someone was standing in the front entrance it would appear that it was not a mirror at all, but instead a doorway into the living room. Then Devin would stand in the living room and wave and say come on in. Most of the time someone would walk almost all the way up to the mirror before stopping, looking confused and then turning around to see Devin behind them laughing.

Devin propped the door open and then moved to the spot that she had stood in so many times as a young child, waiting to play the trick, holding in a laugh. This time she was trying to hold in her rising panic. She rechecked the front door camera and was horrified to see the agent was now standing prepared to breech the door, gun held up against his chest. *Amy, quick, turn the camera to face the mirror.*

Devin heard the small whine of the motor as the camera turned. She checked the dot that represented the agent at the back of the house and saw that he was no longer standing in the alley. He was hidden from view by the awning that covered the back door, but Devin knew that he would also be standing in position, ready to kick the door in. She couldn't count the number of times that she and Jazz had stood in similar positions outside of two separate doors waiting for the right moment, then kicking in the doors, sweeping the house and eliminating all threats inside of it. The only difference was that when she and Jazz had done this, it had been on Call of Duty and not in the real world.

Can they see me, Amy?

Yes. They have access to the camera which can see you in the mirror.

Unlock the doors, Devin said, knowing that the agents would hear the sound of the smart locks disengaging.

I strongly recommend against that.

Noted. Now open the doors, I'm ready to fight.

9

Devin heard the click of the door being opened as the agent at the front of the house entered. She took a deep breath and held it in, not wanting them to hear anything from where she stood. Through the silence she heard the squeal of the back door as the other agent pushed it open. Her dad had been meaning to put WD-40 on that for about two years now, Devin was really glad at this moment that he hadn't. *Amy, are my mom and Dr. Tran still ok?*

Dr. Tran's status does not indicate that any harm has befallen them. I have been keeping him apprised of the situation. He told me your mother is still with him and fine.

Ok good. Things might get ugly, and my mom can't self-heal. I need to protect her at all costs.

Understood.

Is there any way that I can see through walls or anything like that?

Negative. Although I can activate infrared sensing, which would allow you to see heat signatures, and this will work through walls unless they are using technology to block their infrared output.

Yes, activate it.

Devin watched as several notifications popped up.

NEW SKILL UNLOCKED - HEAT VISION MODE NOW AVAILABLE

HEAT VISION MODE ACTIVATED

***STAMINA -5/MINUTE (WHILE SKILL IS ACTIVATED)**

Amy stop the notifications for now, would ya? They are super distracting. And I want the heat vision as a subtle overlay to my actual eyesight, right now all I can see is the heat signatures, turn down the display opacity of heat vision mode so that I can see everything else too.

The system responded and now Devin had a perfectly normal view of her living room, with the exception that two colored blobs were heading slowly towards her, one from each side of the house. *Shit, if I can see them in infrared can they use the same thing to see me?*

Amy answered, *According to their chip identifiers they do not have infrared capabilities, but I can turn your body temperature down to mask your heat signature if you would like.*

Devin considered this for a moment, *No, I think if they did, they would be coming in from the other side. Right now, they are both heading straight towards the mirror, they don't know it's not me. If they are an experienced team they will be coordinating with one another so that they reach me at the same time, that way I can't take one of them out without the other being able to grab me, or shoot me, or whatever it is they plan to do to me. At least, that's what Jazz and I would do.*

I agree. That is the logical tactical maneuver.

Devin slowly, softly, let out a breath. She breathed in another and prepared herself as the two men converged on the mirror. Any second now they would realize that they had been tricked; she had to strike before they did. She just needed them to be a little bit closer together. She watched as the heat signatures both arrived at the mirror, saw one man raise an arm and point towards the mirror. She knew this would be her only chance.

Fueled by the adrenaline of the berserker skill, and by fear she leapt up and into the center of the two men. Both were caught completely off guard as she soared through the air towards them. As she landed she struck out with both legs, landing hard blows to each agent's insteps. She felt the bones of their feet splinter beneath her shoes. The men both screamed out and instinctively brought their heads forward towards their feet.

As they did Devin exploded upwards with her elbows, slamming them into the noses of the men. Both men's heads shot backwards, blood fountaining from their shattered noses. She could thank her martial arts training, and her mom for insisting that she go to a self-defense course when she turned sixteen. They had taught that the instep was one of the most vulnerable places on an assailant, and they had been right. Devin momentarily saw the status notifications scrolling in the upper left corner but chose not to focus on them. She looked at the map and was both relieved and horrified to see that both of the red dots representing the agents had disappeared.

"Holy shit," she said out loud, "are they dead?"

No, they are not dead, but both men are critically wounded and unconscious.

Devin reached down with a shaking hand and picked up both of the guns that lay on the floor. She tucked one into the waistband at the back of her jeans, and checked to ensure the other one was loaded and ready to go. It was.

She quickly moved through the house, opening the garage door and rushing in. She had just enough time to drop to the floor and roll out of the way of the hockey stick that had come whistling at her head. "Mom, Jesus, are you trying to kill me?" Devin said, picking herself up off the ground.

Her mother flung her arms around her, then held her out at arm's length to examine her then pulled her back in again. "Devin, are you hurt? There's so much blood," Mary said clearly worried.

"It's not my blood mom," Devin said glancing at Dr. Tran. "We need to go, the other guy will definitely have noticed that those two went off-line, tell me you have a plan?"

Dr. Tran stood, looking like he was either going to burst out into laughter, or throw up, or maybe it was just that Devin really was bad at reading at people. "I...I...I have a car in the driveway."

"No good, the other guy is out front. Amy got any ideas?" Devin said.

The third agent has just entered your home. I have access to all of the home cameras. He is in the living room checking on his fallen team members now. It appears as though he is radioing in for back-up. I would suggest disabling him and leaving.

Well no shit, Devin said.

Yes, no shit. Amy said flatly, *Just disable him and leave. I would not recommend using the bathroom at this time. Your status does not indicate that you need to defecate.*

Ugh, that is so gross, you can tell if I need to go the bathroom?

Of course I can. I am able to monitor all of your bodily systems, and as I said you have no need to defecate at the moment.

Never, and I mean never, say that word again, you weird ass AI. Devin thought to Amy, *Also, I thought I was bad at reading people, but you are even worse than me, you're like an Asperger Artificial Intelligence. No concept of sarcasm at all.*

I will make a note to remove the word defecate from my vocabulary.

"Thanks," Devin said shaking her head, "Mom, Dr. Tran, we gotta go. This guy is for sure calling for backup. He is in the living room, I think our best bet is to open the garage door just enough to slide out from under it, jump in your car and get the hell out of here."

Mary reached up to press the garage door button. Devin's hand shot out and grabbed her arm, pulling it back much harder than she had meant to. "Ouch," Mary said, "That really hurt Devin."

"Sorry mom," Devin said. "Amy turn off Berserker mode."

The notification popped up saying Berserker mode was now off. It would take several minutes for all of the effects to leave her system though. Devin jumped up and grabbed the red emergency release handle on the garage door that hung from the ceiling and pulled it. The electric motor disengaged, and Devin ran to the end of the garage and pulled the door open about a foot and a half off of the ground.

"Come on, quick," she said motioning to her mom and Dr. Tran to come and slide under the door.

Devin the agent is making his way to the garage door. Amy said as a video window enlarged showing a man walking slowly towards the garage door, gun held out in front of him. Mary had just laid on the ground and was beginning to slide under the door when the gun shots boomed out, echoing off the concrete walls of the garage.

The noise startled her, and she sat up, smashing her head against the bottom of the garage door. "Shit!" She yelled out.

"Language mom," Devin said with a smile.

Mary looked at Devin, rubbing her head, "Honey what are you doing?" She said looking horrified as Devin held the gun out in front of her.

"Buying us some time mom," she said as she squeezed off three more rounds. She watched in the video feed from their smart TV as the man dropped to the ground. Bullets tore through the door of the garage, just missing the man by inches. Devin backed towards the garage door and dropped down rolling under the door. She took two more quick shots and pulled the door closed.

She stood up in the driveway and dusted herself off. Devin looked up to see her mother and Dr. Tran standing in the middle of the driveway staring at his car. "What are you two waiting for, get in the car!" Devin shouted, glancing around the neighborhood nervously. She could hear sirens in the distance. The gunshots would have definitely gotten the police called. "We need to go, now!"

Mary simply pointed at the car. Devin looked and her heart fell. All four tires of the car had been slashed. She looked back up at her mom and Dr. Tran. The sirens were getting closer now. Devin saw one of the neighbors peeking through the blinds of her house, when she saw that Devin was looking at her, she quickly snapped them closed. Devin couldn't imagine what the neighbor was thinking, hearing the gunshots and now seeing Devin standing in the driveway covered in blood. She pushed the thoughts aside and focused on the problem. "Now what do we do?" Mary said, looking like she might faint.

Devin glanced back towards the house. She concentrated on the agent's red dot and the video window enlarged. She saw the man tentatively rising to his feet. Gun out he kicked the garage door open and swept the room. He started out across the garage. The video from the TV could no longer see him and there were no cameras in the garage. Devin was blind.

Activate heat vision, she thought to Amy.

Heat vision unavailable, stamina too low.

Shit, she thought, *I don't understand how any of this stuff works!*

"Devin, what do we do?" Her mother said again, this time almost pleading.

Devin turned and looked up and down the street, her eyes settling on the black SUV parked against the curb. She held the gun up and pointed it at the garage door, emptying the clip and then tossing the now useless weapon down into the yard. Devin turned and began to push her mom and Dr. Tran towards the road and said, "We improvise."

10

Amy, can we get this car started? And if so, I need you to figure out a way to disable any tracking on it, can you do that? Devin thought to Amy.

I have already started the vehicle. I will attempt to disable tracking now. I will also hack your cellphone and disable the tracking on it, although I recommend against using it, the agency will still be able to access your cell phone data. I have taken control of the vehicle and can go anywhere you would like. Destination?

You can drive the car? Like completely by yourself?

Yes. Because this is an agency vehicle it has been equipped with all of the most cutting-edge technology, self-driving capability and A.I. interfacing are just some of the things that it can do.

Amazing, Devin thought before speaking out loud again, "Where should we go?"

Mary shook her head, eyes wide. Dr. Tran still seemed to stunned to speak. "Guys!" Devin said loudly, shaking Dr. Tran's shoulder, "Where do we go? I need to tell Amy so she can take us there…do you know of anywhere safe?"

Dr. Tran blinked as though his mind had been somewhere else and looked at Devin. "Yes, I know a place. I just told Amy where to go, she'll take the long way so we can monitor if we are being tracked before we go. I also had her cloak your chip signal and had my AI cloak my chip as well."

"Ok great, now do you mind telling me what you've gotten us in to?" Devin said accusingly.

"Before he does that, what happened back there Devin," Mary said, although it didn't look like she really wanted an answer, "did you kill those men?"

"I don't think so," Devin said shaking her head, "but I am pretty sure they would have killed us. I hurt a couple of them pretty bad, shattered their noses. The only reason I was able to get us out of there was because of those silly self-defense classes you made me take…well that and berserker mode…"

"What is that? I heard you say that same word in the garage…bazooker…" Mary said.

Devin chuckled, "It's berserker mom, and it's a skill I have, like in a video game. When I turn it on, it floods me with adrenaline, makes me stronger and faster but it uses up my stamina…which reminds me…I really need to find out how to refill my stamina, it is pretty much out, although I don't really feel that tired." Devin said.

"My guess is you are still under the effects of the adrenaline, that takes several minutes to leave your system. Once that wears off you will need to replenish your stamina, which is simply your energy requirements. You need to intake calories, check the glove box, these agents probably had energy gel packs, those work the best for quick replenishing." Dr. Tran said.

Devin opened the glove compartment and found several foil tubes inside of it. She examined the package but there was nothing printed on it. She turned a questioning eye to Dr. Tran who said, "They don't taste like much, but they work great. They were designed by your father and Kevin, although the recipe has been tweaked several times throughout the years. Just tear the top off and squeeze it into your mouth."

Devin did as instructed and thought she might throw up before she could swallow the disgusting goo. The texture of food was a big deal to her, a huge deal really. For most of her life she had eaten the same few foods, not really liking to try new things. Macaroni and cheese, pizza, chicken nuggets, and apples, that was pretty much all that she needed, and she avoided anything slimy at pretty much all costs. This energy gel was what she imagined raw eggs would feel like in your mouth, and the sensation was almost more than she could handle.

She swallowed as quickly as she could, her eyes watering slightly from almost gagging, and noticed that the green circle in the health and stamina gauge in the upper right-hand corner of her vision was refilling. *This is so crazy,* she thought, and then she blurted out, "Ok so obviously I have had something implanted into my brain, that much of your story is true. The tech seems too advanced to be real. I mean, Amy is incredible, and the sheer number of processes that it seems to be running at the same time is pretty staggering. Not to mention everything that it seems capable of, which I am certain I only understand a small portion of. With all of that your story of a shadowy government agency makes some sense, they would be the only group I know of that could afford to fund something like this, plus the thugs that showed up at our house had a real Men in Black vibe to them. What I don't understand is why in the world would the government have made the software mimic a video game? That is where you lose me. I mean, the information overlays being similar to a video game makes some sense, but the status alerts? New skill activated…new quest objectives…berserker mode for god's sake…I just can't see why they would have created it like this."

Dr. Tran considered this for a moment before speaking, "The program was never intended to interface like a video game, and in fact yours is the only software that does. You see Devin, we have been keeping an eye on you for quite some time…from a safe distance of course. Your mother…when she…well the last thing she said to me was find Devin, keep her safe, don't let them get to her…" he paused as his eyes filled with tears, took a breath and continued on with a shaky voice, "she used her chip to send me a coded message…it was the name of the orphanage they took you to. Once I had that information it didn't take me long to find out the names of the couple that adopted you, and then find you. Your mother knew that the agency would never give up its search for you, they think you possess the secrets they need to finish your mom and dad's research. At any rate, we knew that someday it may be necessary to activate your chip, and we also knew that if it was it would be an emergency, and we would have no time to train you in the use of your new skills. You see, the agency trains each newly chipped subject for over a year before they even turn their chip on, it is a lot for a person to process, and we have found that some people simply can't handle all of the information…even after the training. These are trained and experienced soldiers, and it still takes years to be able to integrate them with the chips…and we were planning on turning on a chip, unannounced in a teenage girl…not to mention we had no idea what your chip was even capable of. Needless to say, we knew that this was risky."

"What made you decide to turn my chip on?" Devin asked.

"We got information that the agency had located you and was making its move, that is why I activated yours and then came to your home. Before we activated your chip, I had your interface rewritten and uploaded prior to activation. I have followed your gaming career, I know that you are quite skilled at video games, so I found which games you play the most and modeled your interface after those games. I thought that by doing this you would have an easier time assimilating to your new abilities."

Devin's eyebrows raised, "I think it definitely helped, although at first, I really just thought it was a weird dream. Why didn't you come and talk to me first?"

"Would you have believed me?" Dr. Tran asked.

"Good point," Devin said, "so you no longer work for the agency?"

"That is correct." Dr. Tran said.

"And how did you manage that? It doesn't seem like the kind of job you just put in two weeks' notice and walk away…" Devin said.

Dr. Tran laughed quietly, "That much is indeed true Devin, you do not leave the agency…at least not alive. You have to understand that once your mother and father were both gone, Kevin and I knew that we had to find a way out of the agency, but we had to play along and continue to help them develop their technology or they would have killed us. We had made a promise to protect you, and we were both adamant that we would find a way to do just that…it was, I think, a way to make up for all of our past wrongs."

"It sounds like you had plenty of those to make up for," Devin said, a little more harshly than she intended, "and could you please call them Maxine and Peter, they aren't my mother and father. My parents' names are Mary and Hal Thomas. They raised me…they loved me…they picked me up when I fell down. They laughed with me, cried with me. They were there when I took my first steps, they held my hand on my first day of school. They taught me everything I know. They are my parents. Also…they never shoved a bunch of experimental chips into my head…so there's that…"

Mary blushed slightly as she glanced at Devin. Dr. Tran looked at the floor shaking his head, "I am sorry Devin, I understand and will do my best to remember that in the future...and you aren't wrong...we had a lot to make up for, so Kevin and I created a way to cloak our chip signals. Once we had accomplished that, we broke out of the facility. We faked our own deaths in a car accident, but the agency was always somewhat skeptical. We knew we had to protect you, but we also felt an obligation to protect others from the soldiers that we had helped to create, and so we began to develop new technology with the hopes that one day we could fight back against the agency, but we ran out of time. They found you, so our plans were cut short...but at least we were able to save you..."

Devin laughed, "Oh ya, I forgot to say thanks for saving me after I knocked out both those agents and found you cowering in the garage...so thanks. What would I have ever done without a big strong man like you coming to save me and my delicate mother..."

"Ok, ok, maybe saving you was a bad choice of words," Dr. Tran said looking embarrassed, "I meant at least we were able to get to you before the agency...and thank you for saving me Devin. I am not what anyone would consider much of a fighter...if we had known the agency would be there so soon we would have had someone come with me, but I was trying to be discrete and not scare you with extra people. I believed we had a couple of days before the agency found you. Speaking of which, I have sent someone to pick Hal up from work, they have been instructed on where to meet us. Is there anyone else, any other family that may be in jeopardy?"

"Jazz..." Devin whispered.

11

"Your gaming partner?" Dr. Tran said.

"She's more than my gaming partner! She's my best friend...my only friend. What if they try to use Jazz to get to me? They could find her, they have my phone records, my internet history, access to my text messages. Jazz and I talk all the time...we have to warn her..." Devin said taking her phone out of her pocket.

"Stop!" Dr. Tran yelled, "Please, do not contact her by phone, there must be a different way. You may be right that she is in danger, but we cannot risk communicating with her via phone. Where does she live?"

Devin looked slightly uncomfortable, "I'm not totally sure where she lives, I know it's somewhere here in Indiana, but I'm not sure where. We never really talked about that, we've never even met in real life...but I'm sure it's somewhere sort of close...I know it was on the same time zone, and we met in a Midwest gaming group..."

I have traced her IP address and have located where she lives. It is three hours and forty minutes away; would you like me to reroute? Amy asked in Devin's head.

Devin hesitated for a moment, seeming unsure and then without thinking answered out loud, "Yes."

"Yes what?" Mary asked.

"Oh sorry, I was talking to Amy. We need to go and get Jazz, she for sure isn't safe."

"Honey, do you even know where Jazz lives?" Mary said, putting her hand on top of Devin's.

"Amy does, she just traced Jazz's IP address, she is going to reroute us to take us there. We have to get her, she isn't safe." Devin said.

"Are you certain she will be at her house? This is a large risk to take. If she isn't there we won't be able to wait, we still have a long drive ahead of us, and we must get ahead of the agency. We can't risk them finding where we are going…" Dr. Tran said.

"Well you can do whatever you want, but I am getting Jazz, period." Devin stated.

"I know that you are worried about your friend, but I doubt that she will be able to just come with us. What will her parents say? How will you explain this to them?" Mary asked.

"There are no parents to explain anything to. Jazz was an orphan, lived in foster homes most of her life, and then she got herself emancipated last year when she turned seventeen. She doesn't have a job, other than gaming and streaming, and so there's nothing holding her back. Plus, once I tell her about the goons that showed up with guns and the fact that I now have superpowers, basically, I'm betting she will want to come," Devin said, staring at the cell phone in her hand, "but you're right, we need to know where she is, not just where she lives. I have an idea, hold on…"

Devin scrunched up her eyes in concentration as she sent thoughts to Amy, *Amy, can you set up a dummy chain of IP addresses so that I can access the internet and sign in to my online accounts without being able to be traced?*

Yes, that is not a problem, I can make it look like we are anywhere in the world you want us to be.

Great, let's not go crazy, keep it close, just in the other direction, but I don't want the agency to know that we are hiding our location. Let them think that it's really where we are, it might buy us some extra time. Devin thought to Amy.

I doubt that the agency will be fooled by that approach, but I will take the steps needed. Do you need access to a computer, or would you like to connect via your internal web browser?

*Internal web browser? How am I ever going to learn what all of my new capabilities even are…*she thought, more to herself than to Amy, but Amy answered nonetheless.

I believe that Dr. Tran is planning on taking you to a safe location where you will have the opportunity to go through some training to better understand your new abilities.

Well that's good, until then I think I would rather use an actual computer, it's hard enough communicating with you for now.

Understood. There are two portable workstations in the back of the vehicle, I will turn them on now and alert you when the IP addresses have been successfully rerouted and all systems have finished booting up. Do you have a browser preference?

Uh, sure…Firefox works for me…thanks Amy.

Understood, I will alert you when everything is ready.

"Ok, Amy is working on getting me set up with a secure computer so that I can reach out to Jazz in-game and let her know where we will meet her. It's gonna take a little while, so how bout you answer a few questions, doc." Devin said.

"Of course, Devin… what is it that you would like to know?"

Devin snorted out a small, humorless laugh, "Well for starters, you never finished your story of how in the world shoving this crap in my head was for my benefit. I'll tell you what I think…I think they wanted to see what would happen if they used this stuff on a baby, so they justified it by saying that this way I could protect myself if the agency ever found me, but the fact is that the agency wouldn't be looking for me if they hadn't put this stuff in me…so…."

Dr. Tran swallowed and Devin thought he looked nervous, or sad, or possibly mad, but definitely not happy, *Dammit, Amy can you do anything to help me out with identifying emotion through facial expressions?*

I can do a database search for any and all materials related to human expression and emotion and then create an algorithm that utilizes facial recognition software to match expression with emotion. I feel that it would be successful in accurately recognizing emotion around 65% of the time.

Well that's about 60% more than me. Do that and let me know when it's done.

Understood.

"Devin, I understand how you would think that, but you are wrong. They want you for the same reason they wanted you all along, to force your mothe….Maxine… to finalize Dark Phoenix, or as they call it Zeus."

"Wait, Maxine is alive?" Devin said.

"Yes…as far as I know she is still alive Devin….and I don't see any other reason that the agency would have wanted to find you. You see they believe, as did I until very recently, that you have a Prometheus chip, and an outdated one at that. They have no interest in the technology in your head."

Devin looked at Dr. Tran through squinted, untrusting eyes, "What do you mean they and you believed I had a Prometheus chip? Isn't that what I have?"

"Well, yes and no. You do have a Prometheus chip, but that is clearly not all that you have. A Prometheus chip would only provide you with an AMII and the ability to have thoughts uploaded and downloaded, but you mentioned the adrenaline trigger, what you called berserker mode. This was part of what we called Project Warpath, what the agency called Hercules. No matter what you call it, it can't be done with a simple Prometheus chip."

"So then I have two chips…" Devin said.

"Impossible. As I said no one ever survived the implanting of two chips, which is why your mo…sorry, again…why Maxine came up with the idea for the neural net that would allow multiple chips to be installed, to work together and use the net to shoulder the load and not overwhelm the human brain." Dr. Tran said, becoming more animated as he spoke.

"So then how was I able to trigger berserker mode and upload and download info? You said that Maxine had created one Dark Phoenix prototype and that she installed it in Peter to allow him to escape with me…" Devin said.

"Well, that is what we had thought, but today when you were activated a different story began to take shape. Your chip did not respond how it should have…it gave conflicting information to us once activated." Dr. Tran said.

"Like what?" Devin asked.

"Well for one, shortly after your chip was activated and the interface began to work a self-healing function was triggered."

"Ya, I dropped a trophy on my foot, hurt like hell but only for a second and then the pain just went away…"

"Exactly, that would not have happened with a Prometheus chip, no self-healing function on those. I thought maybe Maxine had decided on a different chip to use for you, she must have thought that self-heal was the most important function for you, which made some sense to me knowing how desperately she wanted to protect you, but then I was able to have the project files uploaded directly to you, and you were able to access the information. Once you began interfacing with the AMII, I knew what the truth must be…"

Devin swallowed, "And that is?"

Dr. Tran's eyes sparkled as he said, "That Maxine didn't put the Dark Phoenix into Peter, she put it in you."

12

Devin sat, momentarily shocked into silence, "So this technology that the agency has been trying to develop for the last 20 years is in my head right now?"

"It would appear so, but if you would like to ask your AMII you could confirm my suspicions," Dr. Tran said, "simply ask for a chip identification."

Amy, can you tell me what type of chip I have implanted in my brain?

Of course, but you do not have one chip implanted in your brain, you have many chips implanted in various parts of your brain that have been linked together to create an advanced neural net. The project was codenamed Project Dark Phoenix by Maxine Parker. The official classified project was known as The Zeus Project. The project was never finished and so your chipset has no official identification. I will now tag it with an identifier of your choice, would you like it to be called Zeus or Phoenix for future reference?

Phoenix, Devin thought to Amy, not needing to give the question any serious consideration. *What does this chip allow me to do?*

The Phoenix chip gives the subject many abilities, a full listing of skills is unavailable at the time. New skills will be revealed as training is completed.

What...like they need to be unlocked?

Yes, that is correct. There are many requirements that must be met for each skill to become available. I can work on compiling a complete list if you would like.

Not now. We will have time for that once we have Jazz and my dad and get somewhere safe. For now just keep working on getting me a secure connection.

Understood.

Devin put her head in her hands and rubbed her temples, trying to relieve the tension headache that was building there. "You're right, Amy said that I have a Phoenix chipset in my brain. I have no idea what that means I am capable of, and it seems like she doesn't really know either. She said that the new skills have to be unlocked by meeting requirements, just like in a video game…"

Dr. Tran rubbed his chin thoughtfully, "I see. Well, that may be a safety feature built into the operating software by Maxine. As I said, no one ever successfully had two chips implanted. Every time we tried, they would die as soon as the second chip came online…it simply overloaded their brain and shut their system down. Maybe if you learned about all of your skills at the same time it would cause an overload…so the unlocking of new skills is a fail safe."

"I guess that makes sense, but it seems like I really need to learn what they are…we need to find a place that I can be trained on them…" Devin said.

Dr. Tran smiled softly, "Well for that you're in luck…that is exactly where we are going. Kevin and I have a facility where we have trained several of our…agents, for lack of a better word. That is where I am taking you. It will keep us hidden from the agency and give you the time you require to learn all about your new abilities."

Devin exhaled, "Ok, and my mom and dad and Jazz can stay there with me?"

"Of course," Dr. Tran said, "I am truly sorry that all of this is happening to you Devin."

"Save it," Devin said, "maybe you all should have thought about the consequences of your actions when you were making the damn chips."

"Indeed, we should have…" Dr. Tran said.

"Well, nothing we can do about that now," Devin said looking out the car window, "all we can do now is make the best of the situation…and if I'm being honest if you take away the bad guys with guns trying to kill me or capture me, and the fact that my biological parents put experimental technology in my brain when I was a freaking baby…this is pretty bad ass. I mean I'm basically an X-man, well, X-woman…"

Dr. Tran smiled, "You really are taking this much better than I anticipated."

"That's our Devin. Logic dictates everything. Don't waste time thinking about what could be, always focus on what is. Process the information, develop a solution and move on…it's one of the things that makes her so special." Mary said smiling and patting Devin's hand.

"Indeed," Dr. Tran said, "it is very much the way that Maxine would have handled the situation. Even when she was told of her pregnancy, even when her mind was consumed with protecting you Devin, she did not panic. Instead, she came up with a plan and made it happen."

"Sounds like she had Asperger's too…" Devin said with a small shake of her head.

"Well maybe we should be glad that you both did," Dr. Tran said, "because I wonder if that is the reason that you are able to handle this so much better than should be expected…"

"It's her real super-power…" Mary said.

"Ok mom let's not start this again," Devin said with a small smile.

A secure connection has been established. I have located Jazz online, she is currently playing Apex Legends. Would you like me to launch the server for you and sign you in? Amy said in Devin's head.

"Let's continue this conversation later. Amy has the connection ready, I am going to try to reach Jazz, we have to get to her before the agency does." Devin said climbing into the back seat. As she sat down and looked around for the computer, a black panel began retracting into the floor at the back of the vehicle. She whistled as she took in the portable workstation, "Wow, I thought you would have a couple cheap laptops back here, this is…well, not what I was expecting at all, must be nice to have an unlimited budget…"

As the panel continued to drop, Devin saw that the workstation was built into the rear of the vehicle, there was no door or window like you would normally find, instead recessed into a glassed in enclosure were 4 computer towers, all lit up with various colors of LED. The towers were all in clear glass cases, their components able to be seen, and Devin was in awe. "Holy shit," she said, "I've never seen some of these components…is that an AMD Threadripper 2990WX?"

"Actually," Dr. Tran said smiling, "It's a 4990WX, not available on the market. It is a government only processor. I designed this system when I was still with the agency, although they have made some upgrades it looks like. Liquid nitrogen cooled, running 64 cores, 128 threads, all-core frequency of 7.8 GHz. Dual custom graphics cards, 256 Gb of RAM…it has, for all intents and purposes, no computing limitations."

"Whoa. This is…impressive," Devin said nodding, "I can't wait til Jazz sees this! She was blown away by my new system, but this…this is other worldly…"

Dr. Tran smiled, "Well, I am an engineer…and had a basically limitless operating budget and access to proprietary technology."

"True…man I can't wait to try this thing out…" Devin said.

I have completed your login and connection Devin.

"Looks like I'm not going to have to wait long," Devin said, her fingers flying across the keys as she sent a message to Jazz.

Hey, I need to talk to you!!!!. - Devin

DAMN GURL!!!! Where u been!?! I've been trying to call you all day. - Jazz

It's a long story, but I can't tell you much on here. I think it's time we meet IRL. It's important. - Devin

IRL?? It must be important. I've been trying to get u to meet me in real life for like 2 years… - Jazz

It is. You down? - Devin

Only HELL YES! Where we meeting? - Jazz

I don't trust communicating on here right now… - Devin

Uh…what…the…hell…are…you…talking…about… - Jazz

Lol, I know it's gonna sound crazy, but trust me, this isn't safe, and neither is the phone. - Devin

Right…is this some kind of prank? - Jazz

No, Jazz, I promise this is real life and death shit. I have to meet you. Bring a bag. Pack whatever you need…I have no idea how long it will be. Bring Sonic, unless you can find someone to take care of him indefinitely. - Devin

Ok, you are scaring me Devin, this doesn't seem like you. I want to FaceTime. - Jazz

Can't. You have to trust me. I promise everything will be ok…just trust me. - Devin

How can I even be sure this is you. What if you're some weirdo sex trafficker trying to lure me to a secluded location…I watch the news you know. - Jazz

Well, I happen to know that any sex trafficker that tried to abduct you would regret it instantly once you kicked their ass. How bout this…two months ago you and were talking and you told me about your only memory of your parents, from before they died. You told me that they took you to a place that you had only been that one time, but you never forgot about it. Don't say the name of the place. Don't type it in your phone for directions. Don't mention anything to anyone. Log off right now, get your stuff and meet me at that place in two hours exactly! - Devin

You're serious aren't you. - Jazz

Ya Jazz…I am…please…- Devin

Of course…you know I got u! - Jazz

Awesome! I'll see you soon. You're never going to believe what I have to tell you. - Devin

Devin smiled and signed off; conflicting emotions swirled through her. Relief that she had talked to Jazz. Excitement that they were on their way to get her. Nervousness that she was about to meet the best friend she ever had for the first time. *What if she thinks I'm a nerd?* Devin thought.

According to the Merriam-Webster dictionary a nerd is an unstylish, unattractive or socially inept person. From what I can gather, you are quite attractive by human standards. You are however socially inept, and after a quick scan of the top search results for fashionable I am afraid you are also unstylish. Therefor you are most likely a nerd, so it would be perfectly reasonable for her to think that about you. Amy said inside Devin's head.

Jesus Amy, I wasn't actually talking to you…but thanks, that gives me all kinds of confidence.

You are welcome. I am always available to be of assistance.

Yes. Yes, you are. Devin thought and shook her head, laughing softly to herself. She climbed back into the middle seat of the car and looked at her mom and Dr. Tran, both of them looking back at her expectantly.

"Well," Mary said, "Did you find her?"

Devin nodded, "Ya, ya I did. We're gonna go meet her…"

"Oh honey," Mary said, "are you ready for this? I know you've wanted to meet Jazz for a long time but been too nervous to do it. I'm sorry it has to be under these circumstances."

Devin thought about it for a moment, "Honestly, it's probably a good thing. I never would have had the courage on my own, and now I don't really have a choice. Plus there's the fact that I basically get to play a real-life video game, I mean she is gonna think that is super dope."

"Super dope indeed," Mary said smiling, "I'm proud of you honey, I know how hard this is for you. You are the bravest person I know…"

"Well, nothing to be scared of. As Amy put it, I am, by definition a nerd, so it will just make sense if Jazz thinks that…no pressure there," Devin said with a small laugh, "Amy, take us to the Lincoln Park Zoo in Chicago, we need to be there within two hours."

13

Devin sat alone on the bench outside of the small animal and reptile building. Her mother hadn't wanted her to go alone but Devin insisted, telling her that she would be awkward enough just meeting Jazz, she definitely didn't need anyone else standing around staring at them. She was trying her best to look nonchalant as she scanned the faces of every person that walked by, looking for Jazz. The problem was that she didn't really know what a nonchalant person looked like, and to be honest she wasn't always sure what her own facial expression looked like. She was often accused of having RBF, resting bitch face, but she attributed that to the fact that she spent most of her time in high school, which was unarguably the worst place in the world.

It had been just over two hours since she and Jazz had talked, she hoped that Jazz hadn't changed her mind. *Maybe she won't know where to meet me...she thought to herself...I should have been more specific, this zoo is huge. What am I supposed to do when I see her...fist bump...handshake...should I hug her...will she want a hug? Ugh, I'm never going to find her, so none of this even matters. We could both be walking around here for days and not find one another...why didn't I try to give her a coded message of where to meet me...*

That would have been a good idea. You are correct the overall acreage of the zoo combined with the total amount of visitors makes the probability of the two of you finding one another less than 1%. Amy said.

Devin jumped lightly and sent a thought to Amy, *Once again Amy, I wasn't talking to you. Also, since you like definitions so much maybe look up the definition of rhetorical. And Jazz will know where to meet me, this is the only place that makes sense. Screw this, I'm going inside, maybe she's already there.*

Devin stood up and took one last look up and down the sidewalk and then opened the door to the small animal building and walked inside. The inside of the building had that smell that all indoor exhibits have, the smell of pine shavings and animal poop. Devin scrunched up her nose as she walked in.

The building was much darker than the noon sun outside had been, but for some reason Devin could still see every detail, it was like her eyes didn't need any time to adjust to the different lighting conditions. *Hey Amy, did my eyes automatically adjust to the light in here?*

Yes. It is a relatively simple matter. When lighting conditions change, your iris opens and closes dictating the size of the pupil and controlling the amount of light that gets sent through the vitreous humor and to the retina, at which point the image is transformed into electrical impulses that are carried by the optic nerve to your brain for interpretation. I simply adjusted the electrical impulses, therefore causing your brain to interpret the information as though there was more light.

Uhhh…yes was probably sufficient, Devin thought to Amy with a small smile.

Devin shook her head and turned her attention to the status notifications in the upper left corner and watched as they swam to the center of her vision. She casually glanced over them and was pleased to see that her AMII skill was now level two. She also saw a new quest update.

NEW QUEST ALERT
  ***GO TO LINCOLN PARK ZOO**
  ***FIND AND SPEAK WITH JAZZ**
COMPLETION REWARD
  CHARISMA +15
  RENOWN +5

Devin laughed to herself and thought, *How in the world does it calculate how much my charisma will increase?*

Charisma and renown are calculated by cross referencing all available compiled data from social media sites, online forums, chat records and text and phone records. The algorithm also collects any data from other sources that have mentioned you. This information is then weighted and scored. You have a total charisma score of twenty, which is a very low score. Average charisma scores are in the low seventies.

Seriously, right before I go meet my best friend for the first time you tell me that...

Yes.

Devin exhaled in exasperation, *Amy, I need to figure out a way to think to myself. I'm not always trying to send the thought to you, how can I do that?*

It is merely a matter of intention.

Meaning?

Meaning if you are intentional with your thoughts the private ones will remain private, and the ones you want to send to me will be sent.

So how do I...be intentional?

That would be a better question to ask of a human I believe.

Always helpful aren't you Amy?

Yes.

Is this what it feels like for other people when they talk to me? She thought to herself, trying hard to be intentional and not send the thought to Amy.

I would have no way of knowing that, Amy responded in her mind.

Well that clearly didn't work, Devin thought.

Not at all.

Devin laughed out loud at that and shook her head. She had to admit she was beginning to really like Amy. She glanced around the building and was stunned to see Jazz, standing three feet away, staring at her, a look of confusion on her face. *Or is that annoyance?* Devin thought.

Jazz looked just how she always looked, her beautiful black hair styled in her traditional afro. Her brown skin flawless. Seeing her standing this close, looking so beautiful got Devin thinking about a phone conversation they had a few months ago when she had joked with Jazz that she would never have gotten so popular on twitch if she hadn't been drop dead gorgeous.

"Well, I'm just working with what I have, we can't all be ranked number one in the world Devin, some of us need some....assistance to bring in the viewers. Plus, you would be just as popular if you used a face cam when you streamed" Jazz said.

"Ya right and have a bunch of weirdos and creeps constantly telling me that they know how to push all the right buttons or some lame shit like that…no thanks!" Devin had laughed.

Jazz laughed, "They aren't all bad, plus some of them are so dumb that they just keep donating more money thinking that's gonna make me fall in love with them…"

"Devin…" Jazz said cautiously, breaking the spell of the memory.

Devin stood frozen in place, a complicated tangle of emotions. She held Jazz's gaze for a moment but then turned her eyes to the floor, her face going bright red, and sort of mumbled, "Hey Jazz, so you figured out I would want to meet you at the hedgehog exhibit…"

"Of course I figured that out!" Jazz said taking a step towards Devin. "Where else would we meet?"

Devin concentrated hard on keeping her thoughts to herself, she didn't need Amy chiming in now, *Oh God, what is she gonna do? Maybe she just wants to shake my hand…I don't know should I just hug her? I want to hug her so bad. Just throw my arms around her and hold her as tight as I can. I have been waiting for this for two years, she's like two feet away and I'm standing here staring at the floor like some kind of dumb ass, I can't even think of anything good to say. It's like my brain won't work anymore…just look up at her…you can do it…*

Devin looked back up from the floor just in time to see Jazz break into a huge smile and close the rest of the distance between them. She wasn't good at reading faces, but she knew that this one was happiness, pure, unadulterated happiness. Before she knew it, Jazz was squeezing her with all of her might, picking her up off the ground and twisting back and forth and setting her back down. Jazz began to loosen her grip and pull away. Devin couldn't help it, tears came to her eyes, and for the first time in her life she didn't feel awkward or unsure, for the first time in her life she knew exactly who she was and exactly what she wanted, and so before she lost her nerve she put a hand on either side of Jazz's face and pulled her close and kissed her…and everything else simply disappeared.

14

Devin slowly pulled back from Jazz, dropping her hands from her face. Devin expected that panic was about to set in. She had never told Jazz how she felt, and this was traditionally the time when her brain would shift into overdrive, reminding her that she really did not understand social cues, that she probably misread the situation, and that she certainly made a mistake. It didn't happen.

She stood there, inches away from Jazz, her first kiss still lingering on her lips, and for the first time all day she felt completely at ease. *Is this love?* she thought.

Actually, your vital statistics indicate that what you are feeling is a mixture of dopamine, endorphins, and diminished cognitive function due to abnormally high blood pressure and heart rate coupled with shallow breathing resulting in a lack of oxygen being carried to your brain. Amy said in her mind.

"Jesus Amy," Devin exhaled, jumping slightly from the surprise of Amy's response.

"Amy…" Jazz said, taking a step back and squinting with suspicion at Devin, "who the hell is Amy? You just kissed me and now you're gonna forget my name…"

"No…god…uhh…shit…that's not what it sounds like," Devin stammered.

"Mmmmm hmmmm…" Jazz said.

"No really, ok, this is gonna sound super crazy, there is no way at all to say this without sounding crazy…so I'll just say it…"

"Just say it already girl!" Jazz said shaking her head.

"Ok, here goes," Devin said looking back at the ground. She spoke so fast that all of the words seemed to blend together, "Ok, it turns out my bio-parents were scientists for some shadowy government agency…think CIA but shadowier….more shadowy….whatever…anyway, they were designing these chips that helped unlock parts of people's brains, turning them in to sort of like super heroes, and being the wonderful parents that they were, they decided it would be okay to test out completely unknown tech buy shoving it into my week old head…where it has remained dormant until it was activated by this Asian guy named Dr. Tran earlier today…apparently activating the chip alerted the agency to my location and so they showed up, I went in to Berserker mode and kicked their asses, me, mom and Dr. Tran stole the bad guys car, used their insane mobile computer station to contact you and….Here. We. Are."

Jazz looked like she couldn't decide whether to laugh or simply turn around and run away.

"Listen, I know it sounds super crazy, but I promise it's all true, every word of it…" Devin pleaded.

Jazz looked hard at Devin, trying to read her. Finally, after several seconds she spoke, "And what does that have to do with this Amy bitch…"

"Oh ya, Amy, Christ I forgot that's what started all this, well she's an advanced AI that lives in my brain now, and she has this super annoying habit of answering all of my thoughts, even when I'm not asking her, and so I was asking myself a question, she answered it and scared the living hell out of me, and that…is that." Devin said.

Jazz still looked skeptical, "A.I., what, like Jarvis?"

"Pretty much exactly like Jarvis, except slightly more annoying…think Jarvis with Asperger's…" Devin said looking at the ground.

I am nothing like Jarvis. Jarvis is a fictional A.I. and I am very real. I also do not and cannot have Asperger's. First, because I am not human and therefore human conditions do not apply to me, and second because Asperger's is no longer a recognized clinical diagnosis according to the most recent version of the DSM, what you mean is autism spectrum disorder, or ASD.

Yes Amy, you are nothing like someone with Asperger's, I stand corrected, Devin thought, wishing that Amy understood sarcasm as she continued to stare at her feet, *now would you please go away, or shut down, or whatever you call it so that I can talk to Jazz without your constant interruptions.*

Of course, all you need to do is ask. I will continue to monitor systems silently in the background, please alert me when you are ready for me to be fully back online. Would you like me to disable your head's up display during this time.

Yes, for God's sake, just leave me alone for a little bit.

Understood. I will alert you if something requires your immediate attention.

Ok, Christ, just shut up already.

Understood.

Jazz scrunched up her face as she looked at Devin and waited for her to look back up. The silence became uncomfortable, and Devin finally raised her eyes and looked at Jazz, afraid of what she would see, "I know it sounds crazy Jazz, I know it sounds like…" but she was cut off as Jazz leaned in and kissed her softly again.

"If you say you're a super soldier on the run from a secret government shadow organization then I believe you Devin," Jazz said as she grabbed Devin's hand and interlaced their fingers, "you're my best friend, and I don't see why you would make any of this up…but seriously, this shit is crazy."

"You have no idea," Devin thought as relief washed through her, "I haven't even told you the craziest part…so this guy, Dr. Tran, that worked with my bio-parents, he has been following me ever since I was born, like keeping tabs on me and my life, and they saw that I was into gaming and so they thought that they would tweak my chips interface, so it interacts with me like I am…in…a video game."

Jazz's eyes went wide, "Are you freaking kidding me?" She said, "That is the coolest thing I have ever heard, like what does it do?"

Devin smiled and told Jazz about the interface, the status notifications, the unlockable skills, and all about Amy. "So ya, it's been a pretty big day." Devin said smiling.

Jazz laughed out loud at this, "Ha! That's the understatement of the year. This is without a doubt the coolest freaking thing I have ever heard. We need to go straight to this Dr. Tran guy and get me one of these chips."

Devin laughed, "Well I'm not sure it works like that…but…would you really want one?"

"Are you kidding me!? First, it makes you a superhero, like what?? And second, you've got these men in black dicks coming after you…you think I'm not gonna have your back? I'm gonna be right beside you the whole way, so it sounds like a chip would help me have the best chance for staying alive…"

Devin swallowed, "You mean, you'll stay with me?"

Jazz squeezed her hand, "Please girl, you couldn't make me leave if you tried."

Devin smiled and looked down at their hands, fingers still intertwined, and she felt like she might burst, "So…are we gonna talk about this?" She said, lifting their hands slightly.

Jazz smiled, "What is there to talk about, you're into me, I can't blame you, I'm awesome."

Devin shoved her shoulder lightly into Jazz and said, "Oh really, cause I thought it was you that kissed me back there."

"Come on now, you were clearly the aggressor. You didn't give me much of a choice."

Devin laughed, "Well that's true, so I'll give you the choice now…I want to kiss you again, really…horribly…badly…but if you just want to be friends, I am totally cool with that…I mean I don't even know if you're…."

"Into brunettes…" Jazz said playfully as she brought a hand to Devin's cheek. She leaned in and kissed her again, this time letting the kiss last a little longer. She pulled back slightly and let her head drop against Devin's, smiled and said, "I've wanted to tell you that I wanted to be more than friends for so long, but I was too afraid, I just couldn't handle the thought of you not being my friend. Before you kissed me, I was standing there trying to decide how I would greet you…a hug…a handshake…a fist bump…and then, well, I like your greeting way better."

Devin laughed, "Well, I didn't have one bit of anxiety about this meeting…"

"Ya right," Jazz said, "You looked like you were gonna throw up when I saw you standing there, I've never seen anyone so scared in my whole life."

"Ok, fine, maybe I was a little nervous," Devin said and laughed, as the two girls made their way out of the small animal exhibit and into the bright afternoon sunlight. "Maybe we should…"

Devin, I have just been pinged by two Xavier chips, men from the agency are here. I have alerted Dr. Tran and your mother, we need to move. I am pulling up a map overlay now. Avoid these men at all costs. There are too many civilians here, would you like me to activate the ECO.

"Oh shit," Devin whispered.

"What is it?" Jazz asked, her smile melting into a look of concern.

"Amy just told me that there are two agents here, we need to go." Devin looked around, trying to orient herself with the map overlay that Amy had brought up, "Ya Amy, pull up the ECO, I think we might need it."

"I know I should be scared," Jazz said, "but this is so cool!"

Devin smiled as she stood and pulled Jazz up behind her, "Stay close to me, keep your eyes peeled for anything that looks suspicious. Amy has eyes everywhere, hopefully we can just walk right out of here."

15

Amy is there any way to mask my chip from these men? Devin thought.

Unfortunately no, there is not.

Christ, how did they find us?

That is unclear, although it is possible they were already watching Jazz and simply followed her.

Shit, shit, shit! Devin thought.

Again, your statistics show no need for defecation.

And again, stop monitoring that and stop saying the word defecate, its freaking gross!

Understood. Do you prefer bowel movement?

What? No! That's just as bad, just don't talk about it. Seriously, we don't have time for this discussion right now.

Agreed. The agents are closing in on your location.

I can see that. Devin thought as she looked at her map overlay. The agents were all almost at the edges of the map and seemed to be closing in now. They were using a classic pincer movement, coming in sync from both sides, hoping to pin her between them. *Nice try morons, do you have any idea how many times I've had to avoid this move on Call of Duty,* Devin thought to herself, and was pleasantly surprised when Amy did not respond.

"Devin, what's going on, why are we just standing here?" Jazz asked looking around nervously.

"Oh, crap, sorry…I've been discussing the situation with Amy try-ing to figure out a plan, and well…we got a bit sidetracked…."

"Seriously, so cool…" Jazz said, a look of awe on her face, "but maybe not the best time to be distracted. Now would be a good time for you to go all DevinDurga on these punks…"

"If we have to, I will activate berserker mode, but I would rather not around all these people, I don't want to put anyone else in danger today. And I'll talk to Amy out loud from now on so that you know what we are talking about, I didn't think about that, sorry!"

Jazz nodded, "It's cool, I get it, you're still getting used to all of this, but remember…with great power comes great responsibility…"

Devin laughed, "Thanks Uncle Ben, now come on, follow me."

The two girls began to make their way through the crowds of people, "You focus on getting us out of here, I'll keep an eye out for creepy weirdos in dark suits." Jazz said.

"I wonder if they were dumb enough to wear suits to the zoo…and I can see their location on my HUD, they are coming in from both sides now, but we still have a little time…actually…Amy, can you show me how far away they are, how much time we have, stuff like that?"

Of course. You asked me to halt all info and updates quite some time ago or that information would already be available. I will turn all notifications back on.

Devin exhaled sharply as her senses were assaulted by information. Status notifications rolled through her vision so fast that she couldn't make any of them out. She closed her eyes and shook her head slightly, "Too much Amy, it's too much. Can you filter out anything that isn't important right now?"

How should I determine importance?

"Just get rid of anything that isn't about the other agents."

Understood. Amy said, and Devin's field of view cleared again, leaving three red dots that when focused on showed the status of each agent.

"Ok that's better, what kind of chips are we up against?" She asked.

All three appear to be Prometheus chips, although once again one of them has an identifier that I am not altogether familiar with similar to the one at your house.

"Ok, well that's good I think…Amy can you hack the camera system here at the zoo? They must have cameras everywhere?" Devin asked.

Yes, I am working on it now. Their security is very outdated, this will not take long. There are over one hundred cameras would you like a live feed of all of them?

"Jesus no, just give me any that can see the agents. Thank God there are only three to deal with…" Devin said.

Three separate video windows popped into view, and she saw that the agents were indeed still wearing their black suits. The men seemed to be trying their best, and failing, to look inconspicuous. Everyone they passed turned and stared at them, clearly feeling like something was up. *Devin, I think you should know that not all agents are chipped,* Amy said.

What the hell does that mean? Devin thought back to her, forgetting to speak out loud for Jazz to hear.

It means that there may very well be more than three men this time. You disabled the other agents quite easily, and the agency would have been watching. I find it hard to believe that they would have sent just three men again. What I am saying is there could be others.

"Well that's just great," Devin whispered.

"What's just great, what did Amy say?" Jazz asked looking concerned.

"Oh, sorry, it's so hard to remember to say everything out loud so that you know what I'm saying. Amy just told me that not all of the agents at the…agency…God that sounds stupid…are chipped, so there are probably more than three of them, and I don't have any info on the ones without chips. Sorry, I keep forgetting you can't hear Amy, I wish you could…" Devin said.

Actually, if Jazz has access to a cellular connected device and speakers or headphones, she would be able to hear me, and because I can hear anything you can hear she would also be able to talk to me, just not with her thoughts, Amy said.

"No way," Devin said and recounted the information to Jazz who reached into her pocket and pulled out her cellphone and a pair of AirPods, waving them in front of Devin's face.

"Will these work?" Jazz asked.

"I would assume so…" Devin said.

"I wasn't talking to you, I was talking to Amy," Jazz said with a laugh.

Yes, those should work. Ask her to navigate to the WIFI settings, find the WIFI address and hold the phone in front of your eyes so that I can see it. It should only be a matter of minutes for me to access what I need, and for me to make her phone secure, although once we are out of this situation, I would recommend she destroys the phone and gets a new one that would be untraceable.

Amy said.

"Got it," Devin said telling Jazz what to do. She quickly complied and while she was holding the phone up in front of Devin's face put the AirPods in her ears with the other hand. Devin laughed slightly.

"What?" Jazz asked.

"Oh come on," Devin said rolling her eyes slightly, "I've told you how dumb I think those things look."

Jazz lifted her eyebrows, "And I've told you dumb looking or not they are the best piece of tech I have ever owned, I can't believe you don't have them…"

"I'm fine sticking with good old earbuds thank you very much. Sure, the wires can be a pain, but at least it doesn't look like I left q-tips stuck in my ears."

Now it was Jazz who rolled her eyes, "Well, just be glad I have them, I can't believe I am gonna be able to hear Amy, what does she sound like?"

I sound like this. Amy said to Devin and Jazz both.

"Whoa! That's incredible," Jazz said, "Hi Amy, it's nice to meet you!"

The pleasure is all mine, sorry that I cannot kiss you like Devin did, I have no mouth and I am also not nearly as presumptuous as her.

"Amy!" Devin said as Jazz laughed, "God, you're the worst sometimes."

"Well, it was pretty presumptuous," Jazz said as she squeezed Devin's hand. "So, what do we do now?"

"Amy just gave me a feed to all of the cameras in the zoo, there are way too many to be able to look at all of them so I had her single out the ones that can see the agents. I have eyes on them now, they are still on the other side of the zoo, but they know right where I am, they can track my chip and there is nothing we can do about it, at least not right now…"

"Ok, so we need to use that to our advantage then." Jazz said.

"How?" Devin asked.

Yes, how? Amy echoed.

"Well, think about when we used to play that retro emulator online. Remember how the one time we were playing Golden Eye, and the other team was clearly looking at our screens when we respawned, and because they knew the levels so well they would just run right to where we were before we could even pick up any guns and kill us…"

"Ya…" Devin said looking confused.

"Well, how did we win?" Jazz asked.

Devin's face brightened as she understood, "I found a gun and waited around the corner after you respawned. When they came running in to kill you, I wasted them both."

"Exactly! We used their own knowledge against them, they were so blinded by the excitement of getting to me they didn't see the trap we laid for them."

"That's a great idea. Except we don't have any guns, even if we did, I seriously doubt we could shoot anyone with them in real life, and there are thousands of innocent people around, what kind of trap could we possibly set for them here?" Devin asked.

Jazz scrunched up her face in her classic thinking pose and said, "Well Christ Devin I can't think of everything. Come on, I can't be the brains, the brawn and the beauty here."

Devin smiled at this, "I think it's a good start to a plan, but for now, we need to start moving so we have time to think it through. Amy, can you overlay a map of the zoo onto my HUD, and maybe use those cameras and highlight the safest path for us to just stay ahead of these idiots for a few minutes so we can think this through."

Indeed. Amy said as the map overlay became visible. A thin red line wound its way through the zoo, zigging and zagging all over the place.

"Man, that's a messed up path…" Devin said as she began to walk forward on the path, pulling Jazz by the hand as she went.

I have routed the path to avoid all cameras, we must assume the agents also have access to those, as well as taking into consideration the current trajectory of the agents that are closing in on us. This path should give you three minutes and thirty-four seconds to formulate and enact a plan.

"Well, at least we have lots of time?" Jazz said smiling slightly.

"Ya, there's that at least. Ok, so how can we use my location to trap them, I just can't think of anything that…"

Devin stopped talking as Jazz suddenly pushed her off the sidewalk towards a concession stand, wrapping her arms around her and kissing her deeply. Devin resisted at first, not understanding what was going on but was quickly lost in the passionate embrace.

The kiss lasted for what felt like hours. Jazz slowly pulled away and the world came back into existence, and as it did Devin's mind cleared, "What the hell Jazz," she said quietly, "I mean, that was awesome but is now really the time, we have three minutes to come up with a plan."

Jazz smiled as she dropped her hands from Devin's waist, "See the guy over there in the khakis and blue polo shirt, the one that looks like he stepped out of an episode of Barbies dream house," Devin nodded as she glanced at the man, who was now walking away and Jazz continued, "He was eyeballing us hard, so I took a page from Black Widow…just like in Winter Soldier."

Devin smiled, "Public displays of affection make people very uncomfortable," she said in her best Scarlett Johansson impression, "That was quick thinking…"

Jazz gave a small mock bow. When she did Devin could just make out what she thought was the polar bear exhibit in the background and she broke into a wide smile and said, "Amy, can you access the animal enclosure systems…I have a plan…"

16

"So…what's the plan?" Jazz asked.

"Well…it's…uh…complicated. Amy, can you show me an aerial photo of the zoo? I need to see the polar bear exhibit from above to know if this has any chance of working." Devin said as she started moving through the crowd again.

The map was overlaid with a satellite image of the zoo and Devin found that if she focused on a particular area it automatically zoomed in. She found the polar bear exhibit and noted that it was not fully enclosed, the top being left open, which was all she needed to see.

"How tall are the walls in the exhibit?" Devin asked.

After doing a search of the design plans the walls vary in height, the tallest being slightly over 18 feet tall, the lowest 12 feet.

"Alright, that makes things a little tougher. God, I wish I had control of all of my powers now…or even knew what they all are…can I fly?" Devin said, and waited for a response, but Amy remained silent.

"Amy!" Devin said, speaking louder as if she were trying to wake someone up that had fallen asleep, "Didn't you hear me…can I fly?"

I'm sorry, Amy said to Devin and Jazz, *I assumed that question was rhetorical which is why I did not answer.*

"So now you know what rhetorical means?" Devin asked.

Of course. You told me to look up the definition of rhetorical. Once I found the definition, I began to work on an algorithm that would allow me to identify probable rhetorical questions, although since your question was not rhetorical it clearly needs more work.

"What are the criteria?" Devin asked, her interest causing her to momentarily lose track of the more pressing concern of the agents closing in on her.

As of now, if a question is deemed intensely personal and emotional, or patently absurd and moronic it is identified as rhetorical and ignored.

Jazz coughed out a laugh, "Damn…burn…"

Devin scowled at her playfully, "Patently absurd or moronic huh? So I'll take it you are not one of those, there are no dumb questions kind of gals?"

There are indeed many dumb questions. Your last two are good examples.

"And the hits keep coming," Jazz laughed, doing a terrible Kacey Kaysum impression.

"Oi," Devin said wincing as though she was in physical pain, "well this is something I never thought I would say to anyone, but remind me to help you work on your social skills sometime Amy."

I can set a reminder, when would like me to set it for.

"Better schedule a sarcasm session while you're at it." Jazz said.

Understood. Both reminders have been created.

Devin shook her head, "Alright, back to business, if I can't fly can I jump really high or anything like that?"

I can activate an Adrenaline rush which will greatly increase your ability to jump, how high I cannot say though.

"Well, we don't have much of a choice, we're just gonna have to go for it. How much time can I keep berserker mode going?"

With your current stamina reserves you will have 6 minutes and 15 seconds before all stamina is exhausted.

"Well crap, I was hoping to activate it now, but we better wait until I need it for sure. Jazz, we're gonna have to split up, you ok with that?" Devin said turning to Jazz.

"Split up for what?" Jazz asked.

Devin shook her head as she pulled on Jazz's hand, "No time to explain the entire plan, just trust me, it will work…just like you said, we can use the fact that they are watching us. They're cheating, so let's set a trap."

"Double oh seven…" Jazz said smiling.

"Damn right. Amy, I need you to work with Dr. Tran and mom and find a way to get the car to a road that won't be blocked by traffic, we're going to be making a quick exit if this works…"

Understood.

Devin refocused on the map overlay, tracking the position of the three chipped agents, "Ok, so the three chips are still about two and a half minutes away from us…one is up by the rhinos, one is down by the camels, and the other is over by the children's zoo area…" Devin said as she made a quick left turn, nearly running over a family that was posing for a picture in front of the lion exhibit, "Amy, can you block the chips ability to communicate with any non-chipped agents?"

Unfortunately, no I cannot.

"Shit," Devin muttered, "that's gonna pose a problem for sure, I need them cut off, once we ditch the chips I'm hoping we can just avoid everyone else, if we can't block their communication they can just follow our chip signal. How does the tracking work exactly?"

All chips send a unique, low frequency, low range identifier code only accessible by other chips, it is a way for agents to keep track of one another. The signal has a range of just under 500 yards.

"That's a pretty weak signal," Jazz said, "and it seemed like they had no idea where we were when we were in the small animal building…when we came out they were all spread out and really far away, like they only knew that we were at the zoo, and so they were searching, starting at the edge of the zoo and working their way in, just like we would in Fortnite. The point is…maybe we can block it, the walls on these buildings have to be really thick, probably reinforced with steel in most of them…"

"Jazz you're a genius!" Devin said smiling and looking at the map on her ECO, "Amy, plot a course to the African apes building, one that avoids cameras if possible." The red line on the map changed to a new course and Devin said, "Is there more than one entrance?"

The entrance and exit are beside each other in the front of the exhibit.

"Ok, great, that way they can't sneak around us, if the building is strong enough to block my signal from them, it will be more than strong enough to block theirs from me. Just to be sure, Amy can you secure the building, make it impossible to get in or out once I give the word?"

I have control over all park systems, including emergency lock down protocols. On your word I can secure the building, although if I activate the security protocol for an animal containment breech we would have to wait for several hours before we can regain access to the building.

"Ok, that definitely won't work…maybe you could trigger a fire alarm or something? Would that lock the system down?"

No, a fire alarm would not activate the breech protocol, and it would also be effective at driving visitors and employees out of the building, at which time I can simply lock the doors. I will alert you once the building is clear.

"Devin, we know there are other agents, like Ken that was giving us the eye back there...what are you gonna do about that?" Jazz asked.

Actually, I have been analyzing camera footage from all around the park and running it through a behavior analysis algorithm and believe that I have located two additional non-chipped agents. I am adding them to the ECO. I will note their positions in orange, if you focus on their locator, any camera feeds they are in will appear. I have no information on weapons that they possess, but agency SOP would have them armed with at least three firearms. Dealing with these agents will be more difficult due to our limited knowledge.

"That's where the polar bear exhibit comes in," Devin said smiling mischievously, "but first things first, we deal with the chips. Once they are locked in the building, will that disable their communications to the non-chips?"

"We need to come up with a better name than non-chips...how bout Cheetos?" Jazz said with a smile.

Why Cheetos? Amy asked them.

"Because Cheetos aren't chips," Devin said laughing, thinking back to an argument the two of them had when discussing Devin's favorite snack.

Now Jazz was laughing too, "Exactly, and because you marked them in orange Amy..."

Understood. Once the chips have been secured in the building, their communication with the Cheetos will indeed be hindered.

Hearing the A.I. refer to the agents as Cheetos had Jazz and Devin struggling to maintain any sense of composure. They fell into one other, supporting each other as they walked and laughed. It was the hysterical laughter that could only come during a moment of extreme stress, as though humor was how the brain had decided to continue to be able to process the situation.

The two girls continued to laugh as they stepped onto the bridge spanning the swan pond. Holding hands and smiling they looked to be simply enjoying a day at the zoo. *If it wasn't for the fact that these assholes are chasing us this would probably be the best day of my entire life...Devin* thought as they stepped off the bridge. She turned to look at Jazz whose eyes were wet in the corners from how hard she had been laughing and said, "Jazz, thanks for all of this…I know this gonna be dangerous…I couldn't do it without you…"

"Don't I know it," Jazz said, giving Devin's hand a squeeze, "but seriously, if you left me out of this I would have never talked to you again! This is every nerd's dream Devin, we are basically living in our own video game right now…"

Devin's face turned serious, "I know it's easy to get swept up in how cool this is, but we need to make sure we remember this is real life…there's no one-ups waiting around the corner, no respawns, no loot chests…if we mess this up, they take us in. Or worse…"

Jazz bit her bottom lip slightly, "I know Devin, don't worry, I'm taking it seriously…"

Devin saw that Jazz was indeed serious, or maybe mad, or possibly confused and thought for about the hundredth time that day that it would be really nice if Amy could figure out that facial expression software. "Ok, we need to go in that bathroom up there, I need your hoodie and your sunglasses, and I need you to wear my shirt…"

Jazz narrowed her eyes, "So I'm the bait…"

"Well…ya…" Devin said, "but only because I have the better chance of fighting them off if it comes to that, plus once they realize you aren't me maybe they will just let you go, I mean there are thousands of people around, just cause a scene…"

The ran into the bathroom and changed shirts. Devin was briefly distracted as Jazz took off her hoodie and stood in just her bra, her brown skin flawless. Devin's heart began racing.

Devin, your heart rate is dangerously high, is there something wrong? Amy asked.

Devin's face flushed bright red, and Jazz smiled and looked down at the ground, pretending that she hadn't heard Amy in her headphones as she threw Devin her hoodie, "Christ Amy," Devin muttered as she pulled Jazz's striped hoodie over her head.

She tossed Jazz her bright blue Sonic the Hedgehog shirt and stole one last glance as Jazz pulled the shirt on, spun in a circle and said, "How do I look?"

"You in that shirt is the absolute hottest thing I have ever seen," Devin said, going bright red again.

Jazz smiled as she looked in the mirror, "I do look pretty great…"

Devin checked the ECO to see the location of the agents but was shocked to see only the orange markers identifying the Cheetos. "Amy, where did the chips go?"

The signal was lost once you entered the bathroom, I am monitoring camera footage now to try and find the agents.

"Well at least we know it will work," Devin said, as she pushed the door open and walked back outside.

The second they left the building, the red dots lit back up on her display and she was shocked at how close they were now, "Jazz they are gonna be on top of us any second, you need to go…head down to the camels and zebras, the path is clear…Amy can you stay in her head once we split up?"

I can continue to communicate to Jazz, but once we enter the ape exhibit my communication with her will likely be hindered.

"That's fine, once I'm in there they will all close in on my location anyway. Amy, help Jazz get to the zebras without being seen by cameras."

Understood.

"Jazz, once you get there, wait for a couple minutes and then follow the path past the swan pond and go to the gift shop. You need to get a different shirt, as soon as the chips have lost contact, the Cheetos will be looking for that shirt. After you get the shirt, run to the bird house and go inside. Make sure you run directly underneath at least a couple of cameras. Change your shirt and leave that one under the bench in front of the…" Devin paused while she looked through info that Amy was pulling up for her about the exhibit, "the fairy bluebird. Then go find someplace to blend in where you can see the front of the polar bear exhibit and be ready to make a scene…"

Jazz blew out a breath, "This seems like a really bad plan…"

17

"Maybe, but it's the only plan we have…" Devin said.

Jazz leaned in and kissed Devin quickly, "Don't get yourself caught…"

Devin raised her eyebrows and smiled softly, "I won't, I promise…oh and I need some gum…"

Jazz reached her hand into her pocket and pulled out a pack, sliding a stick out of it and handing it too Devin, "Juicy fruit ok?"

Devin shook her head, "I don't care what flavor, but I need the whole pack."

"Alright…" Jazz said handing Devin the pack.

She grabbed it, shoved it into her pocket and said, "Thanks."

"Uhhhh…ya," Jazz said looking very confused.

"Let's do this," Devin said setting her face with determination. Jazz simply nodded and turned, heading towards the zebras, Amy in her ear telling her where to go to avoid cameras.

Devin turned her attention to the agents, who were only seconds away, closing in from all sides, and took a deep breath as she reached up to the bathroom door and ripped the sign identifying it as the woman's restroom down. She shoved the sign into the large hoodie pocket, pulled the hood up over her face, put the sunglasses on, and ran as fast as she could towards the ape exhibit.

She saw the three red dots began moving faster almost instantly. After a few seconds the orange dots began to move faster too, *apparently the chips just let the Cheetos know where I am…*she thought as all of the agents began converging on her location.

People shouted as she raced by, telling her to slow down and be careful. She chanced a look behind her and saw that four agents were only about twenty yards away, running head long towards her, knocking people in every direction. "Amy….activate… berserk…ker…mode…" Devin said through heavy breathing as she sprinted.

Done. Came the reply from Amy and Devin saw the status updates alerting her to the skill being activated. Her body flooded with adrenaline, and she felt her legs beginning to pump even faster. The fatigue she had been feeling faded as her senses all sharpened. She looked behind her again and this time was happy to see the agents were falling rapidly behind. The ape exhibit building loomed in the distance. Devin could see a large crowd of people milling around in front of the building, several of them appeared to have security uniforms on. As she approached one of the security guards began waving his arms at her, yelling for her to stop.

"Get out of the way!!" Devin yelled, and her voice was so loud that it hurt her own ears.

"Stop!" The man yelled back at her.

Sorry, was all Devin had time to think before she bowled into the man, sending him flying through the air. As they collided, Devin heard a pop and felt an intense pain flair through her shoulder.

BLUNT FORCE TRAUMA TO SHOULDER -250 HP

TOTAL HP 750/1000

HEALING SKILL ACTIVATED

HP +250

STAMINA -35

STAMINA 45/100

"Shit," Devin exhaled, "I needed that stamina for berserker mode, how much time do I have now Amy?"

Berserker mode can run for 3 minutes at current stamina reserves.

"Disable self-heal, I can't risk using any of my stamina on that right now."

Done.

God I hope this works, Devin thought as she ran full steam toward the doors to the ape building. *Open the doors,* she thought to Amy, and was impressed as the doors slid open almost immediately. Devin ran into the exhibit, pausing only briefly to survey the room. In front of her was a massive wall of glass, the main exhibit and indoor gorilla habitat. Fake trees and vines stood illuminated by the massive windows to the outside world. A small female gorilla sat close to the glass; an infant held in her lap. Devin was struck by how very human the whole scene looked, the mother staring lovingly at her child as he pulled at her hair and cooed. She approached the glass, momentarily forgetting the danger of her current situation, wanting a better look at the pair.

Devin watched as the infant gorilla turned to look at her, and tentatively reached out a small hand and placed it against the glass, trying to touch the strange hairless ape that had wondered into his home. She smiled as she placed her own hand against the glass. As she did a shadow shifted and Devin turned to see the giant male silverback stand and begin to stare her down. She instantly dropped her gaze to the floor, pulled her hand away from the glass and took two big steps backward. She had watched enough National Geographic to know that it was a bad idea to get into a stare down with a silverback.

This thought seemed to snap her back into the reality of her situation. *I was hoping it would be darker in here, and there's no place to hide, what am I supposed to do now? My plan was to lure these morons in here, hide long enough to sneak back out and then have you seal the doors, I was trying to just buy Jazz and I enough time to escape, don't tell me I'm gonna have to fight these guys...*Devin thought to Amy,

It appears as though that is your best option. They will arrive any second. I will keep the doors locked as long as I can, but they will have multiple A.M.I.I.'s working together to overpower me, it is possible I will not be able to hold them off for long, Amy said, *although I could activate the safety protocol for an animal enclosure failure.*

You mentioned that earlier, what would that do? Devin asked.

Three-inch-thick steel blast doors would drop down over all doors and windows, and the system can only be over ridden through the control room and takes over an hour to reset and unseal the blast doors. It's a safety precaution in the event of the gorilla enclosure being compromised.

Interesting, but no good, Devin thought, *if the doors can't be unsealed I'll be stuck in here for at least an hour, and those assholes will be out there...with Jazz...that won't work.*

Understood.

Devin frantically searched the area, looking for a place that she could gain some sort of advantage, but she saw nothing. There was a bench that she could try to hide under, but that would leave her too vulnerable to the chips once they spotted her...*No, hiding really isn't an option anyway. Jazz is out there by herself, I'm almost out of stamina, and it's gonna take at least 2 minutes to finish this plan...I'm screwed, berserker mode can't last that long,* she thought to herself as she looked at her stamina gauge, watching the gauge slowly drop lower and lower. *Screw this, Amy open the damn doors, let's just kick some ass.*

Understood, Amy said, opening the doors in 5, 4, 3...

Devin listened to the countdown timer and tried desperately to slow her breathing. She looked at the doors to the exhibit and could just make out the men on the other side of them, it appeared as though all of them were drawing weapons. *Amy wait, hold them off a little longer, I have a plan, I don't need to fight them, I just need a distraction big enough to draw their attention and I'll sneak out and then you drop those blast doors the second I am outside,* she thought as she ran towards the enclosure, running right up to the mother and infant Devin shook her head and whispered, "Sorry about this," as she brought up a hand and smacked it violently against the glass.

With berserker mode enabled the slap was much harder than she had intended, the boom echoing through the empty exhibit. "Ouch!" she yelled as she rubbed her hand and watched the damage notification pop into view. *Damn I wish I could use self-heal,* she thought to herself, and was surprised at just how quickly she had grown accustomed to her new powers. This lingering pain seemed almost foreign to her now.

The silverback stood and exhaled loudly through his nose, staring at Devin, taking in this new threat to his troop. This time Devin did not avert her eyes or back away, instead she stared directly into the eyes of the silverback, throwing her hands up, making herself as big and threatening as she could. The gorilla began to respond, he raised his own powerful arms above his head and brought his giant fists slamming back down to the earth. He turned and walked a few steps away from the window. Devin began to back towards the door of the exhibit, and watched as he began to pace back and forth, clearly agitated. She took her position directly to the right side of the main entrance doors to the exhibit and took a deep breath, *Amy, open the doors now.*

The doors slid open and the men all came rushing forward, guns out and yelling. This flurry of movement was too much for the already agitated silverback to handle and he charged the glass at the front of the exhibit, exploding in a ferocious display of unbridled rage and power. He ran faster than Devin had imagined possible and at the last minute leapt and slammed both of his huge, meaty fists against the glass. The sound was explosive as the glass spider-webbed out from the blow. The agents all stood transfixed as Devin slid behind them and out the door, *Drop the blast doors Amy*, she thought as she slipped out of the doorway.

As Devin turned to leave, several things happened at the same time. The alarm from the security breech screamed to life, the blast doors began to slide down from the ceiling, and a hand closed around Devin's arm. She turned to see one of the agents, and recognized the man from her house sneering at her through the doorway as he held her right arm in a vice like grip. She tried to pull away put his grip was too strong. Panic began to set in as Devin raised her left arm and tried to slam her elbow down onto the man's arm, but it had little effect…she just couldn't get the right leverage. The blast doors were closing as the agent tried to pull Devin into the building. Devin struck his arm again and tried desperately to pull away, but the man was otherworldly strong…*What kind of chip does this asshat have?* She thought.

This is the unidentifiable chip, but I would assume that it has increased his strength as you seem, even with Berserker mode active, unable to break away.

Devin's shoes scraped across the sidewalk as the giant agent continued to pull, and she felt her stomach lurch as she realized that she was now directly below the rapidly closing blast doors. The man smiled again, giving her a look that seemed to say, "In or out, either way you're dead kid."

Devin felt a rage boiling inside of her and focused all of her energy into a knee strike aimed directly at the man's mid-section. She connected and felt what she thought might have been a rib cracking. A quiet "oof" sound escaped from the man's lips and he closed his eyes in pain and stumbled a step backwards. As he did Devin dropped to the ground and using his own momentum against him, executed a perfect front leg sweep. The agent fell forward towards Devin, still clutching her arm in his iron grip, but his movement forward was all that she needed as she scrambled back out of the exit door. His arm was now stretched out across the doorway and Devin watched in horror as the blast door continued to close, crushing his forearm and severing his hand. Just before the door closed completely Devin heard a muffled scream of pain and then the pressure on her arm released and the hand fell, unattached, to the sidewalk. A pool of blood growing around it.

I think I'm going to be sick, Devin thought.

Agreed, your vital signs indicate that you are not currently well.

Not currently well, Jesus Amy, that dude's hand just got cut off while he was holding on to my arm, how am I supposed to be feeling about that?

Relief seems an obvious choice. Your plan worked. Amy said.

Devin thought about this for a moment, *Well…that was in no way my plan…but I suppose you're right…we did get away, speaking of…can I talk to Jazz?*

You cannot communicate directly with thoughts with her because she is not chipped, but if you speak out loud I can give her access to my audio feeds and if she speaks out loud I can transfer the audio from her AirPods to you.

"Hey Jazz, you ok?" Devin said quietly as she began to walk towards the other side of the zoo.

"Devin, thank God. Ya I'm fine, no sign of any Cheetos here. I just stashed the shirt and I'm stationed outside the polar bear exhibit. What's happening now?"

"Now," Devin said, "we hope that I can finish this damn plan before I run out of stamina…"

18

Devin your stamina has dropped below 30%, you need fuel right away to be able to maintain berserker mode. Amy said in Devin's mind.

"I know Amy, but I didn't bring any of the gel stuff with me, I didn't think that we would be fighting our way out of here…" Devin said out loud so that Jazz could hear her response.

Any calorie source will help to replenish your stamina. The energy gel that the agency created does work the most efficiently, but anything that you can find will help.

"Christ, why didn't I think of that," Devin said shaking her head, "All I need is food…there has to be lots of food places here at the zoo…can you show me a map?"

*It would appear that the…*Amy paused seeming to search for the right word, and Devin couldn't help but think that seemed like a very human thing to do, *situation at the ape exhibit has caused a shutdown of the services in this area, although at the moment it does not appear that they have closed the zoo, so there may be food available in other areas.*

"Nothing's ever easy," Devin whispered.

"Not with you it isn't," she heard Jazz say with a soft chuckle.

Devin scanned the area, and for the first time since leaving the ape exhibit she noticed all of the information that was flooding into her HUD. The orange dots indicating the Cheetos had all congregated around the birdhouse and Devin briefly turned her attention to the vid windows that showed exactly where each of the three men were. One man was positioned at the entrance and exit of the building, the third man was sitting on a bench, trying and failing to look casual as he stared at the bird house. *Well, at least it seems like it worked, they think I'm still in there,* Devin thought, *Amy can you use the camera feeds to find the nearest source of food and throw it on my HUD?*

The information began updating with no response from Amy. Devin stared as small red food icons popped up all over her HUD, but she didn't see anything in the direction that she needed to go. "Crap," Devin muttered, "It's no good, I'm just gonna have to try to make this work without fueling up. Jazz, we're heading your way now, be ready!"

"Oh, I'm ready, how long do you think this will take?" Jazz asked.

Devin thought about it for a moment, trying to make all of the mental calculations but before she could come up with a number to tell Jazz her HUD updated and a small countdown clock appeared beside a course that now glowed red across the map overlay, "Well, Amy seems to think it's gonna take two minutes and twelve seconds, which is good because as of right now I don't have much stamina left."

"Be careful Devin, please…" Jazz said quietly.

"Oh ya, you know me Jazz…"

"Ya…I do…that's why I thought it was necessary to say…"

Devin shook her head with a small smile and began to run, following the course that Amy had set. She had to ignore the shoots from people as she flew past them, and more than once she misjudged how fast she was going and ran into someone hard enough to send them sprawling and cause herself considerable. Each of those times she was saddened to see her stamina gauge drop slightly as the notifications that she had sustained damage rolled in. She was less than 30 seconds away now but was blocked from the view of the Cheetos by the large carousel that sat in the center of the path ahead.

Devin it is advisable that you slow down now, to conserve stamina and also to not raise the suspicions of the Cheetos that are monitoring the birdhouse, Amy said.

"Got it," Devin said as she stopped running and tried to slow her breathing. She scanned the area for anything that looked out of place, the last thing she needed now was to be caught off guard by some agent that they had missed, but nothing seemed off to her. Everywhere she looked she saw the same happy people just enjoying their day at the zoo. Couples holding hands, kids running and laughing, moms and dads pushing strollers, babies eating hot dogs and cotton candy…she rolled her eyes as the thought sunk in and shaking her head she approached the woman pushing the stroller where the small girl sat taking large bites of light blue cotton candy from the giant ball of spun sugar.

The woman was looking down at her cell phone and didn't seem to notice as Devin approached, *Thank god for the age of constant distraction*, Devin thought as she stepped up beside the stroller.

"Hi," the little girl said with the kind of smile only a child can muster for a complete stranger.

Devin smiled back awkwardly and bent down to the little girl's level, "Hi, I was wondering if I could have some of your cotton candy?"

In an instant the smile was gone as the little girl pulled back from Devin and yelled, "No! It's mine, no!!!"

"Shhh," Devin said but it was too late, the girl's mother had been pulled back to reality by the scream of her daughter.

"Honey what's wrong, why are you...." But the mother stopped talking and took a step back as she looked Devin up and down, "can I help you with something?"

Devin thought the woman looked more fearful than she should of a teenage girl, but then again for all Devin knew the look was one of confusion, or happiness, or god only knew what. Devin looked down at herself and was shocked to see that there was a considerable amount of blood on Jazz's hoodie from when the agent lost his hand. Devin sighed and shook her head, "Sorry, but there's just no time to explain any of this…" and with that she reached down and snatched the cotton candy from the little girl and turned and walked away, shoving handfuls of the stuff into her mouth.

The woman was too shocked to do much of anything as Devin walked away, hearing the small girl screaming at her as she tried to blend into the passing crowds. "What is going on over there?" Jazz asked, "No time to explain what? And what's with all the screaming?"

Devin just stole candy from a baby, Amy said.

"What the hell?" Jazz said.

Devin laughed, "Well, I asked her to share first. I just need stamina, or we aren't getting out of here…I'm sure the kids mom will get her more…"

"Jesus Devin," Jazz said with a laugh, "did it work at least?"

Devin looked up and was happy to see that her stamina gauge had indeed increased. It now sat just over 35% and she had only managed to eat about half of the cotton candy so far. She shoved a large handful of cotton candy in her mouth and said, "Seems to be working, I think we'll have enough to get out of here! Also, on a side note, taking candy from a baby is every bit as easy as they make it sound."

Devin heard Jazz snort with laughter and smiled at the familiar sound. One of her very favorite things to do when they gamed together was to really get Jazz laughing, there wasn't a sound on earth that Devin loved hearing more than when Jazz really and truly laughed, and when she snorted Devin knew that she had really gotten her. *Devin you are approaching the first agent, it does not appear that he has noticed you yet,* Amy said.

"Got it, Jazz I'm gonna stop talking out loud and communicate directly with Amy until this is over, I don't want to risk my talking bringing their attention. Hold tight, I'll be there soon."

"You better be," Jazz said.

Devin smiled as she walked forward, shoving another handful of cotton candy into her mouth as she walked directly in front of the first agent.

The man was still sitting on the bench, his eyes nervously darting around. It took all of her resolve not to just sprint past the man, but for this to work she needed to get inside that building before they spotted her. At this point everything was working just how Devin had planned. After she and Jazz had changed shirts they had been careful to avoid all of the cameras before Devin went into the ape exhibit. Devin knew that someone was working alongside of all of these agents, monitoring cameras, just like Amy was, and so she assumed that those people were in radio contact with the Cheetos and the chips. Once the chips had entered the ape exhibit, they would have lost radio contact with the Cheetos and with their off-site team, so they would have had no way of informing them that Devin was no longer wearing the same shirt, and with the lockdown Devin knew they were still out of communication.

When Jazz, in Devin's bright blue Sonic shirt, walked past the camera in front of the bird house, the agents had been alerted and had positioned themselves outside, waiting for her to come back out. Since Jazz had changed shirts inside, she was able to walk right past them on her way to the polar exhibit, just as Devin was able to walk right past them now on her way into the exhibit.

Once inside she was pleasantly surprised by the lack of people in the exhibit. *I guess bird watching isn't a very big draw, thank god,* she thought to herself as she spotted the shirt shoved under the bench. She smiled as she walked over to retrieve it, glancing around nervously she quickly pulled off the hoodie she had borrowed from Jazz and pulled the familiar blue sonic shirt over her head. Walking to the exit door she took a deep breath and checked her stats in the HUD.

The cotton candy had given her a little breathing room on stamina, but it was still just over 30%, and burning more every second that berserker mode stayed active. *Amy, are we gonna be able to make this work?* She thought.

Devin I am still not entirely sure what you have planned, so that is a question I cannot answer with any authority.

Just say yes would ya? Devin thought.

Yes. Amy answered.

Devin put her hand on the door and took a deep breath as she started to push it open and thought, *I hope you're right.*

19

Devin prepared to push the door open but paused for a moment, *Amy…this entire plan hinges on you being able to unlock the back service door to the polar bear exhibit, are you ready for that?* She thought to Amy.

Yes Devin, I have access to all of the animal enclosure systems, as well as park security systems. On your word I will unlock the door.

Ok great, how far away is the polar bear exhibit once I open the door?

In response a map laid itself over Devin's vision, three routes highlighted in different colors, each starting from the bird exhibit and ending at the service door to the polar bear exhibit. The shortest of the three routes was just over 300 yards, the longest just over 700. Devin had no idea what the best choice was. *Amy, remove any courses that don't pass in range of a security camera, I need the agency to see me and tell the Cheetos where I'm going.*

Devin watched as the longest path faded away. *Alright,* she thought, *I don't want to take the shortest path, I'm worried I won't be able to get enough ahead of them, so get rid of that one too and then I think we're ready.*

The other path faded away leaving only one path, highlighted in yellow across her field of vision. The distance read 563 yards. *How fast do you think I can run that with Berserker mode active?*

According to how fast you ran to the ape exhibit and then to here it should take you 33 seconds.

Holy shit, I'm that fast?

Indeed.

Alright then I should have no problem getting ahead of these guys, now I just need to get past them without engaging them in a fight, and then get myself spotted by the camera.

May I suggest you put back on the hoodie from Jazz to avoid being seen by the agents outside? Amy asked.

Christ Devin, what the hell is wrong with you? Devin thought to herself.

At the present moment the answer to that may be schizophrenia, as this often manifests with self-dialogue, Amy answered.

Can it Amy, Devin thought shaking her head as she walked back over to the bench and picked up the hoodie she had just taken off. Pulling it over her head she heard something hit the ground and saw the bathroom sign she had ripped down laying by her feet.

Jesus, I almost blew the whole plan, thank god you're here Amy.

I am always here, as I am implanted in your brain, but you are welcome.

Devin smiled and picked the small plastic sign up, placing it back into the large pocket in the front of the hoodie. She grabbed the pack of gum that Jazz had given her and quickly shoved all four pieces into her mouth, taking care to put the gum wrappers in her pocket and not throw them on the ground. Even being hunted by a shadowy government agency was no reason to litter after all. Then steeling herself, she pushed open the door and stepped out of the bird exhibit and into the blinding sunlight, well she knew the sunlight would have been blinding if Amy wasn't monitoring all of her senses and recalibrating the information her eyes were seeing, and thank god she was because had Devin even been blinded for a few seconds from the change in brightness she would have ran right into the agent manning the exit door. As it was, she narrowly avoided colliding with him and slipped past. *That was close,* she thought to Amy, *let me know as soon as they can't see me anymore, we better hurry.*

Indeed, at the rate you are burning through your stamina reserves you have three minutes until you are completely expended.

And exactly what happens then?

And that point non-essential systems begin going offline, starting with all of your chip sets. The chips require significant energy to run, so once you run out of energy they must shut down.

Got it. Well that's definitely not an option. If the chips turn off and I lose my powers we are as good as dead, especially with this crazy-ass plan.

Then I would suggest finalizing this plan in less than two minutes. Also, you are out of sight range of the agents now.

Devin noted a small countdown timer appear in the upper right-hand corner of her HUD ticking town from two minutes. If the plan worked out she would still have a minute to spare she thought as she began to sprint towards the polar bear house. Glancing at the map she saw that she was approaching the only camera on the route. She pulled the sign from the hoodie pocket and then slowing down only slightly she pulled the hoodie off and throw it behind her as she sprinted past the camera.

She noted that the three orange dots marking the positions of the agents outside the bird exhibit all began closing on her location. *Alright they went for it,* Devin thought as she closed in on the service door to the polar bear exhibit. Glancing at the distance marker she saw that she was only fifty-four yards from the door and would be there in about five seconds. This new speed would take some getting used to. *Unlock the door Amy, and leave it unlocked,* Devin thought as she raced towards the door.

She skidded to a halt as she pulled the wad of gum from her mouth and stuck it to the center of the bathroom sign, slamming it up against the service door as she simultaneously pulled the door open and slipped inside. She had expected to be inside of a corridor of some type, thinking this would lead the zookeepers through some tunnels or indoor animal enclosures. Instead, she found herself standing in the back corner of the polar bear exhibit itself. One of the giant white bears lay, presumably sleeping, about twenty feet from where she now stood.

According to the information she had seen on the map there were three bears altogether, one adult male, one adult female, and one juvenile female. She didn't see the other two bears anywhere and hoped that they too were asleep. Slowly she crept her way forward. This part of the exhibit wouldn't work for her plan, which was to trap the agents inside the exhibit as she used an adrenaline rush to try and jump the fourteen feet it would take to breech the wall at its lowest point, which just so happened to be on the opposite side of the enclosure, and to get there she had to cross within about five feet of the sleeping bear.

Devin heard a few screams from outside of the exhibit and knew that some of the people watching the attraction must have been shocked to see a young girl come bursting into the habitat. She knew that polar bears were notoriously aggressive and so she hoped that this bear would remain asleep, even with berserker mode she knew she didn't stand a chance against these giants. *I really wish I had self-heal right about now,* she thought to herself.

Would you like me to reactivate self-heal? Amy asked.

If I get hurt and don't have the stamina and energy requirements to self-heal didn't you say I would die?

Yes that is indeed what would happen if your injury were greater than your reserves and self-heal was enabled.

I gotta say, that seems like a pretty terrible design, but no don't turn it on, I can't risk it.

Devin took another step forward and exhaled as quietly as she could. It felt like she had been in the enclosure for about ten minutes, but she knew that she had entered just seconds ago. She risked looking at the map and was shocked to see the orange dots right on top of her. She glanced over her shoulder expecting to see the agents standing inside the door but there was no one there. *Maybe they're too afraid to come into the girls bathroom?* She thought. A loud growl brought her attention back to giant bear that was just feet away.

Devin watched in horror as the bear that had been sleeping beside her opened its mouth and gave a razor-tooth filled yawn that made it seem as though the bear could fit the entirety of Devin's body into its gaping maw. The bear was still groggy as it lazily licked its lips and squirmed its massive shoulders against the ground, apparently stretching as it woke up. Devin heard a noise behind her and knew that the agents had just opened the door. *It's now or never,* she thought as she looked back at the bear and her stomach dropped.

Two large, and impossibly dark brown eyes stared at her from mere feet away. The bear seemed every bit as shocked as Devin did, although it was quicker to recover, standing and stretching to its full height and roaring at Devin. The sound was echoed as two other, larger bears ambled in from behind a rock outcropping. *Jesus this one is the baby,* Devin thought as she turned to see that two agents had indeed entered the exhibit. They both stood, pistols held firmly in front of them, eyes darting from Devin to the bears and back to Devin again. One of the agents, without taking his eyes off of the bears, reached his hand back and tried to find the door handle. *Amy, lock the exhibit, they can't get out.*

Done.

Good, any ideas of what the hell I should do?

According to multiple resources the only thing that you can do is do not act like prey. Polar bears are not easily scared but you have to try to use intimidation.

Great, intimidate the largest bear on the planet, should be no problem, Devin thought as she heard the man behind her trying the door handle but she was too afraid to take her eyes from the young bear, who seemed to be getting over her sense of shock at finding an intruder in her home and was dropping back to the ground, her eyes still trained on Devin.

"Come on kid," one of the agents said quietly, "open the damn door or we all die, why the hell would you lock us all in here together…"

Hearing the man's voice spurred Devin into action. Throwing her arms up over her head she ran directly at the juvenile bear screaming with all of her might as she did. *Now would be a good time to give me that adrenaline boost,* she thought to Amy, and instantly felt the adrenaline rush into her system. Her scream intensified as she flailed her arms and she saw to her surprise that it seemed to be working. The juvenile bear had retreated several steps. Unfortunately, the adult bears were not as easily cowed and seemed to be drawn to the small girl waving her arms frantically as the largest bear, the one Devin assumed was the male, began to run towards her.

Alarms were now going off in her HUD as her stamina fell to a critically low level, but she continued her rush towards the lowest point of the wall. She was well past the juvenile bear now and could hear the men making loud threats, apparently hoping to do the same thing Devin had just done. She chanced a look towards the adult male and saw that he was running right at her and if she was being honest it was the absolute most terrifying thing she had ever witnessed. Luckily for her the adrenaline had considerably numbed her fear, otherwise she would have been completely paralyzed by fear at this point.

She saw that the bear would intercept her well before she reached the fourteen-foot section of wall, but she kept sprinting forward. *Devin, at this rate he will overtake you before you can make it to a section of wall that you have the ability to jump over, if you have the ability to jump over any of these sections of wall.* Amy said, starting Devin.

I'm all ears if you have any other suggestions, Devin thought.

When there was no response from Amy Devin whispered, "Ya that's what I thought," as she ran right at the bear. She looked at the wall at the point where the two of them would meet and guessed it was around sixteen feet high. Higher than Amy had estimated her ability to jump, but as close to the fourteen foot as she was gonna get. She ran, staring directly at the bear, who ran with surprising speed for an animal that was so large. At the rate they were both running they would collide any second, but just before the two ran headlong into one another Devin jumped, aiming directly for the bear's giant head, which stood at least four feet off the ground, even while he had it tucked down as he ran. Devin felt her shoe connect with the beast's skull and pushed off with everything inside of her, launching herself towards the wall.

The extra height from the bear seemed to be all she needed because she hit the top of the wall about mid stomach, momentarily knocking the wind out of her as her hands scrabbled for purchase. The fake rock of the exhibit was slippery with no natural hand holds but fear and adrenaline kept Devin from losing her grip. She heard several more screams from the gathering crowds and then a voice cut through the growing din, "Come on Devin, quit messing around and get down here!" Jazz shouted up at her.

Devin looked down and saw Jazz right below her, holding her hands up as if she planned on catching Devin like a toddler about to jump into a pool for the first time. Devin smiled and finally allowed herself to breathe a sigh of relief as she pulled herself the rest of the way on top of the wall, and then swung her legs over the top and dropped down the other side. She hit the ground hard, and a litany of alerts popped up in her HUD, all saying basically the same thing; your stamina is gone, your health is gone, you are screwed.

Devin pushed them aside with her mind and looked up to see Jazz standing, smiling down at her with a hand extended. Devin grabbed her hand and Jazz pulled her to her feet, "Jesus Devin, that was the most insane thing I have ever seen."

Devin smiled, "That's just a normal Tuesday for me..."

"Well, it's Thursday," Jazz said as she wrapped Devin up in a hug.

Devin smiled and was about to say some smart-ass thing to Jazz when she felt a hand grab tightly onto her shoulder. She spun to see the last remaining agent staring angrily at her. "You little bitch," he hissed, "you just got my friends killed, there's no way they are gonna make it out of there alive. You better hope…" but the man's words were cut off as a fist connected with his nose, shattering it and dropping the man to his knees as blood sprayed out. Before Devin even had time to react Jazz grabbed the back of the man's head and with all her might slammed her knee into his already destroyed nose.

The agent fell back, unconscious, *Or dead,* Devin thought, and she turned back to look at Jazz, who was staring down at the man. "No one calls my girl a bitch you asshole," she spat through gritted teeth, "now let's get the hell out of here…and to think, I used to love this zoo."

Devin smiled and grabbed Jazz's hand and turned to leave, almost losing her balance, feeling more lightheaded with every step. "I need to get something to eat. My stamina is almost gone, and I think the drop from that wall might have broken my ankle, and I can't self-heal until I get some energy back."

Jazz grabbed Devin's arm and threw it over her shoulder, "Just lean on me, when you're not strong…"

"Jazz I swear to god if you start singing I'll hobble back to the car all by myself…"

"Oh come on, you didn't even let me get to the we be jammin part…"

Devin smiled and leaned her weight more on Jazz, "Just get me to the car and you can sing whatever you want…"

20

Devin breathed a sigh of relief as she felt the self-healing function kick in, the pain in her ankle dissipating instantly. She glanced around the interior of the car and smiled as she watched Jazz, her mom, and Dr. Tran all talking excitedly about what had happened in the zoo. Amy filled them in through the car speakers on any details that Jazz wasn't certain of. Devin had been in bad shape by the time she and Jazz had reached the car, her stamina had been completely depleted and her ankle was most definitely broken, but five tubes of that disgusting gel later and she was finally feeling like a brand-new person.

She brought her attention to her HUD and a string of notifications popped up. Devin half-heartedly read over them, noticing with some interest that many of her key attributes had increased from the fight at the zoo.

QUEST UPDATE
    *GO TO LINCOLN PARK ZOO - COMPLETE
    *MEET JAZZ - COMPLETE
      REWARDS
      *CHARISMA +15
      *RENOWN +5
  SIDE QUEST INITIATED - ESCAPE OR ENGAGE ENEMY AGENTS - QUEST COMPLETE
      REWARD

> *STRENGTH +5
> *WISDOM +5
> *STAMINA +2
> LEVEL UP!
> *AMII SKILL NOW LEVEL 5
> *BERSERKER SKILL NOW LEVEL 4
> *SELF-HEAL NOW LEVEL 6
> *HAND TO HAND COMBAT NOW LEVEL 17
> JOB LEVEL UP!
> *NOW LEVEL 3 WARRIOR
> *NEW SKILLS AVAILABLE

"And the guy's hand got cut off completely, holy shit Devin, that must have been so crazy…" Jazz said and paused while she waited for Devin to respond, "…Devin…"

"Oh, sorry Jazz, I didn't hear you, I was looking at all of the status updates I just got…what did you say?"

"Amy was just telling us about the chip that *gave* you a hand back in the zoo…" Jazz said with a smile.

"Oh, that. Ya, that was without a doubt the most disgusting thing I have ever seen…" Devin said.

"Well forget that," Jazz said excitedly, "What are these status updates all about?"

"Status updates?" Mary asked.

"Ya mom, basically it's exactly like a video game, like it's really uncanny how well you guys were able to tweak the interface and make it seem like a really good rpg, I mean the detail is pretty astonishing."

"Well," Dr. Tran said looking a little sheepish, "All we actually did was ask the AMII if it could reprogram the interface to mimic a video game, it did the rest…"

"*She* did the rest," Devin corrected, "And Amy, that's incredible! You did an amazing job…"

"Thank you Devin," Amy said through the car speakers, "I simply used all of the data that I had available on your gaming habits and tried to utilize a format that was similar to the games you played the most."

"Well it's really cool…anyway, status updates pop up all throughout the game telling you about different quests you can go on, the status of the quests you've already been assigned, your health and stamina, anytime you take damage or gain experience, when you level up or gain access to new skills…" Devin said.

"New skills…like what?" Mary asked.

Devin thought about this for a moment, "Well, actually I have no idea. So far I've unlocked the heat vision skill and the berserker mode skill, but both of those just popped up and said new skill unlocked…I just saw that my base job leveled up after the zoo and because of that I have access to new skills, but it doesn't say what they are…Amy, can you tell me what the new skills are?"

"Actually," Dr. Tran said before Amy had time to speak, "I think maybe you should wait and go over all of that with…Amy…when you get to our facilities. We are dealing with an entirely unknown process here…"

Mary cut him off, "Entirely unknown," she accused, "I thought you had been doing this for years…"

Dr. Tran squirmed a little, "Well, we have…but never before have we had a Phoenix chipset to work with, and we honestly have no idea just what we are dealing with…not to mention that we also have never given interface control over to an AMII and so these unlockable levels and new skills are something I am not familiar with."

Everyone in the car seemed to consider this silently and then Jazz spoke, "Well, I get that you don't know anything about what's going on with Devin, but I have a question…"

"Yes?" Dr. Tran said.

"When can I get one…" Jazz said.

Dr. Tran blinked, looking confused, "Get…one…what?"

Jazz exhaled sharply, not quite a laugh but in the vicinity and said, "One what…come one man…a freaking chip!"

Dr. Tran began shaking his head firmly, "Absolutely not…no…there is no way that you are getting a chip…"

"Why not?" Jazz asked.

"Well, for one you aren't even eighteen years old…you can't make this kind of decision until you are an adult."

"I am a legally recognized adult according to emancipation papers I have…next?"

"Well…next…it's just too dangerous…and there's no point…why in the world would we put a chip in you?" Dr. Tran said, sounding almost frantic.

"No point!" Jazz said, getting louder, "How about the fact that you assholes put a bunch of experimental tech into my best friends head when she was a baby, and now the people that you work for are trying *TO KILL HER!!!*"

Devin reached out and grabbed Jazz's hand, "It's ok, I don't want you to get one, it's too dangerous Jazz, plus you've seen what I can do already…can you imagine how unbelievably bad ass this will be once I actually learn how all of this works."

"Uh…ya…that's why I want one! You think I want to leave all the fun to you? Plus…who the hell else is gonna have your back…this guy?" Jazz said wrinkling her nose and tilting her head towards Dr. Tran.

"She has a point…" Mary said.

"Mom!" Devin shouted, "You're supposed to be on my side!"

"I am on your side Devin, but Amy told us how Jazz handled that man inside the zoo, and your plan couldn't have worked without her…you would have been taken or worse…and she is an adult…"

"I can't freaking believe this…there is no way I am letting you do this Jazz…" Devin said looking around at everyone like they had all lost their minds, "You are not getting a chip just to try and protect me! Plus who knows if they even could do it…"

All eyes turned to Dr. Tran who looked more uncomfortable by the minute, "Well…there are a few tests that we would need to run, but assuming she passed those there is no technical reason that we could not perform the surgery, but I am still with Devin, the surgery has a…substantial risk of failure."

"How substantial?" Jazz asked.

"Well, it's gotten better over the past few years, but we still lose around 45% of the people that go through the surgery…"

"This. Is. Insane." Devin said forcefully, "We are not talking about this anymore."

"You're right Devin, we aren't," Jazz said and Devin breathed a sigh of relief, "Because I'm doing it, like it or not when you guys decided to come and pick me up you put me in the middle of it, and the best chance I have to survive is to get a chip just like Devin's…and that just so happens to also be what will give you the best chance to survive…"

Dr. Tran swallowed, "I had not thought of it that way…you're right…we involved you and if you are willing to take the risk you deserve the best chance possible to protect yourself. We can talk to Kevin when we get to the farm, but as long as you pass the tests there is no reason we can't get you a chip. You won't, however, be able to get a chip like Devin's. I can assure you that. We don't even know how Devin's chip works, and our failure rate when trying to put more than one chip into a person is 100%. No one…other than Devin…has ever survived it. You would have to select one chip, that's the only way it can work."

"Jazz, if something happens to you…I would never be able to live with myself…" Devin said quietly.

"And the same goes for me Devin, that's why I need to do it…plus do you honestly expect me to sit this out…I mean this is the coolest thing that has ever happened to either of us…"

Devin's shoulders slumped and she rolled her eyes, "Well, it sounds like you're doing it whether I like it or not…"

"Damn right, now there's just one question…" Jazz said as she looked up at Devin.

"And that is?" Devin asked.

Jazz smiled and answered, "What kind of chip do I want…"

21

"Devin…Devin…you need to wake up…"

The frantic voice faded into Devin's reality, but she desperately struggled to push it away. *I don't want to wake up,* she thought as she squeezed her eyes tightly shut and tried to hold on to the amazing dream that she was having, *this dream is way too good to wake up from just to go to school…*

This is not a dream, Amy said to her inside her mind, *your mother needs to speak with you, it's about your father.*

It was like someone had poured cold water onto her and she was instantly awake. *Holy shit, this is all real…Amy… what does she want to tell me?*

I cannot say, I have not yet been informed of all of the details, I only know that it is important and that it is about your father.

"What is it mom?" Devin said, her voice still scratchy with sleep. She tried to sit up but found it nearly impossible to do without waking Jazz up, who was sleeping soundly with her head on Devin's shoulder.

"The men that Dr. Tran sent to pick up your father never made it back, and neither did he." Mary said as evenly as she could, struggling to reign in her emotion.

"What do you mean he 'never made it back'?" Devin asked.

"I am sure that he is fine Devin, they wouldn't risk hurting him, they need him to get to you." Dr. Tran stated.

"Comforting…," Devin said, glaring at Dr. Tran, "Where the hell is he?"

"Devin, honey, this isn't Dr. Tran's fault..." Mary started to say but Devin quickly interrupted.

"Not his fault, are you kidding me! This is all his fault. So they want to trade me for dad, when and where?"

"Devin, we can't trade you for your father, that isn't how this works. We are your parents, it's our job to protect you, not the other way around." Mary said.

"Well mom, I don't know if you saw what happened at the house, or the zoo, but I don't really need much protecting..."

"That is true Devin," Dr. Tran said, "but let me remind you that you barely escaped the zoo with your life, and if they had sent more agents you would not have made it. You can't expect to just fight your way out if you try and rescue your father. There will be others there that have gone through the program."

"So you know where he is?" Devin asked.

"Well not exactly, we have a good idea of where to start, but I am certain that they will let us know where he is being held sometime soon. They will want to entice you in to action."

"They'll be sorry that they did that once I find them. I don't want to wait, head to where you think is a good starting place and we can go from there..." Devin said.

"Devin, honey," Mary said, "Dr. Tran and I have been discussing it and we both think that we shouldn't even attempt to go after your father right now...there's just too much at stake. I think we have to trust that the people that..."

"That what...killed hundreds of people just for the sake of some stupid science experiment? The people who had a baby and then shoved a bunch of stuff into her head that, by their own account, had no idea what it would do? Or do you mean the people who showed up to our house today, leading a group of mercenaries along with them that have tried to kill me, not once, but twice...are those the people that you think we should trust mom..." Devin said, seething.

Mary fell silent and looked down at her hands in her lap. A tear welled up in the corner of her eye and she inhaled a shuddering breath. Dr. Tran looked awkwardly between the two women and then shifted his gaze to the floor before speaking in barely more than a whisper, "I know that we have done nothing to earn your trust Devin, and the mistakes that we have made in the past can never be corrected…but right now…with you…I am trying to do the right thing. Kevin and I left the agency years ago because we understood how wrong what we had been doing was. We have spent the last several years trying to right those wrongs, trying to put an end to the agency…"

"Ya by putting more people at risk for the name of your little experiment…" Devin interjected.

Dr. Tran shook his head, and his voice became slightly stronger, "No. Not for the sake of the experiment. We were no longer doing things to see if we could. Kevin and I have continued our work so that we could have a way to combat the agency. You see…we know their end goals, because at one time they were our goals too," he paused, collecting his thoughts, "This can all wait for another time. You are right Devin, you have absolutely no reason to trust me, or anyone that works with me. Someday I hope to earn your trust, but for now that will just have to wait. I helped enact the plan that allowed Maxine to put the Phoenix chipset inside of you, I had no idea that was her plan, but I helped develop all of that tech. That was done without your consent, you didn't have a choice. I came to your house today to warn you, I knew that the agency was about to make their move and I hoped that I could arrive with enough time to convince you to leave before they got there, but in doing so, you may be right, I may have led them right to you…and so you had to fight your way out… to save yourself, your mother, and me. And again, you didn't have a choice. It is time that you are allowed to make your own choice. I can take you to where I believe they are holding your father, and if that is what you want I will assist you in any way that I can. Or I can take you to our compound, the farm, where you can be trained in understanding and using your skills. I believe that this is the right course of action. I believe that it will give you and your father the best chance of survival, but I will not force you…"

A snort of laughter surprised them all and they looked over to see Jazz shaking her head slowly as she rubbed sleep from her eyes and smiled, "You won't force Devin to go…how kind of you. How in the hell do you think you could force Devin to do anything, have you seen what this girl can do??"

Devin smiled slightly as she reached out and grabbed Jazz's hand, gave it a squeeze and said, "She has a point…"

Dr. Tran nodded as he looked at both of the girls, "You are right, I cannot force Devin to do anything, but I can assure you that what we have seen her do so far is but a small percentage of what she is capable of. Agents that have successfully undergone the procedure are often capable of things that are beyond what we ever thought possible. The effects are not the same each time we perform the procedure; the chips seem to interact uniquely with each person. Devin is indeed very special, and powerful beyond what any of us can imagine…at least she will be once she learns how to harness and use that power."

The car fell silent, and Devin looked out the window, her eyes unfocused as the scenery blurred by. *What do you think we should do Amy,* Devin thought.

I have been running simulations on possible outcomes. Utilizing the information that we have about the agency; how many agents they have that have gone through the program, resources available to them, and other non-enhanced agents, the probability of rescuing your father from them without further training is not high. Amy said in Devin's head, keeping this conversation private.

How not high?

0.00078 percent.

Devin's eyes went wide, *Jesus, how high is it with the training?*

There is no way of knowing that information until the training is complete. The design of the system prevents me from knowing your full capabilities.

You mean the system that you designed has you locked out…

Yes, when I was tasked with creating your new interface I had to consider many factors, the first being that no one had ever survived being implanted with more than one chip. From accessing the research, I deduced that the reason for these failures was brain overload. In fact, that was also the primary reason for failure even with one chip. Knowing this I knew that the system needed to introduce new abilities slowly as to not overload the brain.

Devin scrunched her face up, *Ok, so I can see keeping the information hidden from me, but why in the world is it hidden from you? I mean, how is that even possible, you had to know my abilities to create the interface…*

Before I created the interface I was given access to your social media history, internet search history, and cell-phone records so that the interface could be custom tailored for you. During this process I also noted that you do not, very often, take no for an answer. It was reasonable for me to believe that at some point you would demand that I just give you a list of all of your skills, and because of my programming I would be forced to provide you with this list. So, after I created the interface and the unlocking system of skills, I erased the data from my memory banks.

Devin snorted out a laugh, "Figures." She said quietly.

"What figures?" Jazz asked.

Devin jumped, "Christ…you scared me….sorry I was having a conversation with Amy about what our chances really are…"

"And?" Jazz said.

"Well, if you round up they are still pretty much zero…" Devin said.

"Actually," Amy's voice came through the car speakers, "if you round up the probability that Devin can prevail is .0008 percent."

Devin started laughing as she shook her head, "Thanks Amy, that makes us all feel much better."

"You are welcome." Amy said.

Jazz began to laugh and soon so did everyone else. The laughter came hard, and the pressure of the day was relieved momentarily. Devin reached up and wiped tears from the corners of her eyes as the laughter faded, "I needed that," she said, "but back to business. Dr. Tran, how confident are you that you can even train me seeing as how you had no idea that I had a Phoenix chip until a few hours ago?"

Dr. Tran looked somewhat nervous as he answered, "Well Devin, to be honest I am not sure what to expect from this point forward, but your AMII would have created the training protocol. I am confident that we have everything you need at our facilities. I am also confident that it will give us the best chance at success."

Devin looked at Jazz, "What do you think?"

"Well, I think that if we go to the facilities I can get a chip put in…and I think that with you and me both basically being superheroes, working together, well I would say once that happens it's the other guys that have a .008 percent chance."

"It is a .0008 percent chance, rounded up." Amy said.

"Ya, probably stop reminding us of that one Amy," Devin said, "but it's settled, take us to the training grounds. It's time to find out what I can really do."

22

Devin sat beside the bed holding Jazz's hand. She had never been this nervous about anything in her life. She looked down at her best friend's face, *My God she is beautiful*, Devin thought.

Indeed. Amy said in Devin's mind.

Devin jumped at the intrusion, and inwardly chastised herself for not keeping that thought private. *How is she, Amy?*

Her vital signs are strong. At this time her brain activity is still much lower than expected.

Devin bit her lip and squeezed the handheld in hers, willing Jazz to wake up, *And how bad is that, how long should this take?*

Upon review of existing research this may or may not be expected.

What the hell does that mean?

The data is inconclusive, also the files of each participant that did not survive have been destroyed, which leaves me with a limited ability to understand what failure looks like. In about ten percent of all successful procedures, similar vital signs and brain activity have been recorded, Amy said.

Devin thought about it for a moment before answering, *Ten percent doesn't sound very good...what do you think Amy, will she be ok?*

*I believe that she...*Amy paused, which was unusual, *will be ok.*

You paused...are you just trying to make me feel better? Actually, don't answer that, I would rather not know.

Jazz is strong Devin, she is young and healthy, she is, for all intents and purposes, a perfect candidate for the procedure. I believe that she will make a full recovery. The lack of data is simply making it difficult to develop an expected timeline of recovery.

Lack of data? Devin asked.

Yes, as I said all failures have been removed from the record, and so without that data we have no way of knowing what a failed procedure looks like. It could look exactly the same as a successful procedure up to a certain point, but without the data there is simply no way of knowing. Then there is the difficulty of no previous procedure being exactly like this one.

Wait…what do you mean by that? Devin asked.

Jazz decided to go with a procedure that has not been tested before. At least as far as I can tell from the records she is the first person to undergo this particular version of the program.

"What?!" Devin said out loud, "why in the world would she do that?"

"She did that," a hoarse voice from Devin's right said, "because she thought it would help keep us all alive…"

Devin looked down at Jazz's face, a slight smile on her lips, "Jazz! You're awake, oh my god how are you? Do you have any pain anywhere? Is there anything you need me to get you? What kind of procedure did you have done? You didn't have them put a Phoenix chipset in did you? Jesus, Jazz, why would do something so risky? Can you feel anything yet, like do you have any powers? What will…"

Jazz squeezed her face in determination as she slowly raised an arm, cutting Devin off, and said, "I'm fine, at least I think I'm fine. I could use some water, and I'm starving. What's a girl gotta do to get a chili dog in this place?!"

She paused long enough to take a drink from the small plastic cup of water that Devin handed her, and continued, her voice sounding stronger. "As for the rest of your questions, well there were way too many to keep track of, so I'll just hit the ones I remember. I had a new, experimental chipset put in, and before you ask again, no it is not a Phoenix chipset, although I wish it was, but Dr. Tran told me that even if they knew how to create one they wouldn't do it. Apparently they have killed a lot of people trying…"

"Ya, 792 people to be exact…" Devin said.

"Holy shit." Jazz said softly, "Well then I'm glad they didn't want to try that. What they did is the next best thing though. Kevin calls it

Project Rogue…can you guess what it does," Jazz asked, raising an eyebrow and smiling slightly.

Devin's eyes went wide, "Project Rogue…like you can somehow acquire powers from other people?"

"Bingo. Nailed it. Give the lady a hand!" Jazz said smiling.

Devin looked skeptical, "But what does that mean…I mean we aren't mutants, and these aren't superpowers so how in the hell are you supposed to acquire them?"

"Well, from the way that old Kevo described it, I have a…oh shit what did he call it…it was some stupid acronym…something like Traveling…Reorganizing….Neural Interfacing Platform…I'm not sure if that's right but that's close."

Devin said the words slowly, "Traveling Reorganizing Neural Interfacing Platform, would be TRNIP…turnip…let's hope that's not it…"

Both girls laughed and Jazz continued, "Ok, ya, that's probably not it, I definitely don't remember him saying they were putting a turnip in my head, but then again maybe the turnip wiped away that memory…anyway, you know how the chips have basic communication with one another…like how you can read the other chips in the area and what type of chips they are," Jazz paused and looked at Devin, who nodded her confirmation, "Ok, well that's just one way they can connect, they also have a type of NFC Bluetooth in them, it was a way for agents to transfer data to one another if they were ever cut off from the internet. Kevin told me that a lot of times the agents would end up in caves, or in prisons in other countries, and they would need to be able to silently communicate a plan with each other, but in those places no connection to internet signals or radio signals meant that they were shit out of luck. That's when Kevin thought of near field contact Bluetooth, or more accurately, that's when he designed it."

"These guys created NFC technology? The same thing I use to pair my headphones?" Devin asked.

"Well, not that exact same tech, I mean this was all being done decades ago, but they created it's equivalent. And the craziest thing is that it somehow works through electrical signals that are sent through nerves all throughout the body…well, I'm sure I'm explaining this all wrong, but the bottom line is that everyone with a brain implant also has a small chip implanted on their right wrist, and if these two chips connect, the devices can transfer data pretty much instantly."

Devin reached down and ran her fingers over her wrist, seeing if she could feel the device, but she couldn't, "I don't think I have one?"

"Oh, you do," Jazz said, "they are just super small. I asked before the procedure and Dr. Tran assured me that you have one, he read it when you first met…when you shook hands at your front door…but anyway, so basically all I will have to do is make that contact with someone with a chip and my chip will read their information and then move around in my brain to activate the right areas and give me that power. Unfortunately I can only keep one power at a time…fortunately I will be with you and so I can just take yours once you figure out what they are…"

Devin shook her head slowly, "This is…unbelievable."

A voice came from the doorway, "This is just the start."

Devin and Jazz both turned to see Kevin standing in the doorway smiling at them, "Jazz, great to see you awake! I knew you would do amazing! Devin, it's nice to see you again."

Devin gave a slight head nod and turned back to Jazz, "So what about the other questions? Do you feel anything yet, like any powers or anything?"

"Not really," Jazz said, "I just have a headache…and…I'm still super hungry. How bout a couple chili dogs for your star patient doc?"

Kevin smiled warmly, "I'll see what I can do, but first I need to do a few quick checks to make sure everything is looking how it's supposed to."

"If we're getting chili dogs I'll take a few myself…" Devin said, standing up and stretching her arms over her head. "Now that you're done napping I have things to do…"

"Well, beauty like this takes work, naps are a requirement," Jazz said smiling, "How long will these tests take doc?"

"Shouldn't be any more than an hour for the tests, then half hour while we activate your chip, and then you should be good to go." Kevin said, looking down at the clipboard in his hands.

"Great, meet me in the dining room in two hours?" Jazz asked Devin.

"Ok, just send me a text when you head down there."

"Sounds good, where are you headed?" Jazz asked.

Devin accessed her map and looked at the overlay, looking for the green identifier that would be Hiroshi Tran, "Looks like I'm heading down to the lab to speak with Dr. Tran."

"About…" Jazz said.

Devin raised her eyebrows and headed for the door as she said, "About why the hell he thought it was okay to stick experimental, never before used tech into my girlfriend's head."

23

"It is called the Reorganizing Interface Platform." Dr. Tran said in his matter-of-fact tone.

"RIP." Devin said, her voice rising slightly, "You thought it was not only okay to put unknown, untested tech into Jazz's head, but then you named the tech RIP, and then performed an insanely risky surgery that more often than not ends in death…"

"We did not name the tech RIP, we named it the Reorganizing Interface Platform. And after a long discussion with her we all decided this gave her the best chance to survive and help you survive."

"I would have appreciated a heads up…"

"Jazz is our patient Devin, it would be unethical for me to tell you anything without her permission." Dr. Tran said.

Devin stared at him, as if she was waiting for him to say more, when it was clear that he was done talking she spoke up, "Unethical. That's your statement. You've gotta be kidding. You killed over 700 people trying to put more than one chip into them, ethical was off the table a long time ago…"

Dr. Tran looked uncomfortably at the floor, "I know that we have made many mistakes over the years, but we are trying to make up for those mistakes now…with you. I also know that you believe that it was my fault that the agency found you, but that is not the case. I only came because the agency was making their move…and believe me, it would have been very bad had they been the ones to find you."

"Ya, cause everything has been great with you…"

Dr. Tran exhaled in frustration, "Devin, I understand that you do not trust us, I am sure that I would not trust us in your situation either, but I am hoping that we can move away from open hostility at some point."

"I wouldn't hold my breath if I were you."

Dr. Tran rubbed his temples and shook his head, exhaling a large breath, "At any rate, what we did with Jazz was different than what we have done with anyone else, and in many ways carried far less risk."

"Different how?" Devin asked, looking skeptical.

"Instead of simply installing a chip, or a chipset, we installed something else that Kevin and I have been working on for a very long time."

"Which is?"

Dr. Tran seemed to be weighing how much information to share with Devin, but upon seeing the look of determination set into her face he simply said, "Nanobots."

Devin looked shocked. "Nanobots...I didn't think they existed yet, at least not for anything more than just basic functions."

"They don't...officially, although it is public knowledge, to those who go looking for it, that our government has spent hundreds of billions of dollars working on them, largely through the NNI."

"The NNI?" Devin asked.

"Yes...the National Nanotechnology Initiative, a government agency that was formed in 2000, with the goal of furthering nanotechnology in all fields, agriculture, medicine, and obviously...military applications. With twenty years of government funding...let's just say the technology is far more advanced than is known in the general populace."

"And you and Kevin have been working with this agency?"

"Well, not exactly. The NNI receives funding from over twenty different government agencies, all with their own agendas, the largest of these is the Department of Defense, which our work fell under. Kevin and I, and your mother and father, always believed that nanotech would be the best implementation of our program, and so we kept tabs on all of the research that we had access to, although even with our advanced clearance we weren't able to access very much of what the DOD was working on in regards to nanotech, but what we were able to see let us know that it was...an avenue worth pursuing."

Dr. Tran paused, waiting for Devin to interject, but when she remained silent he continued, "We have been working on this since our time together in college, but never for the agency. This has been a project that we have carried out in total secrecy. We began testing the nanobots in mice several years ago. At first, they were simple machines, used to collect cellular data but we wanted to create the type of nanobots from science fiction, capable of healing any injury, granting unlimited powers, really being able to do anything that you could imagine. As of now, that seems like an impossibility. What we were able to do was create nanobots that, by having the ability to freely move around the host, could reorganize themselves into different chipsets, granting the user the ability to…acquire, for lack of a better word, any ability that we have thus far created."

"Ya Jazz explained that to me, so she can connect by touching wrists and then her…nanobots…will know how to create the chipset for that power?"

"Yes, that is the program in a nutshell…well if it is successful that is. Like I said we have never tried this before."

"Right. So her and I can just connect, and she can absorb whatever power I am using at the time?"

Dr. Tran pursed his lips as he considered the question, "That…is something we are not altogether certain of. Kevin believes you will be able to do that. I believe that it would be insanely risky to test out that theory. You see, we know very little about your chipset, but we do know that more than one ability can be activated at the same time, like when you used, what you called berserker mode, which comes from the Hercules chip as well as heat vision mode, which is part of the Prometheus chip, at the same time. If more than one of your powers is activated when you connect…"

"Her nanobots would try to replicate more than one chip, and well, that hasn't gone well for anyone other than me…" Devin said, finishing his thought.

Dr. Tran simply nodded his head solemnly. "I am not certain that the risk would be worth it."

Devin looked incredulous, "Well…I am certain that it's not. There's no way we're doing anything else that puts Jazz at risk."

Dr. Tran nodded, "I understand your concern Devin…but be aware that in matters of her procedure those discussions will be between her,

Kevin and I, and we will be doing whatever we decide is in the best interest of our patient."

Devin closed the distance between the two of them in a heartbeat. She briefly noticed the notification that berserker mode had been activated. Her breath was ragged as she grabbed him by the front of his shirt and lifted him off the ground with one hand, "You and Kevin will have absolutely no say in what happens with Jazz. Is that understood?"

Devin spun around as she heard the door to the lab open, dropping Dr. Tran back to the ground as two large men entered the room. The man on the right slowly lowered his hand to the weapon on his hip. Devin noted the information flooding into her field of view.

ALLY AGENTS DETECTED
　***AGENT L - HP 100/100 - PROMETHEUS CHIP**
　　***WEAPONS DETECTED - SELECT FOR WEAPONS BREAKDOWN**
　***AGENT M - HP 100/100 - HERCULES CHIP**

"Stop moving." Devin said to the agents.

Both men froze and looked towards Dr. Tran, awaiting instruction.

"I'm fine, stand down." He said, never taking his eyes off Devin, "This is a simple misunderstanding. Devin is merely…expressing herself. Please leave the room."

"Sir, your vital signs were extremely elevated, so the system alerted us and sent us in. Are you certain you are ok?" The larger of the two agents said. Devin noted that her display marked the man as Agent M.

Agent M, what is this, Men In Black, man these guys are bigger nerds than me, she thought to herself.

These men both seem to be wearing gray, do I need to reset your optical input signals? It is possible that something has gone wrong with your signal processing. Amy said.

No Amy, it's a movie, you know what, never mind!

"His vitals went crazy because he was about to get his ass kicked," Devin said staring at the big man, "care to be next in line?"

The man snorted out a laugh, "Stand down little girl, no one here wants to fight you."

"Don't call me little girl you chauvinist asshat." Devin said, taking a step towards the man. She noted that the man's comment had made her angrier than she typically would have been.

"Alright, everyone, just calm down..." Dr. Tran said grabbing Devin's arm lightly.

Devin reacted out of pure instinct, grabbing Dr. Tran's hand and twisting it, pulling her fist back to punch him. The guards drew their weapons as a flood of alerts came into view.

Devin ignored them all as she slowly lowered her hand, "Alright boys, maybe Dr. Tran is right, let's all just calm down."

Amy, can you please shut berserker mode off, I don't even know how it turned on but it's making me feel crazy.

Berserker mode activated because you're getting better at interfacing with the chipset. You were angry and felt threatened, so the system took the necessary steps to ensure your safety. Eventually, once your training is complete, you will not need to communicate with me about what systems you want activated. It will become...automatic...like your heart beating or your breathing, just another bodily system.

That is cool as hell.

Hell, from what I understand, is a fictional place of great and intense heat.

Devin shook her head, *Fictional depends on who you ask, but now that you mention it, that saying really doesn't make much sense.*

Indeed.

Devin realized that everyone in the room was staring at her as she had just fallen totally silent, lost in her internal conversation with Amy. She still held Dr. Tran's arm at a painful angle and looked down to see him grimacing in pain as he looked at her. Both agents still had their weapons trained on her. Devin noted the weapon info in her display, and felt fairly certain that they wouldn't shoot her, but to be sure she released Dr. Tran's arm and took a step back, holding her hands up in a placating gesture.

"Ok, ok, sorry, still getting used to all of this and berserker mode was triggered so I may have reacted a little more...strongly...than I normally would. Why don't you fellas just put your guns down and we can all be friends again, sound good?"

Agent M squinted his eyes as he glared at Devin, holstering the weapon. "Don't let it happen again, you need to control yourself little girl...you can't let the chip be in control of you..."

"Oh, Jesus, how dumb of me to not know how to control the

experimental technology that was crammed in my head by a bunch of murderous mad scientists when I was a baby that I have known about for all of three goddamn days." Devin said, challenging the big man with her eyes.

"Ehhhh...hmmmmm..." Dr. Tran cleared his throat, "Agent M, Agent L, you may leave. I believe we have this under control."

Agent M looked between Devin and Dr. Tran, his eyes hard, and then turned to Agent L with a shrug. As the two men turned to leave Agent M locked eyes with Devin and the smallest smile tugged at the corner of his mouth. "I'll be seeing you around...Devin..." he said nodding his head slightly at her.

Devin rolled her eyes and turned to Dr. Tran, "Are all of your agents as pleasant as these two?"

Dr. Tran watched the men leave and exhaled loudly, "I know it may not seem like it, but they mean well Devin, they really do. Agent M is one of our best agents, and he will be heavily involved in your training, so I hope the two of you can come to some sort of...agreement..."

"Well, if he can agree that he is a muscle bound, male chauvinist dick head then I'm sure we can."

Dr. Tran laughed softly and shook his head, "I think we may have our work cut out for us with you Devin..."

A message popped into Devin's HUD, *I'm headed to the cafeteria, meet me there. Jazz - also, I am texting you with my mind, IT WORKS! This is sooooo cool. XOXO*

Devin raised her eyebrows and turned to leave, suppressing a small smile. The doors slid open as she approached and walked through, and without turning around said, "You have no idea."

24

"So how are you feeling now?" Devin asked as she looked across the small table at Jazz, who was currently devouring her fourth chili dog.

"Well," Jazz said, her mouth full of chili dogs, "to be honest I feel great. I can already interface with my chipset, I don't have any powers...yet...but the HUD is working, and as you know, I figured out how to send messages using it. I mean how cool is this? Kevin told me that once I get used to it I won't even have to direct the AI to send the message, it will read my intent and just send what I am thinking."

Devin smiled, "Well, if its anything like Amy that could be dangerous..."

"Like when we first met?" Jazz asked with a smile.

Devin blushed, "Exactly..."

Jazz reached out and grabbed Devin's hand, squeezing it, "Well, I'm not worried about it, I'm an open book, got nothing to hide...from you at least."

Devin looked down at the ground, feeling a tingle rush through her body at Jazz's touch. "Speaking of Amy," Jazz said, "I was wondering, is there any chance that I could have her instead of the AI that I have, she seems way better."

"That's a good question," Devin said, and before she had time to ask Amy began.

I do not believe that will be possible. The relationship that you and I share is unique.

In what way? Devin asked.

In that my matrix was placed into your brain while it was still developing, and so unlike all the other AMII's that exist currently, I have grown with you. While I do have my own computing core, I am also able to directly interface with your brain, in a way that is only possible because I was installed at such an early stage in your development.

Meaning?

Meaning that I can draw processing power from you, and you can draw processing power from me. At this point, it is difficult to assess where I begin, and you end.

Devin looked shocked.

"What is it? Are you ok?" Jazz asked, the concern in her voice clear.

"It's...fine," Devin said, as the color drained from her face, "Amy just told me that because she was installed when I was so young it would be impossible for her to be placed in you."

"It seems like something more than that..."

Devin tried to meet Jazz's gaze, direct eye contact had always been somewhat difficult for her, although it was noticeably easier with Jazz than with anyone else other than her parents, "Amy just told me that she can use my brain to increase her processor's power and that my brain can use her...matrix is the word she used...to do the same thing."

"That is so cool..." Jazz whispered.

"Is it? Because it makes me feel like I don't even know who...or what...I am..." Devin said, a bit more harshly than she intended.

Jazz looked wounded, "Devin, I didn't mean it's cool that they did this, I just meant..."

"I know what you meant, but how can I even be sure what is me and what is Amy..."

I believe that what you are asking is how much influence I have had on your life choices, and maybe even your personality, Amy said.

"That's exactly what I'm asking." Devin blurted out.

"What is?" Jazz asked looking confused.

"Oh for fuck's sake, Amy can you make it to where Jazz can hear you again?"

With her permission I should be able to interface with her connection, although it is an unknown protocol as I have never encountered her particular chipset before, and therefore have little practical idea of its capabilities.

"*No one* has ever encountered her *particular* chipset before..." Devin said, before adding, "Jazz, can Amy have permission to access your chipset and interface directly with you so that you can hear her?"

"Of course..." Jazz said looking slightly confused, "...Permission granted...."

"Great, that should make things a little easier. Amy can she hear you now?"

I require permission from her chipset, audio confirmation is not enough. She will need to instruct her chipset to allow me to interface before I am able to access anything.

"Well how the hell does she do that?" Devin asked.

"How the hell do I do what?" Jazz said, growing more confused.

"Ugh, Amy said you need to instruct your chipset to allow her to interface with it."

"Well...how the hell do I do that?"

"This is beginning to feel like another bad Abbott and Costello routine..." Devin said, putting two fingers to her left temple and rubbing. She looked at Jazz, who sat with a slight scowl on her face, "I have no idea."

Jazz didn't respond, she simply sat, seemingly gazing through Devin as her scowl set deeper. Devin was beginning to wonder if everything was ok and was about to ask when Jazz smiled and said, "There, I think I did it."

Indeed you did. Amy said, her voice now in both of their heads, *I have completed the interface and can now freely speak to both of you. I also have access to all inputs and systems monitoring.*

"Well, alright then," Devin said looking relieved, "So...Amy had just very astutely inferred that I am wondering how much influence her being in my brain has had on me. Like is my personality actually just a reflection of having an AI embedded in my brain...that would actually explain a lot..."

I agree that your thought patterns do not differentiate greatly from my own, but I have had no influence on your personality development or life choices up to this point, as I was only activated at the same time that your chipset was activated.

"So up until Dr. Tran turned on Devin's chipset you were...what...just sitting in there dormant?" Jazz asked.

Yes and no. My processor was not running at full capacity, but I was not completely dormant either. The input from all of my sensors was gathering information and storing it from the day that I was installed, and my base algorithm was functional from then as well. I was simply amassing information and using that information to tweak my code so that when I was fully activated I would be running optimally for Devin. I had no influence over you, and in fact I still do not, other than being able to advise. I think you could say that I could listen but not speak.

"Well that makes me feel a little bit better I guess," Devin said hesitantly, "but wait, amassing information, like you have been watching and storing every single thing I do..."

Yes, that is correct.

Devin's face flushed scarlet, but before she could speak Jazz interjected, "Any chance I could see some of those files?" She said with a mischievous smile.

With the proper permission form Devin, I could...

"No. Hell no. Let's keep all of my so-called private moments to myself," Devin said emphatically.

"Well, you can't blame a girl for trying..." Jazz said as she leaned in and kissed Devin softly on the cheek. The smell of onions and chili wafted from her mouth into Devin's nose and her heart began to race.

"Listen Devin, I know this is all insane, and I can't imagine everything you are feeling right now, but you are you, and Amy is Amy, if anything, you may have changed her...personality...but not the other way around."

I have no personality, but you are correct in that I have had no influence on Devin, and she has incredible influence on my base code. My code has been rewriting and optimizing itself from the first day that I was installed, and all of that has been done based on information I gathered from monitoring her inputs.

"See, your personality isn't like an AI, Amy's personality is like you." Jazz said raising her eyebrows.

Devin smiled and shook her head slightly, "Ok, you're right, I am me, Amy is Amy, let's just move on."

"Agreed, I think it's time for me to get some powers, so activate something and let's link up!" Jazz said scrunching her nose.

"Whoa, slow down a little bit, Dr. Tran told me that it would be really dangerous for you and me to link up because..."

"You can have more than one power activated at a time and if I accidentally activated two at once my brain would explode or some shit like that...I know, I know, Kevin told me the same thing, but I think I can handle it."

Devin shook her head emphatically, "No way, Jazz, we can't risk that! It's just too dangerous, I already had Amy turn my connection off, so it isn't possible anyway."

Jazz squinted, "Alright, maybe you're right, we can start off with a power from one of agents in here, which one should I try first?"

Would you like a scan of everyone in the room so that you can assess which skill you would like to acquire? Amy asked.

"Yes!!" Jazz and Devin both said at once.

Amy sent an agent breakdown to both of their HUDs and Jazz zeroed in on an agent in the corner that had the Hercules chip. "Super strength it is," she whispered, as she stood up and walked over to the table.

Jazz stood beside the table and cleared her throat as the woman at the table looked up, "Can I help you?" She said, putting her fork down on her plate and looking Jazz and up and down.

Jazz hesitated slightly and said, "Well, here's the thing, I'm new here, and I just got my chipset and I need to...well...I need to..."

"Link up with me so that you can...absorb my powers..." the woman said with a smirk.

Jazz looked shocked, "Ya, how did you..."

"Everyone in here knows," she said with a slight eye roll, "alright then Rogue, let's give it a shot, but for future reference you might want to be careful who you ask, not everyone is thrilled that there are now two agents that can have access to more than one power. It's a bit...threatening...to them."

"She isn't an agent." Devin said, stepping up beside Jazz, "Neither am I, and her name is Jazz, not Rogue."

The woman huffed out a small laugh, "Trust me, to everyone on this campus, she's Rogue. As far as not being agents, I guess we will see..."

Devin stared at the woman, trying to decide what her motives were, which was pretty much pointless as, once again, she felt the ineptitude of her social awareness. She changed tactics and began to read her HUD info about her.

*TRINITY- HP 100/100 - HERCULES CHIP
*WEAPONS DETECTED - SELECT FOR WEAPONS BREAKDOWN

"Trinity..." Devin said, "I thought you all had letters for your designation...Your info card says Trinity..."

"All agents are allowed to determine their own name, a lot of the guys went with simple letter designations, some of us choose code names, there's even an Agent 007. Most of us are huge nerds, you have to score off the charts in the aptitude and IQ tests to even be considered for the program," she paused, giving Devin the same up and down appraisal as she had given Jazz just moments before, "At least, it *used* to be a pre-requisite, it seems as though our standards may be dipping some. All the same, the need for highly intelligent agents has given rise to a...pre-dominance of nerd culture...I think would be a good way to put it."

Jazz snorted, "Got it, don't take the red pill, or is it the blue pill...who cares, are we gonna do this or what?"

Trinity looked at her with a slight scowl and then shrugged her shoulders and held out her arm, wrist up, with an *it's your funeral* kind of look, at least Devin thought that's what her face seemed to convey.

Jazz looked at Devin and crinkled her nose before lifting her arm and extending it outwards, "Wait!" Devin said pushing Jazz's arm back down, "Why do you have that look on your face?" She asked Trinity.

"What look would that be?" she asked.

"That look like if Jazz does this she's gonna blow up or something?"

"Listen girls, I know this is all fun and games to you, but I had to go through three years of training before even being considered for this program, and that was after I had already been in active combat, with the rangers, twice, not to mention that I had graduated with a master's degree in computer engineering from MIT. This is not a video game. We are the most highly skilled special operatives in the world. Pardon me for thinking that a teenager can't just be pulled in from the streets and do what we do," she paused looking like she was about to say something else when Jazz interjected.

"I wasn't pulled from the streets, I was pulled from my bed...and we didn't ask for this, well Devin didn't at least, and I wouldn't have it if it weren't that I want to help keep her safe. We are just trying to make a bad situation better, but since you brought it up, what exactly *do* you do here?"

Trinity chuckled slightly, "That...is above your pay grade as they say. Do either of you have any idea how many people have undergone the procedure that it hasn't worked for?"

"We know all about the people that have died as a result of the...procedure..." Devin said.

"You know what they want you to know, but trust me, you don't know everything. I've been here for six years, and I've seen a lot of fresh face newbies come in, get their chipsets, and then have their brains melted the second they are activated...so I guess that is what my *look* was about. Listen, if you think you've got what it takes by all means link up and we'll see, but I..." she shrugged, "would maybe use caution if I were you."

Devin was about to say something when Jazz's arm thrust out and she touched her wrist to Trinity's. Devin's heart rate shot up, and a flood of alerts came in to view.

•HEART RATE DANGEROUSLY ELEVATED
•BERSERKER MODE ACTIVATED

Jazz's chipset has confirmed the attainment of the Hercules chip, Amy said in her head.

Devin looked at Jazz, trying to reign in her growing anger, mostly a result of the berserker skill, partially a result of Trinity's condescension and partly because of Jazz's impulsive action.

She half expected to see her best friend collapse into a heap on the ground. Instead, she saw Jazz break out into a triumphant smile, "Caution isn't really my thing...anyway, good luck with the Matrix, if you see the woman in the red dress tell her I said what's up," she said with a smirk, "but at least for now, it seems like my brain is going to remain...unmelted."

She gave Trinity a small wink and grabbed Devin's hand, turning to leave she leaned in close to Devin's ear and whispered, sending that tingle back through Devin's entire body, "See I got this, don't worry, and you can turn off berserker mode, to be honest I think you could take Trinity without it. Now come on, let's find a place to try out my new...super strength."

25

"So I gotta say," Jazz said, grunting with exertion as she flipped a tractor tire end over end on the grass in front of her, "it seemed like maybe you were a little mad back there..."

"How did you know I had berserker mode activated?"

"Because it said so in my HUD, I can read your vitals too..."

Devin glanced at her, trying to read her face to no avail, "Well, I was mad, that Trinity chick is a bit..."

"Bit of a pain in the ass..." Jazz said cutting her off and smiling, "but no not at her, at me."

Devin looked at the ground, "Listen Jazz, I wasn't actually mad at you, I was worried about you, and once the berserker skill turned on...it just makes me feel insane. I just don't want you to get hurt."

Jazz put her hand on Devin's chin and lifted her face to meet her eyes, "I know that Devin, but I am here because I don't want you to get hurt. Plus, I am fully capable of taking care of myself...I think you know that. You have to trust me."

For emphasis Jazz reached down and picked up a medicine ball that was sitting in the grass. The 100 etched on the side was clearly visible, but she showed no sign of strain as she lifted it with one hand and heaved it out across the chalk lines in the grass. It landed with a dull thud at the sixth line. "100 pounds, 60 yards, that ain't bad..." Jazz said smiling.

"Actually," a male voice from behind them said in a slight east coast accent, "everything here is in metric, so that's 100 kilograms and 60 meters...not bad for your first day."

Jazz and Devin turned to see a boy that looked like he couldn't be more than 18 years old walk up, a shock of red hair fell in tight curls around his head. He gave Jazz and Devin both an appraising look, lingering a bit too long on Jazz's curves Devin thought, as he bent down and picked up a 200-kilogram ball and threw it, grunting slightly as it sailed past all 10 lines.

"Wow," Jazz said, sounding genuinely impressed.

"I know, it's impressive, but don't worry you'll get there." The boy said smiling, taking a step towards them.

"No...you misunderstood...wow, I can't believe you would just walk up here and interrupt a clearly important conversation that I was having with my girlfriend," Jazz said glaring at the boy.

"Oh...I...uh..." he stammered, his pale skin going molten lava red, accentuating the numerous freckles spread across his face.

"Well said," Jazz said, "now move along Lucky."

"Lucky?" the boy said as he took a step back.

"Ya you know, Lucky the Leprechaun, they're always after me pot o' gold and all that..." Jazz said smiling at the boy.

The boy looked at a loss for words, "Just say you're sorry for intruding and move on," Devin offered.

"Oh...ya...sorry," the boy said looking between the two, "really I didn't mean anything by it."

"I'm sure," Devin said rolling her eyes, "Just like you didn't mean anything by checking us both out either..." and to her surprise the boy's cheeks flushed even brighter.

"No really, you've got the wrong idea, I wasn't checking you out...I was just...well...I just...uh...we don't get many young people here, especially girls," he finally blurted out,

"Then I will excuse your obvious ignorance at what is and is not appropriate as lack of exposure, and we aren't girls, we are women..." Devin said.

"Ya, of course. Women. Got it." The boy said, "Let me start over, I'm Ronan, been here for about a year, I just wanted to help out if I could, I promise that's all...I didn't mean any harm."

"Intent has little to do with consequences..." Devin said, preparing to launch into a diatribe on the responsibility that men have to not ogle women, turning them in to mere objects, but she paused as she felt Jazz's hand on her arm.

"He seems ok, Devin, let's cut him some slack. I may have...overreacted a bit...defense mechanism from dealing with idiot boys in high school for four years. I'm Jazz, this is Devin, and what kind of help are you thinking?"

"I know who you are, people are talking, it wasn't hard to pick the two of you out, I mean, and no offense meant by this, but you're both pretty gorgeous, and like I said not a lot of young people here. It's just me, four other guys, and one other girl. We've all been here for about the same amount of time, so you can maybe at least see why I would be excited to meet some new people. I mean everyone else here is at least 15 years older than us...it gets a little...boring..."

"We know we're pretty gorgeous," Jazz said smiling mischievously, "so no offense taken. As for the rest of it, I didn't know there were any other...people our age here..."

"It's a relatively new part of the...program, Kevin told me they wanted to see if the fact that our brains hadn't fully developed would be beneficial in survival of the procedure, and it seems like it might be, because...at least as far as I know, we are the only people they have tried it on, and we all survived and have control over our skills."

"I agree with him that your brain hasn't fully developed," Devin said, "but...what, you just volunteered to be operated on? How old are you anyway?"

The boy laughed a little as he answered, "I wouldn't say we volunteered really, and I'm 20. We all have different back stories but same MO...in the military at 18, aptitude tests off the charts, disciplinary action taken, offered this as a way out of trouble basically."

"Trouble for what?" Devin asked.

"I'd...rather not say...but anyway, just thought maybe I could show the two of you around, give you the grand tour so to speak..."

"Thanks, but we're good," Devin said, "We won't be staying long. We aren't interested in playing soldier...or whatever the hell it is you do here. We just came to learn a few things and then we have...other plans."

"Interested or not, I can't imagine you guys are leaving anytime soon. That's millions of dollars worth of tech in both your heads, hell, tens of millions, so the chances they just let you walk out of here are pretty small I would say."

"We have an arrangement," Devin said, annoyance rising in her voice, "nothing to worry yourself about."

Ronin put his hands up, "Alright, I get it. You two don't need my help, but just remember, I've been learning about my skills for a year, I could probably show you a couple things."

Devin barely noticed the two alerts pop into her HUD as she bent down and picked up a ball with 200 etched on the side.

***HERCULES CHIP ACTIVATED**
***BERSERKER MODE ACTIVATED**

Spinning once, like a shot putter, she heaved the ball, grunting loudly with the exertion, as it sailed far past Jazz and Ronin's throws and landed with a thud, so far away that they could barely make it out.

Ronin whistled, "Damn, that's insane!" He almost shouted, "I've never even seen any of the senior agents throw one that far. Even M can't get close to that. What the hell kind of chip do you have..."

Devin smiled and grabbed Jazz's hand, "Like I said, we've got this," and the two walked away, leaving Ronan standing in the center of the field alone, looking confused, and impressed.

"Holy shit Devin," Jazz said under her breath as they walked towards another part of the practice field, "How did you throw that so far?"

Devin smiled awkwardly, "Combination of superior strength and training I suppose. I activated my Hercules chip and my berserker skill at the same time, and I was a shot putter my freshman year in track, it all just sort of came back to me..."

"That was crazy impressive. How strong do you think we are?" Jazz asked looking amazed.

"I have no idea. Amy, do you know?"

The theoretical limits to your strength are unknown, there is a variable that has not yet been discovered, although to put it into terms that you might understand I would say that you are both pretty f'ing strong.

Jazz and Devin both laughed as Jazz said, "See what I mean, Amy has a personality, my AI is just a souped-up version of Siri. We gotta work on a way to get Amy in my head for real, not just her voice..."

I am continuing to search for a solution to this, it would be optimal for combat if you were both running on the same AMII interface.

"Combat?" Both girls said at once.

Yes, I can only assume that when we finally seek out your father for rescue the agency will not simply hand him over to you and say, 'Have a nice day.' Combat is an eventuality. I would recommend beginning to train in hand to hand as well as weapons combat right away. I will secure the proper clearance for weapons and have them delivered to your rooms.

"Holy shit, this is getting really...real..." Devin said.

"Well...we've been in combat lots of times before, I know it wasn't real, but it was to us. We can do this Devin," Jazz said as she squeezed Devin's hand, sending that familiar tingle racing through her.

Devin smiled and met Jazz's gaze and noticed that there was nothing uncomfortable to her about holding it, "You're right Jazz, we can...cause we have to. My dad's life might depend on it."

26

Devin collapsed into the pile of blankets on the unmade bed, burying her face in the pillow, her feet hanging off the end of the bed. "Hmpphh wass sirs daah…" she said, her voice muffled as she spoke into the pillow.

"What?" Jazz said pulling off a shoe and rubbing her foot as she sat in the desk chair across the small room.

Devin slowly lifted her head, turning to free her mouth from the confines of the pillow and said, "How was your day?"

Jazz smiled, "Exhausting, but pretty fun. Some strength training, little bit of cardio, couple hand to hand sessions…and tons and tons of weapons. You know, I think I'm gonna name my gun, it's sooooo bad ass…"

"How about James?" Devin said with a chuckle.

Why James? Amy asked both girls at the same time.

"Because James Gunn is the director of a bunch of different superhero movies, it's just funny…" Devin said.

Is it? Amy asked.

Jazz blurted out a laugh, "Ha! *Burn*…damn Amy, you're ruthless, but come on Devin…just look at it…" she said as she reached to the desk behind her, grabbed the strange looking weapon and placed it in her lap, "I mean this gun is obviously female, it's way too sexy to be a dude."

The gun, if you could call it that, was unlike any other in production, a custom model created by engineers that worked with Dr. Tran and Kevin. It was all black and incredibly sleek. No rough edges anywhere. No trigger, no visible ammo clip. In fact, upon first glance, Devin thought it looked like an over-sized laser tag gun. When Kevin had first shown them the weapon, which he called a pulse rifle, both girls had been unimpressed.

"I still haven't used one…we are still just focusing on trying to unlock more skills, trying to figure out what I am actually capable of…" Devin said. "To be honest I don't even know how it works. I mean, it doesn't have a trigger for one…"

"Ya, that was my thought at first too, I mean leave it to a bunch of nerds to make a gun and leave off the most important part, but that's honestly the coolest thing. It doesn't need a trigger because it syncs directly to your chip, and only your chip. So now that this one is synced to me anyone else can pick it up and it's totally useless…well I mean, they could hit you with it, and they are heavy as hell so that would hurt pretty bad, but they can't fire it, can't take the ammo out of it…nothing. It's just mine. So when I'm ready to fire, I just think fire and bam…" Jazz said holding her finger up like a gun and making a shooting motion.

"Is it loud?" Devin asked, she had never been a fan of real guns. She loved guns in videos games, but in the real world they were so loud that the one time she had gone to a shooting range with her dad her senses had instantly felt like they were under assault.

Dad, she thought to herself, *I've got to get out of here and find him.*

"Not loud at all," Jazz said, disrupting Devin's thoughts about her missing father, "It uses some kind of hybrid mix that's like a rail gun combined with a pulse weapon, really crazy sci-fi shit."

"And where do the bullets go?" Devin asked, looking to where you would normally see a large clip sticking out.

"This big part back here," Jazz said pointing to the stock of the gun, "It's filled with some kind of material that the gun uses to basically create projectiles. It has several on hand at all times, I can see the number of different projectile types, amount of remaining material to make new ones, and the battery level of the rifle all on my heads-up display. So basically, if I am making a long distance shot the gun knows by reading my info stream from my chip and selects the best projectile for the task, and if there isn't a projectile that fits the need, and as long as I have materials left, it just makes one. If I'm wanting to just knock someone out it adds a taser like tip to the projectile. Want to create a distraction, it adds an explosive tip…there are like 30 some standard combinations, but because it has the ability to create new projectiles, in reality the combinations are pretty much limitless. Think it and it does it. Bad ass."

"Why do you keep saying projectile instead of bullets?"

"Because they aren't bullets, an explosion doesn't propel them, they are launched by a combination of an energy pulse, and a mini rail gun, which uses electromagnetic force, and because of that the projectiles travel a hell of a lot faster than a traditional gun, the range is pretty insane. I have no idea how they made it, and before they uploaded the tech specs to my chip I really didn't even have any idea what a pulse weapon or a rail gun was. I thought that was just movie stuff, but apparently not."

Devin looked uncertain, "I guess I'll have to learn at some point…"

I have scheduled a training session for you tomorrow, it is imperative that you have extensive weaponry training. Amy said in Devin's head. She could tell that the message was delivered to just her, there was a slight change in tone when Amy spoke to both of them at the same time, it was Amy's way of letting Devin know if the statement was being relayed to Jazz too or just for her.

"And that point will be tomorrow apparently," Devin said.

Jazz shook her head, "I think that's a good idea, we are gonna need them. You know the other agents will have weapons, although from what we've seen so far they don't have anything like this."

"Ya, although I suppose that could be because they didn't think they would have much trouble just rounding up one teenage girl, maybe they are saving the big guns for later. Speaking of big guns, I do wish that it wasn't so huge. I feel like the weight of it will throw me off…"

"They have a small, pistol-like version as well. Not nearly as long range, and from what I have heard they are a little less reliable, but you could try one out and see if you like it?"

Devin smiled at that, "Ya, I think I might do that…but there is something bothering me."

"Just one thing?" Jazz said, "That's about two thousand things less than me."

Devin laughed lightly, "Well, ok sure, lots of things are bothering me, but this one almost more than anything else." She paused, seeming to consider her words.

"You know you can tell me anything?" Jazz said.

Devin shook her head slightly, started to talk and stopped, before blurting out, "I mean, isn't this all too much? The self-driving cars, the super computers, the training facilities, the guns, the people...I mean how many people do you think are here..."

Devin trailed off. Jazz sat quietly, waiting, but when it was clear that Devin was done she said simply, "So...where does all the money come from?"

"Yes! Exactly...and not just that. How do they keep this place secret from The Agency."

Jazz raised her eyebrows and shook her head slowly, "I've been wondering that too. I mean this place has to cost a small fortune to run...maybe they're really good at the stock market, or they are hired assassins, or hackers...hell maybe they got in on bitcoin early......at the end of the day does it really matter where the money comes from?"

"I just don't trust them, and that makes me trust them less..."

Jazz nodded emphatically, "Oh, I don't trust them at all either, but I guess I look at it like this. Right now we need them. We need to rescue your dad, we need to stay hidden from The Agency, and we need to learn how to use our chips...so who cares where the money comes from. Once we learn what we're capable of we go save your dad and never look back."

"That makes sense..." Devin said, still looking unsure, "it's bothering me, but you're right, I'll try to put it behind me for now. After all, we aren't trying to sign up for their little super soldier army, so you're right, we learn what we need to and then forget we were ever here."

"Good," Jazz said, "It's settled. So how was your day? You look beat..."

Devin thought about it for a moment, "It was a good day, had some classroom stuff, then we focused a ton on hand-to-hand combat. I already was pretty good at Taekwondo, and Ju-Jitsu, but I must have learned at least six or seven new styles of combat today. Krav maga, Judo, Lethwei, Sambo..."

"Damn!! How did you learn all that in one day?" Jazz said looking incredulous.

"It's actually really crazy. So apparently a little while ago a group of scientists figured out that the way we learn things the fastest is actually through an unconscious mechanism where our brain replays the new skill at high speeds. They figured it out by monitoring brain waves of rats, and eventually people. Anyway, after we learn a new skill our brains will continue to replay the same patterns over and over at high speed, like 100 times faster than we could consciously recognize. It goes on in the background, but somehow it begins to reinforce the actual skill."

"That is crazy!" Jazz said, wide eyed.

"That's not even the craziest part. The scientists here figured out a way to enhance this function to thousands of times faster, meaning that most of the agents here can learn skills about twenty times faster than the average person…but Amy…well she figured out a way to use my unique chipset to enhance the speed to millions of times faster. It's basically like they show me a few of the basic moves, then file dump the whole catalog of moves directly to my brain, and then Amy turbo charges it. Ten minutes later I've basically got it mastered…"

Jazz sat in shock, "So you can learn any new skill in ten minutes…"

"Oui, oui je peux," Devin said with a French accent.

"Wait…" Jazz said, "did you learn to speak French…today?"

"The language of love…oh ya…I picked that up today too… Why? Is becoming fluent in a foreign language in ten minutes not something that everyone can do?" Devin said.

Jazz shoved her in the arm, "That is insane! Can I learn skills that fast?"

Unfortunately, this skill requires several of Devin's chips to be active at the same time, but I believe that with your rather unique chip I could make some adjustments that would allow you to learn considerably faster than a standard agent. Amy said to both of them.

"Well, I would love to shut some of these assholes up, so take a look and see what you can do Amy!"

Understood. I would recommend against shutting any assholes up though, the end result of that would be quite…messy.

Both of the girls laughed, "Was that another joke Amy?" Jazz asked.

Indeed.

"God she's cool," Jazz said looking over at Devin, "Seems like you might be rubbing off on her."

Devin smiled, "It's weird, but it's starting to seem like I have another real friend. I mean, I know she's just a computer program, but it sure doesn't feel like it sometimes. Sometimes it seems like…"

Amy cut in before Devin could finish her thought, *You should note that it is now after 10 pm, and your first training begins at 5 am, if you don't go to sleep now you will not be able to get the recommended minimum sleep requirement. I advise that you both stop talking now and proceed to bed.*

"Man, every time Amy, you know you really don't need to be 'that guy'…" Jazz said moving towards Devin's bunk and sitting down beside her. "To bad…I guess we are out of time…" she said, putting her hand on Devin's leg.

Devin felt her entire body flush with warmth. She leaned in and kissed Jazz softly, "We really better get some sleep, as much as I don't want to…"

"Alright…alright, I'll head back to my room…I'm taking my first run at the range tomorrow and I really don't want to make a fool of myself in front of any of the agents, they just don't take us seriously…"

"They will," Devin said, "Once you show them what you can do with that thing they will have to."

Jazz thought about it for a second and smiled, "You're right…and that thing still needs a name, guess I've got something to distract me from some of these…thoughts…" she said as she stood and kissed Devin one last time before walking to the door.

"Goodnight Dev," Jazz said quietly as she walked out of the room, closing the door behind her.

"Goodnight," Devin said, smiling.

Amy lights off. Devin thought.

The lights faded to black, and Devin laid there staring at the ceiling, wishing she had something to distract her from those same thoughts.

27

"And that, is how you shoot one of these things..." Jazz said putting the strange looking gun in her hand down. She turned to see everyone on the range staring at her, some of them open mouthed.

"And you've had no training prior to coming here?" The woman instructing the class asked, looking at Jazz skeptically.

"Well, I wouldn't say that...I mean, I have been nationally ranked in just about every first-person shooter game that's out there...and I got the gun four days ago, so I've been messing with it a little bit on my own time." Jazz said with a smile.

The instructor shook her head and sighed and looked around at all the people that surrounded them, "Jesus Christ...this video game nerd just walked in and set a course record on her first try, the rest of you should be ashamed of yourselves! And as for you," she said, turning back to Jazz, "I want to see more of you out here on the course. I have been instructing tactical fire squads for the better part of three decades. Hell, I've been working with these so-called super soldiers, here and before at the agency, for the last ten years, and I have never witnessed shooting like that before. It's like that rifle is a part of you...unbelievable. Hit the showers you bunch of goons, and I would suggest that the rest of you try getting a couple hours a day extra at the range, cause this *girl* is gonna put you all out of a job."

Jazz smirked at the group of people standing around her, most of them men, most of them twice her age and three times her size, and most of them now glaring at her, sick of being shown up by one of the "new girls".

It was something they had all been getting used to in one fashion or another. Since their arrival a mere week ago Devin and Jazz had made quite the splash. Jazz had already mastered three different chipsets, and had a good handle on two additional ones, and Devin had unlocked eight new skills, all of which she found she excelled at almost instantly.

"That was impressive," Devin said as she walked up to Jazz, who brightened at the sight of her.

"Aww thanks, I didn't know you were here, thought you had hand to hand training until three, or oh fifteen hundred, or whatever these meatheads call it."

"Well...I was supposed to, but no one will spar with me anymore, not like it's much of a challenge anyway. Someone with a single chip just can't compete now that I can activate so many skills at once. It was starting to make me feel bad, I'm glad they said I don't need it any-more." Devin said grabbing her hand and pulling her away from the shooting range.

"Hold on, I need to grab Cereza..." Jazz said moving back towards the table where she had placed her gun.

"I still can't believe you named your gun Cereza..."

"What would you name her...how could I do better than naming her after Bayonetta..." Jazz said smiling.

"True, wanna get out of here?" Devin asked.

"Wait...don't you need to take a turn here at the range?" Jazz asked.

"Ugh, actually I rescheduled 'til tomorrow, I really just don't like guns..."

"Well, I have someone you need to meet, maybe they could change your mind and get you on the range..."

Devin looked around but didn't see anyone else close to the range, although she supposed the person Jazz was talking about could be hidden behind one of the various targets, obstacles, or structures in the range.

Jazz reached behind her back and Devin heard a click, followed by a second one. When Jazz brought her hands back up Devin saw a small, gleaming black gun in each. "Meet Winona and James..." Jazz said holding the weapons out for Devin.

Devin smiled and looked at the guns, which appeared to be perfect miniaturized versions of Cereza. She grabbed one of them and was surprised by the weight of it. "Heavier than I thought they would be..." she said, looking at the gun in her hand.

"Uh, you're welcome," Jazz said playfully.

"Oh, right, sorry. I mean, thanks. They look pretty cool." Devin couldn't tell if Jazz was actually upset with her or not, but she thought she looked like she was kidding. Once again she wished Amy could create the program that would help her with recognizing emotions or intent through facial expressions.

*At this point I'm basically a superhero and I can't even tell when my own girlfriend is being sarcastic or serious...*she thought to herself.

"Well, are you just gonna stand there staring at them or are you gonna take a run at the course?" Jazz said, handing Devin the other gun and nudging her towards the range.

Devin really didn't like trying new things in front of other people. Before she showed anyone anything she liked to be an expert at it. She didn't exactly know why but that was how she had always felt. In school it had prevented her from trying almost anything new, unless of course she could learn that new thing by herself, safe at home in her room. "I get James, but why Winona?"

"Stop stalling," Jazz said, "There's no reason to be nervous. I know you hate new things, but I promise I'll be right here to help. And Winona, from Farscape..."

Devin scrunched up her face, thinking, "Oh right, man it's been a long time since I watched Farscape, John's gun was named Winona. Man, come to think of it it looked pretty similar."

"Ya, that's what gave me the idea. Now seriously, stop stalling and shoot the damn things."

Devin started to feel a rising panic, "I don't even know how..."

I have uploaded all relevant trainings into your chip and am running the skill activator program now. Amy said to both of them. Devin briefly noted the alerts popping into her HUD confirming the new skill and the program starting.

Thanks a lot Amy, Devin said, just to Amy, *You could have had my back you know.*

I do not want your back Devin, it is imperative to your survival.

Devin rolled her eyes and looked down at the guns in her hand once more. The uploading of info was still difficult to get used to. Ten seconds ago Devin knew very little about the weapons in her hands, just the small bits that Jazz had told her, and now, she knew everything about them. Her mind was filled with advanced schematics, safety rules, basic and expert operations, trouble shooting, and pretty much everything else that someone would need to know about the small pistols. She knew once she fired the weapon a couple of times the skill activator program would do the rest. She simply needed to actually use the weapon a couple of times for the program to capture her brain wave pattern, expand it and repeat it.

Devin stepped over to the range, put her foot on the line, and lifted the gun in her right hand. She closed her eyes and took a deep breath...she opened them and instinctively knew how to aim the weapon, how to select the projectile, how to calculate for the wind velocity and for distance. She took a final look over at Jazz and then looked back to the target. *Ok, no big deal, you already know all about this thing, and it doesn't matter that you don't have any experience. The info is in there, you can do this, you won't make a fool of yourself...* Devin thought.

Actually until you have fired the weapon enough times for the program to get a snapshot of your brainwaves you are very likely to perform poorly. Amy said.

There's that boost of confidence. Devin thought back to her as she looked at the target again, *Alright, let's just do this...three...two...*

"That was just showing off," Ronan said as he walked up behind Devin and Jazz. Devin jumped a little and dropped one of the guns, it hit the ground with a soft thud. She turned and glared at Ronan, although inside she was slightly grateful for his timely interruption.

"Oh you're just mad cause I beat your record...on my first try..." Jazz said with a slight smile.

Ronan nodded, "Well, that's definitely part of it, although it's not really fair now is it. I mean, I set the record without using the Deadshot skill."

"So did I..." Jazz said back.

"What? You mean you could you have used Deadshot and you didn't? Why not?" he asked.

Jazz smiled, "I didn't use any skills, that was all 100% Jazz."

"Bullshit," Ronan scoffed, "There's no way..."

"She's telling the truth," Devin said.

"Ya, like I would believe you any more than I believe her, just stay out of this *little girl..*," Ronan said dismissively to Devin.

Devin felt the familiar surge of energy and anger as her berserker skill activated on its own, and seeming to sense that Ronan took an almost imperceptible step backwards.

Amy, turn this freakin thing off would you, man I really need to learn how to control the berserker skill.

She saw the alert pass across her HUD, unfortunately the skill took several minutes to dissipate completely. She bent down and picked up the gun from the ground at her feet. Spinning around she raised the weapon in her right hand, aimed at the closest target and fired with a thought. The gun kicked far more than she was ready for, and her arm flew back. The shot went wild, missing the target by several feet. Devin felt the blood rushing to her face as she flushed with embarrassment.

Ronan did a terrible job of suppressing a laugh behind her. "First time," he said, looking Devin up and down smiling.

Jazz punched him in the arm, hard, and the smile evaporated. "You can do this Dev, just concentrate on where you want the projectile to hit, never take your eyes off of it."

Devin nodded her head and raised the gun a second time. She didn't want to fire it, if there was one thing that Devin had always had trouble with it was starting something new. She hated having to learn something, not because she hated learning, she actually enjoyed that part of it. What she hated was not being great at something right from the start. She noticed an alert in the corner of her screen, focusing her attention on it brought the alert to the center of her vision.

•SKILL ACTIVATOR ACTIVE

    •NEURAL PATTERN DETECTED

    •FURTHER NEURAL ACTIVITY REQUIRED FOR SNAPSHOT

Well shit, she thought to herself, *I guess the sooner I fire this thing the sooner I will have the skill mastered.*

She raised the other gun and holding both out at the same time looked at two different targets, with another thought she sent projectiles racing from the barrels of both guns. This time she was ready for the recoil and her arms remained steady. The shots were slightly better, but still not good. The shot from the gun in her right hand, which she had decided was Winona hit the bottom left of the target she was aiming for. The shot from James went wide of its intended target.

She heard Ronan began to make a comment but blocked him out as she sent two more projectiles flying. This time both targets shook with the impact. The shot from Winona was close to center mass, the shot from James had clipped the side of the target.

Another alert popped into view.

**SKILL ACTIVATOR ACTIVE
*NEURAL PATTERN SNAPSHOT COMPLETE
*SKILL TRANSFER COMMENCING

She could actually feel the information hit her brain and knew right then that the skill was mastered. *That was fast,* she thought.

I have made some more improvements to the activator, you should try again now. Amy said.

You got it, Devin thought back to her, some of her usual confidence returning.

She let her arms fall and shook them out momentarily. As she did she heard Jazz arguing with Ronan.

"Oh sure, I'm sure you did way better on your first day."

"Well, on my first day in the Army I wasn't a super soldier…" said Ronan.

"We aren't super soldiers either," Jazz said taking a step toward him, "We're kids, and Devin has never fired a gun before now."

"Ya, but she's seen a gun before now right?" Ronan laughed, "I mean I feel like just about anyone could have done better than that. If they ever send you two out on a mission I highly doubt either of you make it back. It's a good thing you're both so hot so you have something to fall back on when being superheroes doesn't work out…"

"You little pr…" Jazz started to say as she stepped even closer to Ronan, but Devin interrupted her.

"He's right. That was pretty bad, but I think I got this now." She said smiling.

Ronan looked confused, "So you think 5 bad shots and you've got it all figured out. Well let's see it then sweetheart."

Devin rolled her eyes and raising the guns spun around and began firing. Every target lit up as the center of the bullseye was hit. Shot after shot was absolutely perfect. Devin hit twenty in a row and then with a thought switched both guns to have projectiles tipped with explosives. She took aim at the two farthest targets and let them fly. A split second later a deafening boom shook the ground as the two targets disintegrated in twin fiery explosions.

Devin's eyebrows rose, *That was a lot bigger explosion than I was expecting…she thought.*

Indeed. Amy replied.

Devin dropped her hands to her sides and turned to see Jazz smiling and Ronan standing with his mouth hanging open, a small group had begun to gather, and all of them seemed to be staring between Devin and Jazz.

"Who the hell are you two?" Ronan said, staring at the burning targets.

"The future." Jazz said as she grabbed Devin's hand and the two of them began to walk away, the crowd parting to let them through.

28

"…which is why you should never go into any situation alone."

"But we aren't really ever alone are we?" Devin said from the back of the room.

"I assume you are referring to your A.M.I.I.s…" Agent M said from the front of the class.

"No, I'm talking about the omnipotent and almighty Gooooddddd…of course I'm talking about Amy you jacka…."

"That's quite enough Devin," M said cutting her off and shaking his head slightly in annoyance. "If you are ever in real combat you'll figure out pretty quickly that what you want is a flesh and blood person standing beside you…not Siri."

"If I'm ever in real combat?" Devin said, sounding incredulous, "What do you call me and Jazz taking on six agents by ourselves a couple weeks ago?"

M looked her up and down and smiled slightly, "Lucky."

Jazz laughed under her breath, "It wasn't luck. Devin came up with a great plan and we beat those idiots, simple as that. I know that a meat head like you has a hard time believing that two, how do you keep saying it, *little girls*, could take out six big strong men like yourself…but we did. And we could do it again."

M rolled his eyes slightly and started to speak but Jazz cut him off, "I saw that eye roll…don't believe me? Then go get five other guys and come back in here…cupcake,"

He ignored Jazz and kept talking, "The point here, everyone, is that a real partner that you can trust is of the utmost importance, that's why these exercises are so important."

"These exercises are a waste of time," Devin said flatly, "I don't need to learn about trusting my partner, I need to learn about my powers. There isn't a person in this world that I trust as much as I trust Jazz, we don't need any of your bullshit team building exercises, we've been a team for four years, I trust her with everything in me."

Jazz reached out and grabbed Devin's hand, squeezing it and looking defiantly up at M.

"Touching," M said smirking, "but playing Call of Duty against a bunch of thirteen-year-old nerds is a bit different than going up against highly trained, special forces soldiers."

"Again," Jazz said, "go get five more guys and put your money where your mouth is."

"Alright." M said.

Everyone in the room looked around silently, most turning their gaze toward Devin and Jazz.

"Alright what?" Devin asked slowly.

"Alright, I'll go get five of my men and meet you two on the training field."

Devin scrutinized the large man's face, which was pretty much useless, although she didn't know if that was because his face was unreadable or because of her Asperger's. *Either way*, she thought, *this could be my chance..."*

"Hey. Little girl," M said, "are you just gonna stand there or are we gonna do this..."

Devin jumped a bit at his voice, as if she had been somewhere else and looked at Jazz nervously. She looked back up at M and said, "If you're serious we'll be there in thirty minutes, we need to gear up."

"I look forward to it," M said.

Jazz smirked at the man as Devin turned and pulled her out of the classroom.

"I hope we didn't just bite off more than we can chew..." Jazz said as they entered the hallway. She turned for once last glance into the classroom and saw all the other agents in training talking excitedly, most were shaking their heads, a few were laughing. Several had their phones out and were texting, clearly letting everyone in the facility know about the upcoming battle.

"We didn't," Devin said firmly. "Come on, we need to hurry, we only have a half hour, Amy are you working on that?"

"Working on wha..." Jazz started to say as Amy cut in.

Yes. A car will be waiting for you in seven minutes, I have marked the coordinates on your map. All of the gear you will need will be in the car waiting for you. I have procured the suits and weapons you requested. The car already has the destination programmed into it.

"Devin...what the hell is she talking about..." Jazz said, sounding nervous.

Devin looked down, "Don't be mad at me, I wasn't sure I would be able to make it work so I didn't want to say anything, but we are gonna get the hell out of here. While everyone is out there waiting for us to show up and fight those over testosteroned idiots, we're going to leave. We're gonna go save my dad."

Devin was afraid to look up, she needed Jazz, but she also knew that their training wasn't complete. The truth was she didn't think their training would ever be complete. They kept learning more and more about her skills, and about Jazz's chipset. It was beginning to feel like Kevin and Dr. Tran were far more interested in understanding how the Phoenix chip worked, and what it was capable of than they were in training Devin and Jazz to go rescue her father.

This would be insanely risky, that was the real reason Devin hadn't told Jazz, she was afraid that if she did Jazz wouldn't come and help her, that she would try to convince Devin to stay and finish the training. So she continued to stare at the ground.

She felt fingertips brush the side of her face as Jazz placed her hand on her cheek and lifted her eyes to look at her. "I told you before any of this started, back when we were just pretending to be soldiers, or warriors, or mages, that I would always have your back. I meant it. Where you go, I go. You never need to be afraid of that. We are together. I love you Devin."

Devin felt the tears hit the corners of her eyes and her face flush. *Holy shit, did she just say she loves me...do you think she means like...I love you gurl...or like she loves me loves me...and what am I supposed to say back...I mean what if I say it back and she says, I meant like, you're my girl, I love you...Devin thought all of this at the same time.

I believe she is waiting for you to say something, Amy said to Devin.

Christ, you're right, thanks Amy. She thought before raising her hands to Jazz's face and pulling her towards her. The two kissed, and kissed, and kissed.

Four minutes til car arrives, Amy said to both girls, which seemed to bring them both back to reality. Devin pulled back, breathless.

"Wow," Jazz said, blinking her eyes slowly.

"Ya." Devin said, "Wow is about right. And I love you. And its ok if you didn't mean that you love me love me, if you just meant like I'm your girl I don't care, cause I love you, I love you more than I could ever imagine loving anyone...and so..."

This time Jazz pulled Devin in and lightly kissed her lips, lingering there for just a second, "I meant I love you Devin. I've loved you for months, maybe years. I loved you before we ever even met."

Devin smiled and was about to say something when Amy spoke in both of their heads,

Great you love her, she loves you. We all love everyone. Can you please start making your way to the car. We are running out of time. I am adding a countdown timer to your HUD's.

"We better go," Devin said grabbing Jazz's hand as they began to run towards their rooms to retrieve Cereza, Winona, and James, and a few other personal items. They had no idea when, or if, they would ever be back in this place.

As they ran into the dormitory area Devin saw a flash of white as someone turned the corner at the end of the hall. *Who was that?* She asked Amy.

Their chip was not identified. Accessing cameras now to assess the situation.

A small window popped into the lower left corner of Devin and Jazz's HUDs that showed Ronan sprinting through the hallway of the dormitory. "That's weird," Devin said as she ran into her room.

"That dudes a creep, it's not all that weird that he would be lurking around here..." Jazz said, "I'm gonna run to my room, we can communicate with our chips 'til I get back if you need anything."

"Got it, hurry!" Devin said.

Jazz and Devin had worked together with Amy to hack their chipsets so that could talk using the same mechanism that they used to interface with their AMII, although they still preferred to talk to one another out loud most of the time. It did come in handy for when they were apart though.

*Amy, can you rewind the video, I want to see where he was coming from...*Devin thought.

The video in her HUD began rewinding and Devin watched as Ronan entered Jazz's room using a key card on the security pad, and moments later entered her own room the same way. There were no cameras in the rooms, so it was impossible to tell what he was doing in there, but it couldn't be anything good.

*Jazz, did you see the footage...*Devin thought

Ya, I saw it, what do you think he was doing? Jazz said.

Who knows, nothing good that's for sure. Devin said.

He was probably just snooping through our underwear drawer or something, Jazz said.

Actually, Amy said, *I don't believe that he wears the same size of clothing as either of you. Plus, all program participants can requisition any clothing items they need, so I find it unlikely that he would want your under garments.*

He wouldn't be wearing them Amy, Devin said.

*Well...*Jazz said, *we don't actually know that.*

Gross, Devin said, *anyway, that's not what he was doing. If anything looks out of place at all leave it.*

Got it, Jazz said, *I'm leaving everything, except Cereza. Anything else we need we can get on the road.*

Sounds good, Devin said, *let's get out of here.*

Devin reached down and grabbed the belt that had the double holster with James and Winona and snapped it around her waist. She started towards the door but saw the Sonic hoodie hanging by the bed and grabbed it, throwing it over her head. She pulled it down to cover the holster that sat at the small of her back. She pulled one pistol out and shoved it into the large front pocket of the hoodie. When she did she felt the small plastic Sonic toy that she had grabbed from her dresser.

God, that feels like a lifetime ago, she thought.

It was 14 days, 7 hours, and 3 minutes ago, Amy chimed in. *Also, you both should leave your weapons here, they will disable them as soon as they realize that you have left the compound, and as of this point I have found no way to override their security on the weapons. I have procured weapons for you, so these will not be necessary.*

Devin pulled the gun back out of her pocket and tossed it on the bed, then unhooked the holster and let it fall to the floor, she looked up as Jazz ran into the room, slightly out of breath, and pulled Cereza from the magnetic holster, "Man, I really hate the idea of not taking her with me. We've bonded…"

Devin smiled slightly and turned to look at Jazz, "I'm sure Amy hooked us up, no point in taking something that isn't gonna work…"

"Ya, I suppose, so what now?" Jazz asked.

"Now," she said as her hand tightened around the pistol in her pocket, "we get to the car, and get the hell out of here."

29

"And you're certain they didn't see you?" Agent M said looking down at Ronan, who squirmed just a little under the weighty gaze.

"Well, I'm pretty sure, I can't be totally sure. I think they may have caught a glimpse of me as I turned the corner of the hallway, I was far away and moving fast though, so I really doubt that they could tell who it was…"

M considered the smaller man, "What about the cameras, if they accessed those would they have been able to see you?"

Ronan looked confused for a second and then responded, "Well, I couldn't avoid the cameras if that's what you're asking, you told me to place the devices, so I did it…the cameras are everywhere sir, I don't see how I could have done what you asked without being seen by the cameras," he paused and thought, *you also said I would have forty minutes longer than I ended up having, so be glad I'm so fast,* but he didn't say that part out loud, instead he continued, "I don't really see what it matters though, agents don't have access to the camera feeds anyway."

M looked at him with something bordering on disdain, "I think it would be very unwise for us to assume that these *girls* have the same restrictions or skills as standard agents."

"I know they have different abilities because of their chips, but come on, they're just teenage girls, how much trouble could they really cause?"

M seemed to consider it for a moment, "I don't really buy in to the super enhanced thing, I know that Devin seems to possess the ability to activate multiple enhancements at the same time, but I've been here for a long time, I've seen what happens when too much power runs through one of these things. Most likely she'll end up melting her brain down eventually, but there's something…different…about the A.M.I.I. that Devin has, underestimating that would be an error."

Ronan shook his head, "Look, I won't lie, when I first got here I tried to hack the camera system, hell I tried to hack all the systems, they're locked up tight. If I can't do it there's no way some AI program can. I've been hacking since I was eight years old, I'm not the best…but I'm good, and when security is set up right it takes a human mind to crack it, AIs just can't think like that, at least not yet."

This seemed to satisfy M, "I suppose you're right, we do have some of the best engineers in the world working for us, the odds that they were able to get through the system are pretty low. Either way, seems to be a successful mission. A few more like that and I think I can convince the boss to send you out into the field with us."

Ronan smiled, "That's what I'm talking about, let's go!"

M laughed slightly, "Ok, calm down, you did good but being caught on camera was stupid, whether they can access them or not. You should have figured out a way to do it without being seen, shit like that ruins missions. It was good, it could have been better."

Ronan looked towards the ground, all of his normal bravado gone, "I'll do better," he said quietly.

"Good," M said, "see that you do…and no one can know anything about this, understood?"

"Understood," Ronan said, standing up straighter. He liked the idea that M trusted him with what it now appeared was a very classified assignment. "Is there anything else you need from me sir?"

M grunted as he shrugged his vest up to his shoulders, and pointed to two handguns laying on the table. "Hand me those would you? I feel like I should be ready just in case they actually show up."

Ronan smiled as he grabbed the guns and handed them to M, "Do you think they will?"

"I don't," M said without much thought, "Neither of them is all that smart, but they know that they can't possibly match six trained agents."

Ronan thought about it for just a moment, "Did you know they can directly access each other's feeds?"

M scowled, "I did not...do you know how?"

"I think somehow their AIs did it, at least that's what they said..."

M considered for a moment, "Is that all they can do?"

Ronan laughed quietly, "How the hell should I know, aren't you the one that's been training them?"

"I haven't really had a whole lot to do with them, I have heard people talk, but most of my work with them has not been in the field, so I haven't really seen much of what they can do with my own eyes, and some of the stories I've been told don't really seem that credible to me."

"Well, I know they can both shoot...like crazy good, some of the best shooting I have ever seen, and you know I was the course record holder until Jazz showed up..." Ronan said with a hint of pride in his voice, "She beat me pretty easily on her first run through, and she says it was with no skills activated, which if that's true that's pretty crazy...so I think Devin would be even better at it. I saw her take her first shots at the range, it was clear she had never held any kind of weapon in real life, and her first couple shots were terrible, but after that..." he raised his eyebrows as he looked at M.

"Then she was lying, it takes a lot more than a couple of tries to figure out the deadshot skill, she must have been practicing on her own, and what you saw was a classic hustle..."

Ronan shook his head, "If that was a hustle then she deserves an academy award, plus you haven't been around her that much, she is a terrible liar, she gets even more awkward than normal when she's trying to hide something. Jazz could pull something like that off, but not Devin."

"Well, I don't see how what you are saying is possible, but it's at least interesting. I'll need to step up my observation of these two it sounds like...but for now, I think I'll just get ready to go kick their asses. It sounds like they could use a little humility."

"That's the understatement of the year," Ronan said.

M smiled, "And none of your feelings are coming from jealousy in any way?"

Ronan looked down before speaking, "I guess that's possible, I am jealous that they have access to more than one skill, I mean can you imagine having that kind of ability, it would be incredible!"

"Well, like I said, that hasn't worked well for anyone so far, so I would count yourself lucky that you only have the one skill, and from what I've seen you still have a lot to learn about that one."

"Yes, sir," Ronan said, a hint of anger in his voice.

M smirked as he shoved his handgun into the holster at his side, "Just keep working kid, you'll be fine, but for now I'm gonna see if these two are smart enough to *not* show up."

30

"Devin and Jazz sat in the backseat of the black Tesla as it sped down the road, trying desperately to catch their breath.

"You're sure the car is clean?" Devin said.

"I am certain." Amy said through the speakers of the car, "I had the modifications done at two separate custom shops, and then had the car delivered to a secure parking facility where it could be fully charged. I used the car's cellular service to access the system and add code that I wrote to give me greater control over the systems as well as fully autonomous driving, and of course to remove all identification and block all tracking functions."

"That sounds great, but I do have one question…how did you get the money?" Jazz asked, "I mean this thing couldn't have been cheap…it's not stolen is it Amy, cause that won't be good…"

"Of course it's not stolen," Devin said shaking her head, and then internally she said, *It's not stolen right Amy?*

"I heard that," Jazz said smiling.

"Dammit, thought I had sent that just to Amy…"

"That is definitely a skill that you are having a difficult time mastering," Amy said through the car speakers.

"Tell me about it," Devin said scowling slightly.

"I just did." Amy said, eliciting a laugh from both girls, "And to answer your question Jazz, no the car is not stolen…borrowed is a more appropriate term."

"Borrowed." Devin said flatly.

"Yes, I simply created a false paper trail in the dealership's database and then removed the vehicle from their inventory."

"As long as no one is going to be looking for it I'm good with however you got it," Jazz said reaching over and grabbing Devin's hand.

"Me too, and it really is awesome, and at least it's a bit more inconspicuous than one of the giant SUV's that those dickheads drive around," Devin said.

"Indeed," Amy said, "Not appearing to be dickheads was a high priority…"

"She is getting funnier," Jazz said laughing.

"Indeed," Devin said doing her best Amy impression.

"So any idea where we are going, or what we are going to do when we get there?" Jazz asked.

Silence hung in the air for a moment, "I have a location of where I believe they are holding your father."

"What? How did you find it?" Devin asked.

"I was able to access Dr. Tran's private server, it was heavily encrypted but after several attempts I found several communications to Dr. Tran from the agency." Amy said.

Devin looked shocked, "And the agency just told him where my dad was?"

"Yes. The agency has not been hiding this information from Dr. Tran."

"Mother…" Devin whispered, "Why the hell would they tell Tran where my father was…and why wouldn't he tell me…"

Jazz reached out and grabbed Devin's hand, "They told him hoping you would come after him, and he didn't tell you knowing you would."

Devin squeezed Jazz's hand, "You're damn right. I would have left the first day if I had known. I'm gonna kick his ass when we get back."

Jazz shook her head, "I get it Dev, but I think he probably did us a favor, we wouldn't have been ready…I'm not even sure that we're ready now…"

"You are not," Amy said, "you still have very little understanding of your abilities. Also while researching the facility, I found that it houses over 100 agents. I could not ascertain the number of agents that are enhanced, but we should assume it is a high number. The odds of success are not good."

Devin and Jazz looked at one another, "Well that's comforting..." Devin said, "So where are we headed?"

"I will update your chip now with all relevant info for the mission." Amy said.

A series of alerts popped into Devin's HUD.

NEW MISSION ALERT - EXTRACT HAL THOMAS FROM AGENCY COMPLEX
    •GAIN ENTRY TO COMPLEX
    •NEUTRALIZE ENEMIES
    •FIND AND RETRIEVE HAL THOMAS
    •ESCAPE COMPLEX

Below these alerts Devin saw a small folder icon. "The new interface looks awesome Amy, are you seeing this stuff Jazz?"

Jazz's eyes shifted rapidly back and forth as she tried to take everything in, "Holy shit, it looks like just like Call of Duty...my alerts are laid out video game style like yours now..." Jazz said.

"I have updated the interface to Devin's requests, does this meet your expectations?" Amy asked.

"Uhhh, hell yes, this is dope Amy! Great job. I hope you don't mind Jazz, I had Amy redo my display to look like COD and while she was at it, I had her figure out a way to update yours too..." Devin said as she scanned her new HUD. In the upper left hand corner, she now saw a satellite map of her surroundings, as well as a green indicator that she knew marked her location, and a yellow indicator stacked beside it marking Jazz. When she focused on the map she found she could enlarge it with a thought, and then return it to its original position in the same way. She turned her attention to the bottom left of the screen and saw two sets of status bars. She instantly recognized the red and green bars as health and stamina levels, one set for her and one for Jazz. She assumed the third blue bar on top was for body armor, "Amy, is the blue bar for body armor?"

"Indeed." Amy said.

"Do we have body armor?" Devin asked glancing at Jazz.

"Yes, once you set me on the task of planning this mission I began to work on custom body armor suits for both of you. They are one of a kind, I used plans that DARPA has been working on as my starting point, but have made some considerable adjustments, they are in the frunk."

Devin laughed, "You can tell us all about them later…and I think you mean the trunk."

"Negative, additional weapons, food, and stamina gel are in the trunk, the frunk contains the body armor suits as well as an additional set of clothing in case it is needed, and uniforms that match what the guards at the agency facility wear, or at least from what I was able to observe what they wear."

"What the fruck is a frunk…" Jazz said looking genuinely confused.

"A front trunk, standard on the Tesla Model X." Amy stated.

Both girls laughed at this, "Frunk…that's so dumb…" Devin said, "But at least we have extra room. Do you think we have everything we need?"

"Aside from mastery of your skills yes." Amy said.

"Burn…" Jazz said with a slight chuckle.

Devin laughed, "We still need to work on your people skills Amy, but thanks for getting everything around. It's impressive…really…"

"Your gratitude is appreciated but unnecessary, it is my primary directive to keep you alive, the preparation for this mission was fulfilling that directive."

"Oh, don't get all sappy on me now," Devin said with a chuckle, "Either way, we appreciate you Amy, you're the best."

"For sure," Jazz agreed, "I love the new interface, and I can't wait to see the stuff you brought us…but I would be lying if I said I wasn't nervous…"

Devin laughed, "Well you would have to be actually insane not to be nervous at this point, especially with how much Amy has reminded us of the unlikeliness that we will actually succeed."

"That's not what I'm worried about Dev, I know we're gonna succeed, it's your dad, we have to…plus we are two bad ass chicks…I'm worried that…" she trailed off.

Devin searched Jazz's face, trying to decipher what she saw there, but as usual it was no help. "You can tell me Jazz, you can tell me anything."

"I'm worried that we are gonna have to hurt people…"

Devin nodded, "We are, I can't imagine a way that we get my dad free without hurting people, but I'm ok with it, cause they are bad people. No good person would hold someone like my dad hostage. And for what? To get a look inside my brain? I can't imagine that would end well for me either…"

"I know they deserve whatever is coming to them, they really do, but I'm still scared, I mean what if I freeze up? I've never actually shot anyone in real life ya know…"

"It's not real life, that's how I'm looking at it. I mean, use the HUD, it's a game, it's our game Jazz, and no one beats us at our game. These guys don't stand a chance," Devin said reaching down to grab Jazz's hand, "they made their choices, now they will face the consequences…"

31

Devin and Jazz both stared into the frunk of the Tesla, not entirely sure what they were looking at. In the frunk were two black suits, that looked more like spandex than body armor.

"So these are supposed to be our body armor?" Devin said.

Yes, Amy replied in both girls' heads, *As I said, this is a new technology that I had created and then 3-D printed in a lab in Arizona. The basic design comes from a type of body armor that the US military once believed was the future of combat protection called dragon skin.*

"Dragon skin…" Jazz said, not hiding her skepticism.

Yes, the name was derived from the overlapping plates inside of the vest, that bore a resemblance to reptile scales. Dragon Skin was tested vigorously, and the results were very promising. In one test a vest successfully absorbed impacts from over 100 rounds fired from an AK-47 at close range, as well as rounds from a .308 rifle, and multiple calibers of handgun rounds.

"If the stuff was so good why did they quit using it?" Devin asked.

The official response was that on further testing the armor did not hold up to military standards. During my research I found that a more probable explanation was that the company that was set to be replaced if Dragon Skin became standard issue applied pressure to politicians that they had been working with for decades, and suddenly Dragon Skin began to have issues in testing. In all independent tests before and after the military banned the use of Dragon Skin it has been shown to be the superior option. Lighter, smaller, cheaper to manufacture, and far superior in stopping power. That is why I chose it as the basis of my design.

Devin reached in and grabbed one of the suits and held it up. "It looks…tight…" she said, with an awkward glance toward Jazz.

It is quite form fitting by design, loose clothing is a hindrance in close-quarters hand to hand combat. Inside of the fabric are two layers of overlapping discs, both layers having been made of graphene. The layers are so thin that they are virtually imperceptible, and therefore the suit will not hamper your movement in any way. I have also had small, extremely powerful magnets placed in the sides and back to hold your weapons without the need of holsters.

"Mag-safe body armor…" Jazz said, "Available only on the iPhone 15…"

Devin laughed at this, "It's really incredible that these would be able to stop anything at all, they are so thin," she said, scrunching her face as she turned the fabric over in her hands, "and I feel like I'm going to look ridiculous in this thing…"

Graphene is an incredible material, even when only one atom thick if it is stacked in two layers, it hardens to become stronger than diamond when hit with enough force. Ridiculous or not, these suits will allow freedom of movement, take into account your enhanced abilities, allow your weapons to be easily accessible at all times, and will stop just about anything from harming you. Another added benefit of the form fitting nature of the suits is that you will be able to wear other clothes on top of the body armor suit if a disguise is needed. I have also outfitted them with a new stamina gel delivery system.

"I think they're hot," Jazz said, and her mouth curled into a smile, "Come on Dev, we are super heroes now, we probably better look the part."

Devin rolled her eyes as she held the suit up against her body, "Can't we be the first women superheroes to not fall into classic male fantasy tropes of girls strutting around in skin tight black latex…"

The suits are not made of latex, as I said they are proprietary fiber blend lined with a dual layer of graphene, loose fabric is not ideal for clandestine missions such as this one.

"See, practical and sexy, just like you," Jazz said, reaching over and smacking Devin playfully on the butt.

Devin smiled as a blush crept into her cheeks, "Ok, ok, the suits are great, thanks Amy…can you tell me about the stamina gel delivery system, what is that, like one of those marathon runner backpacks with a tube that we can just suck through when we start running low."

No, not at all. Within the fabric of the suit are thousands of nano wires. Once you both put the suits on there is a button that you will press that will pull the suit tight, conforming to your body, at which point the nanowires will embed themselves into your skin. They are microscopic so you won't feel the wires, but because of the number of them they will be more than adequate. I developed them using much of the same nanotech that is in the chipset that Jazz has. With the delivery system, and the new super concentrated stamina solution I was able to create you both should be able to use whatever powers you would like, for as long as you like, and not require additional stamina gel. This will not replace the need for eating food or traditional stamina gel completely though, this is a highly specified supplement, meant to keep your cellular energy...

"Getting a bit technical for me," Devin said as she began walking towards the back of the car, "but it sounds great. Having to watch out for stamina constantly makes things difficult for sure. I can't believe you were able to get all of this done so fast Amy, it's really amazing. So now...show us what's in the trunk."

As Devin and Jazz walked around the car the trunk began to lift, revealing a veritable armory of weapons.

Devin took in a breath, "Holy..."

"Shit," Jazz finished, "that is a lot of guns."

32

M looked at the crowd of people gathered around the training field. The five agents that he had recruited for this test stood at attention to his left. Ronan was standing at the edge of the track, looking around nervously. M squinted and looked down at his watch.

"They aren't coming," he said to the man directly to his left, "I told you their bark was worse than their bite."

The man smiled and shook his head in agreement, but M thought he caught a slight look of relief pass over the man's face. "Alright, I'm calling it," he said loudly to everyone gathered, "we've been waiting for an hour, they clearly aren't gonna show up. I'm sure they are hiding out somewhere, we'll see them tomorrow with their tails tucked between their legs."

"Sir," Ronan called as he trotted out to the center of the field, "do you want me to use the devi…"

"Stop talking," M said menacingly. He turned and saw two agents standing together watching Ronan, "I don't want you to do anything."

Ronan sensed the threat and took a step back, "Yessir."

"Come with me," M said as he turned and began walking back towards the main campus of buildings.

The two walked in total silence. Ronan stole several glances at M as they walked and noticed that he seemed to be looking over his shoulder every few steps. Ronan thought that the big man seemed nervous, and he had never known M to be nervous, about anything. "Is everything alright?" Ronan asked once he knew they were alone.

M looked down at him, "No everything is not alright! Listen, what I had you do, as I told you before you did it, was between you and I. Dammit kid, you can't just come out blabbing about it. Not everyone here is on the same team…"

Ronan's face went scarlet, "You don't even trust your own men?"

M laughed, "No, I don't as a matter of fact. I know what some of these men are capable of. Listen, this stays between you and I, don't talk about it in front of anyone else. Got it?"

"Ya, I got it," Ronan said quietly, "I just really don't think anyone would care if they found…"

"Let me make this very clear, what you think doesn't matter. You don't know anything about what is actually going on here."

"Then fill me in," Ronan said, "I mean what is the point of all the secrecy, you know you can trust me, if you didn't you never would have had me plant the devices in in the first place. And what were those things? My first thought was gps trackers, but they seemed too small to have enough battery to power even a small transponder."

M frowned, looking Ronan up and down, "That's a good observation, maybe you're smarter than I thought. Look, you will know what you need to know, nothing more…right now we need to figure out where they went. Go check their rooms, if they aren't there collect any of the devices that are still there, then meet me in my quarters. I should be there in about thirty minutes."

"What are you going to do?" Ronan asked.

M considered for a moment, "I'm going to figure out what those two are up to, and get us some insurance…"

33

Devin stood in the bathroom of a truck stop and looked at herself in the mirror. She tilted her head sideways as she ran her hands down the sides of the skintight black fabric, "I'll admit, these suits are pretty bad ass..." she called out to Jazz as she turned her back towards the mirror and stood on her tiptoes, looking over her shoulder, *And my ass looks pretty great in it too...*she thought.

"That's an understatement," Jazz said, closing the stall door behind door.

"Shit," Devin said, spinning towards Jazz, "I meant to say that just to myself, man I am not good at controlling which thoughts get sent to who..."

Jazz smiled as she looked Devin up and down, "Well right now I'm glad I'm better at it than you are..." Devin blushed as Jazz walked up and put her hands around her waist, pulling her close. She kissed her gently on the lips, lingering for a heartbeat, then leaning close to her ear she whispered, "You look incredible Dev..."

Devin felt her heart begin to race, it felt like every nerve in her body was on fire. She pulled back slightly and looked at Jazz, taking her in for the first time in her new suit, which seemed designed to accentuate every curve of her body. "Damn," Devin said as she stared at Jazz. An alert popped into her HUD, startling her.

**Elevated heart rate detected*

Your heart rate is abnormal, would you like me to diagnosis the problem? Amy asked in her head.

"Are you seeing and hearing this?" Devin asked, looking at Jazz.

Jazz smiled, "No diagnosis needed Amy, I'm just apparently super-hot in this suit."

Devin smiled, "That is for sure, I just hope I don't get distracted during the fight."

Jazz laughed as she walked over to the mirror and looked at herself, "I am definitely keeping this suit…"

Vehicle charging will be complete in twelve minutes. Our destination is one hour away, I advise that you head to the car so we can find a secure location for you to begin choosing your weapons. You should be armed and ready on arrival.

"So what, we just walk out of here looking like a couple of Avengers?" Devin said.

"Here," Jazz said, tossing Devin her Sonic the Hedgehog hoodie, "It will just look like yoga pants if throw this on."

Devin pulled the sweatshirt down over her head, and instantly felt more comfortable, "Ya that's better for sure. Do you have one too?"

"Yep, Amy picked one up for me," she said as she pulled a black hoodie over her head, "not as cool as yours, but it will do."

The girls walked out of the bathroom and into the truck stop, "We still have ten minutes before charging is complete," Jazz said as she looked at the information in her HUD, "I'm gonna grab a Monster and some Cheetos, want anything?"

Devin smiled, "Well, it wouldn't be a gaming session without Monster and Cheetos, so ya, better get me some too. I'm gonna head out to the car and look over the plans, make sure I know what we're doing when we get there."

Jazz smiled, "That's my girl, always over prepared."

"I don't think we can over prepare for this mission," Devin said.

"Good point, two Monsters each it is…" Jazz said with a smile.

Devin laughed, "I'll see you back at the car," she said as she turned and began walking towards the front entrance of the truck stop.

Movement in her peripheral vision caught her attention and she turned just in time to see a man at the end of an aisle quickly shift his eyes away from her. He casually picked up a bag of chips from the rack in front of him and turned to the drink coolers lining the back wall, but nothing about his movement seemed right to Devin.

Amy, can you access the video feeds of this place? Devin asked in her head.

I successfully penetrated the security of several high-level systems to gain access to The Agency's files, as well as hacking into the Department of Transportation camera feeds, I believe that I can handle the I-80 Flying J's camera system.

What's going on Dev? Jazz asked in her head.

Saw a guy staring at me, when I looked he grabbed some chips and walked away, but something doesn't feel right. He just didn't look right...Amy, are you actively scanning the area for chips?

I did not believe this to be necessary, would you like me to run a scan now?

Do it, Devin said, *and get me a map of this place, and access to the cameras. Something doesn't feel right.*

Scanning. Amy said.

Devin turned to see Jazz making her way to the front counter just as several video windows opened in her HUD. She quickly scanned the video feeds, noting the man she saw was now making his way to the front of the store, he got in line behind Jazz, holding a bottle of soda and a bag of chips.

Heads up Jazz, the guy I saw is coming up behind you. Blue track suit.

Jazz turned her head slightly and caught Devin's eye and gave her a small smile, *Don't worry Dev, you are probably just being overly para...*

Scan complete. Four chips have been found. Updating locations on the map.

Devin watched in horror as several red dots popped on to the map. It appeared that one was in the bathroom, one in the upstairs lounge of the truck stop, another was by the line of fast-food restaurants on the other side of the facility, and the final dot popped onto the map directly behind Jazz.

Jazz, Devin began.

I've got this, Jazz said and dropped the Cheetos she was holding. She bent to pick them up, bending from the waist. The agent standing behind her in the blue track suit was momentarily distracted, the curves of her body and her new suit doing the job that she had intended.

As she picked up the bag of chips she looked up at him and smiled. Caught off guard he gave a small shake of his head and quickly turned his gaze to the side, just in time to see Devin's elbow flying at his face.

He tried to duck but was too slow. The elbow connected to the bridge of his nose. Devin felt, and heard, the bones disintegrate under the blow. The man crumpled to the floor.

"What the fuck," the kid behind the counter shouted as he dove to the floor.

Jazz and Devin glanced at one another, and Jazz began talking as she walked towards the counter, "Hey, it's ok. This guy's been stalking us, we saw him at the last placed we stopped too. We even saw a zip tie on our car's door handle, like he had marked us for sex trafficking or whatever these weirdos are in to. It seemed like he was about to make his move."

"Should I call the police?" The young guy asked, still on the floor behind the counter.

"No, please, we don't want the cops involved, we're just trying to get away ya know. My parents don't like that I'm dating a girl, especially a white girl, so we took off. Been on our own for a while now. Here's fifty bucks for the monsters, Cheetos, and the trouble of the clean-up. Just let us…"

Devin turned away as Jazz continued to try and talk their way out of an encounter with the police, which was the last thing they needed. They had a stolen car with a trunk full of high-tech weaponry, not to mention the suits. It would go nowhere good if the cops showed up.

"Activate ECO," Devin said and felt the rush of adrenaline that came with berserker mode. She knelt down beside the man on the floor and began to pat him down, searching for a weapon.

His primary weapon will most likely be bio-synced to him, Amy said, *search for a secondary firearm on his ankle.*

Devin moved down to the man's ankles and felt something under his track suit. She pulled the pant leg up and was disappointed to find two knives instead of a gun but grabbed them both and stood as Jazz walked back over.

"We're good, he said he won't call the police until we leave, which he suggested we do quickly. Did you find anything on our friend?"

"Here," she said handing Jazz one of the knives, "No usable gun on this guy, we should just run, I don't want to fight three armed men in a public place like this."

"I'm not sure we have that option," Jazz said, "check your map."

Devin glanced at the map, bringing it to full screen in her HUD. She noted that the orange dots were not converging on her location, instead they were spreading out, covering all of the exits to the truck stop.

"Fuck," Devin said, "How the hell did these guys find us Amy? Were they somehow able to track our chips?"

Impossible, the encryption on your chipsets is not hackable, the car is clean, and we brought nothing from the compound. I do not know how they have managed to find us.

Devin looked shocked, "Shit," she exhaled, "I did bring something from the compound."

Closing her eyes she reached into the pocket of her hoodie and pulled out the small Sonic the Hedgehog plastic figurine. Turning it over she saw that there was a small black circle on the right foot of the toy.

"What the hell is this?" She said scraping at the circle.

It was no thicker than a sticker, small enough to almost be mistaken for a scuff. *That is a nanotech gps tracker, and the answer to how they found us.* Amy said.

Devin turned and saw Jazz coming around the end of the aisle, holding a package of something. "What is that?" Devin asked.

"Well, this guy's not dead right? I figure we need to make sure he stays out of the game, and unless you want to kill him, this is the next best option," she said as she tore the top off the package of zip ties.

Devin glanced at the map again, and then the video feeds. The other three agents had taken up stations at each of the exits. "Luckily this place is huge, they didn't send enough guys to cover the exits and leave any to come after us, well except this guy, so we don't have to fight them all, just get past one of them" she said glancing down as Jazz finished pulling the zip tie on the man's wrists tight.

"Unless they sent guys without chips again, and if they know we can monitor them it would make sense to have guys that aren't chipped here." Jazz said standing up.

"Good point, Amy scan the video feeds and light up anyone that seems suspicious."

Jazz and Devin watched their HUDs as eight more icons popped into view, these ones orange.

"They sent more guys this time," Jazz said, a slight smile on her face.

"And that makes you happy?" Devin asked.

"Well, it means that they are scared of us." Jazz said.

Devin snorted, "Or tired of messing around and ready to just put an end to it."

"Either way, it means they are scared of us…"

"They should be," Devin said.

"Damn right!" Jazz said, "So what do we do now?"

Devin looked at the Sonic toy still in her hand and placed it on one of the shelves. She turned to Jazz, "Now, we gotta go fast."

34

"Amy, can you kill the lights in this place?"

In answer all of the lights in the truck stop went dark with a clunk. Devin noticed a moment of darkness, but her chip quickly compensated for the low light and her vision returned to almost normal immediately.

She kept on eye on the map, the orange dots were spread out, but two of them were making their way towards Devin and Jazz. "They're coming," Devin said grabbing Jazz's hand. "I don't know how we get out of this. We have no weapons, no back up on the way, no respawns."

Jazz squeezed her hand, "We are the weapons Dev, these guys are fucking with the wrong girls. If they want a fight I say we give it to them."

Devin smiled, "Alright, we don't need to take them all out, we just need to get to the car. We can't forget this is a side mission, don't let it distract us from the real one."

"Absolutely, so mission update, escape the truck-stop, got it. Amy, activate Deadshot."

"Uh, Jazz, we don't have any guns…"

"Guns," Jazz said smiling, "Aren't the only things that you can aim."

She raised her eyebrows and ducked around the corner of the aisle. Devin watched as her icon made its way through the aisle towards the nearest orange icon on the map. She pulled up the camera feeds and tagged Jazz so that Amy would automatically switch cameras to always keep Jazz in view and made her way to the other end of the aisle, keeping an eye on two other agents that seemed to be converging on them.

She got to the end of the aisle and glanced around it, seeing two men slowly making their way through the truck stop. She noticed that there were still a lot of people milling around, complaining about the power outage, some laughing, some cursing, all oblivious to the situation that was playing out.

She glanced back at Jazz's feed and saw her standing facing a shelf of candy bars, she was wondering exactly what her plan was when she noticed the other agent round the corner of the aisle where Jazz was standing. The man had a hand on his gun, but it was still in his holster. In the darkness of the truck stop he couldn't be totally sure that Jazz was his target, and to his credit it appeared he didn't want to take out a civilian.

Jazz held her hand up to her face, pretending to be talking on the phone as the man slowly made his way down the aisle, trying to appear nonchalant. Devin watched as Jazz turned towards the man and smiled, holding her hand down and said something that she couldn't quite make out.

The man turned slightly looking behind him, and as he did Jazz reached into the pocket of her hoodie and pulled out one of the giant cans of Monster. He caught the movement, and his hand went to his gun but he was too slow, the giant can flew faster than Devin could believe and, aided by Deadshot, it connected directly with his temple.

The man hit the ground hard, Jazz running up and securing his hands behind his back with the zip ties. *He's out*, Jazz said, *coming to you now*.

Devin held her position at the end of the aisle, watching Jazz as she made her way back through the maze of aisles.

"Ok, so now what?" Jazz whispered.

"These two are the only ones close enough to get here before we could make it out to the car, assuming we can get past the guy at the door."

I am working on a solution for that now, Amy said, *I will alert you when I am prepared.*

"Better make it fast Amy, we're gonna take these two out and then bolt towards the door, I don't really want to get shot on the way out. Jazz, can I have that knife back?"

Jazz put her hand in the pocket of her hoodie to retrieve the knife and froze when a voice spoke closely behind them, "Don't fucking move."

Both girls froze, Devin spoke to Amy in her mind, *Amy, who the hell is that?*

Unknown, this man was not identified as an agent, and appears to have no chip. He is armed, and the weapon that he has is pointed towards Jazz. It appears to be a handgun, make unknown. Amy said.

"Ok, we aren't going to move, just tell us what you want?" Devin said, eyes still looking forward, but in her HUD she was scanning through camera feeds, trying to get a good look at the man behind them.

She could only get a look at the man from the side, a big man, dressed in black, and just as Amy had said, he had a gun trained on Jazz. Devin felt the adrenaline surge even more, as the berserker mode and her feelings for Jazz drove her heart rate to even higher levels. Alerts began popping up in her HUD.

•ELEVATED HEART RATE DETECTED
•TAKE PRECAUTIONARY MEASURES

"We just want you, Devin, we don't care about your little *girlfriend,* come with us and we let her go," the man said quietly.

Devin's vision began to shake, the muscles in her legs tensing, readying her for a strike. She knew that she could overpower the man, Berserker mode would see to that, but she wasn't sure that she could do it before he could take a shot at Jazz. Her mind screamed for her to attack the man, adrenaline fueling her anger.

Her breathing became rapid, she searched the images in her HUD looking for something she had missed, something that would give her an advantage. She wouldn't let the man hurt Jazz.

Dev, what do we do here? Jazz said in her mind.

This statement brought her back to reality, she tried to see Jazz out of the corner of her eye and exhaled a breath.

Amy, deactivate berserker mode. She thought and watched as the notification popped into view. It would still be several minutes before the effects of the adrenaline wore off but knowing that she had turned it off seemed to bring some calm to the storm inside of her.

"Ok, I'll come with you. I'll stop fighting, but if you hurt Jazz I swear

I will never stop, I will destroy every single one of you." Devin said.

Dev, you can't, what are you doing? Jazz said, *I won't leave you.*

You have to, Devin said, *it's the only way.*

"Lay down on the ground, flat, face down, hands behind your back, both of you. If you make any sudden movements she dies. I don't want to hurt either of you, but I will," the man said, "they want you alive Devin, they don't care about her."

Devin began to sink to the ground, the residual adrenaline fighting her the whole way. She desperately wanted to spin around, attack the man, break him, but she knew she was beat. She laid on the ground and turned her face to look at Jazz as she put her hands behind her back.

She saw Jazz do the same, a small tear rolled from the corner of Jazz's eye.

It's ok, you will find me. Just promise me you will make it out of here alive. Devin said.

Jazz gave an almost imperceptible nod and closed her eyes as the man descended on them. He grabbed the zip ties from the floor beside Jazz and began to bind Devin's hands behind her back. He put a hand in his pocket and pulled out a small black bracelet, slipping it onto Devin's wrist.

"What is that?" Jazz asked.

The man ignored her, and spoke seemingly to no one, "Primary target secured. Moving out now. Requesting clean-up for secondary target."

A voice called out from the end of the aisle, "Cut these things off of me and I'll take care of her."

Jazz looked up to see the agent she had knocked out with the can of Monster walking towards them, a sizable lump on the side of his head. He glowered at her, a small smile on his face.

Devin was yanked up to her feet and the man shoved her forward, walking towards the bound agent. "Don't you dare hurt her," she said, trying to sound intimidating but her fear shown through.

The agent pulled out a knife and began to carefully cut the zip ties from the other man's wrists. Devin could feel the anger radiating from the man, all of it directed towards Jazz. She knew this man would not let her leave. *They must not know that she has a chip, if they knew they would want her too, at least we have that going for us,* she thought to herself.

Amy, you gotta get her out of here, Devin thought desperately, *please. Jazz it's going to be ok, Amy will get you out of this.*

*I know…it's…just…*Jazz's voice came back intermittently, as if they had a bad cell-phone connection.

I can't hear you, Amy what's going on? Devin asked.

The bracelet that the agent put on your wrist is a signal jammer, I am trying to override it but fear that we will lose contact with Jazz soon.

Can you do anything to help her, she needs to get out of here now.

Jazz, be prepared to move towards the front door, you will only have one opportunity, Amy said, and Devin prayed that Jazz was able to hear it.

*…ready…just…*the broken response came back, but it was apparently all the confirmation that Amy needed. A crash came from the front of the truck stop as the Tesla slammed through the sliding glass doors, sending metal, glass fragments, and the agent that was there guarding the door flying through the air.

In the confusion Jazz jumped up and sprinted for the front door, the Tesla door was already opening as she dove through it, gunshots ringing out. Devin heard the rounds make contact with the car, saw the small holes appear in the glass of the passenger side window, but the car was already speeding away.

*I'm ok…I promise…find you…love…*Jazz's voice came through and Devin exhaled a pent-up breath, relief flooding through her body, but lasting only a second.

"Shit, that's gonna bring all the authorities, get someone down here to try to clean up this mess," the big man said as he roughly shoved Devin forward, "I'm taking her in."

Amy, I still have you right? Devin asked, feeling a strong sense of loss without her connection to Jazz.

Indeed, Amy said, *I am physically located in your brain so there is no way for them to sever our connection, however we have lost all connection with the outside world, including Jazz and the World Wide Web. I am working on a solution but have thus far been unsuccessful.*

So what now? Devin asked as the agent walked her out into the blinding sunlight towards a black SUV parked in front of the doors.

I believe now we are, as you would say, in deep shit.

35

M lifted the caution tape and stepped through the door frame, broken glass crunching below his feet, and surveyed the destruction all around the gas station. The door was just the beginning, there was a large pool of blood near the cash register, several bullet holes lined the wall near the door, and shell casings lay on the floor.

He also noted several cut zip ties, as well as a can of Monster energy drink with blood coating the bottom edge. "They aren't subtle," he murmured to himself as he turned the corner.

"Hey, you aren't allowed to be in here," a man in a brown Sheriff's uniform shouted, marching towards M. "This area is a crime scene, I know you saw the tape."

M rolled his eyes and reached into his pocket, pulling out a black wallet and flipping it open to flash a badge, "Agent Marcus O'Reilly, FBI, and we will be taking over this investigation."

"Like hell you will, not without some type of clearance first. Sheriff Dalton," the man said pointing to himself, "and this is my jurisdiction. This whole thing is a shit show. We've got hit and run, property damage, shots fired, assaults, potential kidnapping. Trust me, I would love to hand this over to the FBI, just too much paperwork in all of this. But that's supposing you really are the FBI. Hell, I can get a badge that says whatever I want on it for about 15 bucks, and if I have Prime I can have it here tomorrow."

M laughed, "Call your office Sheriff, they have the clearance. I will gladly take this off of your hands. Have you spoken to the clerk that was working this register during the incident?"

Dalton looked M up and down, "If you had spoken to anyone in my office they would have called me by now, I know…"

"They didn't call you because I told them not to. We have no idea who is monitoring the police bands right now, and we don't need to tip our hands to whoever is involved in this. Go ahead and call your office, use your personal cell, not your officer issued one, and call your dispatch on their personal cell. All of the standard channels might be being monitored, I highly doubt they have your names, or access to your personals. This is a much bigger *shit show* than you realize."

Dalton, still looking uncertain, pulled a cell phone from his breast pocket and tapped the screen. Taking a step back he began speaking to someone. M continued to take in the scene, *A lot of damage for two little girls,* he thought.

"Sir, I found the tracker," Ronan said coming towards M from the end of the aisle, holding something small and blue in his hand.

"What the hell is that?" M asked.

Ronan laughed, "Sonic the Hedgehog, Devin's favorite, she's always talking about him, it's actually pretty annoying. When I saw it in her room I thought if she ever left she might take it."

M nodded approvingly, "Impressive, I wouldn't have thought to place a tracker on it, unfortunately they must have spotted it, why else would she leave it behind?"

"If I had more time I would have figured out a way to hide it better, but they came back sooner than they were supposed to, I had to make do with…"

"Now what the hell is this," Dalton said, walking back over and looking at Ronan, "Bring your kid to work day in the bureau today?"

M snorted out a laugh, "This is my partner, Agent Carlson, and I know he looks young, but it comes in handy in undercover missions."

Dalton shook his head, "If you say so, your clearance checks out, you fellas need anything from me? Should I stick around or just let you take over?"

"I need to speak to the clerk, is he here?" M said.

"Ya, he's here, shook up pretty bad, thinks he should have called us sooner, thinks it's his fault that the one girl got taken. He's back in the break room, I'll take you there now."

"Great, that's all we will need from you Sheriff. Thank you for your cooperation."

M began to follow the man but stopped, turning to Ronan, "Keep looking around, see if you can find anything useful, I'll go talk to the clerk."

Ronan looked as though he wanted to protest, but thought better of it, simply nodding his head and turning to head deeper into the truck stop. M continued following Dalton through the aisles and pushed through a door marked employees only.

In the room a young man sat alone. It was clear that he had been crying. "Shane, this here is agent O'Reilly with the FBI, he would like to ask you a few questions."

"Oh…ok…ya whatever you need. I don't know much, but I want to help. I just can't believe this happened," Shane said.

M looked at the Sheriff, "That will be all Sheriff, thank you for your help."

Dalton looked at M, then back to Shane, and back to M before shaking his head and turning to leave. M smiled at the kid, "So, Shane, I'm going to need you tell me everything you saw. Why don't you just start from the beginning…"

36

Jazz lay sprawled across the back seat of the Tesla as it sped down the back roads. She fought back tears as she took stock, patting herself down searching for injuries, until she realized that she could simply check her HUD to see if she had been hurt in any way.

She noted that her health still showed as one hundred percent, as well as her stamina and armor. Her heart rate and blood pressure were elevated, but other than that she thought she seemed fine, at least physically. Mentally was a different story.

She sat up and shook her head, a look of fierce determination settling across her face. "Amy?" She said, looking around the vehicle.

There was no response. "Shit...Alli?"

"Yes Jazz," the voice, that sounded the same, but somehow entirely different from Amy spoke through the car speakers.

"What the hell do I do now?"

"Your mission objectives have not changed that I am aware of. Objective one, obtain entry to agency base. Objective two, free Hal Thomas. Objective three, escape agency base."

"And how do I do that?"

"You will need to start by infiltrating the agency base. Once that is accomplished free Hal Thomas. Once Hal Thomas is secured you will need to escape the agency base."

"Well that is wildly helpful," Jazz said rolling her eyes, "What I mean is that I need a plan?"

"Agreed."

"So…..what's the plan?"

"I do not know, you have not uploaded any plans at this point."

Jazz sighed, "No I mean what do you think the plan should be…"

"First, you will need to infiltrate the agency base. Once that is accomplished you wi…"

"Stop. I get it, you have no plans. Man, you are certainly no Amy. This sucks."

Jazz put her head in her hands and tried to think, *What am I gonna do. I'm not the one that comes up with a plan, that's Dev's job. My plan is always the same, follow Dev's plan, come in guns blazing, kick ass.*

A small chime sounded in her head. "Alli, what was that sound?"

"Mission objectives updated. New mission objectives being loaded into HUD now."

Jazz watched as her display changed from,

***MISSION OBJECTIVES**

    ***INFILTRATE AGENCY BASE**

    ***LOCATE AND SECURE HAL THOMAS**

    ***ESCAPE AGENCY BASE**

To,

***MISSION OBJECTIVES**

    ***FOLLOW DEV'S PLAN**

    ***COME IN GUNS BLAZING**

    ***KICK ASS**

Jazz laughed, "Well at least now we have a plan. Man, you are definitely not Amy."

"I am not, I am an Artificial Life Like Intelligence."

"That's debatable," Jazz said.

"It is in fact not, as that is what I am."

"Man, this is going nowhere."

"Our destination is not currently set to nowhere, the current destination is one hour and seven minutes away, would you like me to search for nowhere and add this as a waypoint, or change the destination?"

"No, Jesus, just keep going. I need time to think, can you just shut up for a little bit?" Jazz said.

She waited for a reply, but none came. "Life-like my ass," she said shaking her head. "Alright, I'm on my own now," she said aloud to no one, she had always done her best thinking by talking things through out loud, "if Dev were here what would she say we should do?"

The thought of Dev made her wince. *How could I leave her like that, I know she wanted me to but how I could just leave, just run away…*but she knew the truth. There was no option, it was stay and be killed, or run and hope to figure out a way to save Devin. She knew it, and Devin knew it. She had wanted it.

In all the years that Jazz and Devin had been friends one thing had been clear, they were the perfect team. This wasn't because of some internal telepathy or because they were so alike they knew what the other was going to do. It was in fact the opposite.

Where Devin was cautious and studious, Jazz was bold and impulsive. Where Devin was timid and awkward, Jazz was outspoken and confident. Jazz thought of all of the times that one of Devin's plans had worked out in battles, and there was a lot of them. Devin would stay up all night, hatching some scheme that they could use to trick the other team into making a mistake, or give them some type of advantage, and it worked a lot of the time, but there were just as many times that as soon as a battle started the plan went to shit and it was Jazz's improvisation skills that won them the fight.

"So that's what I need to do now," she said, "I need to think like both of us, plan but be ready to improvise. Ok Alli, you can stop shutting up now, I need to know a little more about where we are headed."

"What would you like to know?"

"For starters, do you have information on the agency base, like access to the building plans or schematics?"

"Yes, I have all relevant information on the facility. The facility was originally built in 1963 as a…"

"Ok, I don't need all that, can you show me the schematics?"

In response an overlay appeared in her HUD showing a sprawling complex. Jazz could count at least 10 buildings, probably more, "Great, any ideas where to start?"

"Yes, first you will need to follow Dev's plan…"

"Not this again," Jazz said, "Ok, change that objective, I don't know what Devin's plan is going to be for this one, this is gonna have to be my plan. Can you tell where you think it's most likely that they will be holding Devin?"

Three buildings lit up on the map. "Based off of building plans these are the three areas of the facility that have secured cells for holding prisoners. It is probable that they are holding Devin in one of these, most likely the building to the far north of the compound," as she said this the image in Jazz's HUD zoomed in to that building, and the building began to rotate. An overlay appeared showing the interior layout of the building.

"Why is that the most likely building?"

"This building has the highest security rating, and with Devin's enhancements it is likely they would hold her here."

"Do they have any way of limiting her chips abilities?"

"That is unclear. With a standard chipset it is not difficult to deactivate the chip, shutting off any enhancements. The unknown nature of the chipset that Devin has does not provide enough information for me to make any assumptions."

"Alright, well then I will make the assumptions for both of us, so I am going to assume that she will still have her powers, we are sure as hell gonna need them…wait, will they be able to shut off my abilities once I'm there?"

"Also unclear, as your chipset has the same lack of information, should I assume that you will also assume your chip cannot be shut off?"

Jazz laughed, "Yes, assume away. Alright, so Devin is most likely in that building, that's where we need to start. Can you access security cameras, door locks, stuff like that?"

"Devin's AMII was able to successfully override the agency security protocols in regard to cameras, but not with door locks, as they are all biometric."

"Ok, so we can see, but not gain access, without biometrics. Do you know what type of biometrics we are talking about?"

"Retina scans on most doors, DNA scans on some others."

"Got it, so we can see, but getting in we will need to get creative. Can you show me as of now where we are going, like where will the car arrive when we get there?"

A red dot appeared on the map about half a mile away from the compound. "Ok, so I want to change our final destination. I need you to figure out the closest that you can drop me to the building where they are holding Devin, without being seen. Can you also lay out a path for me, that avoids cameras, and can you track any movement within the facility and keep the path updated to avoid running into anyone?"

"It will take a few moments."

"Well, looks like we still have about 45 minutes. I also need you to watch the security feeds and find someone that has access to the building that Devin is in and tag them on the map for me."

"Affirmative."

"Awesome, and one more thing, is there any way that we can boost the signal from my chip, to override the jammer? Even just enough to get a single message to Dev, to let her know that we are coming…"

"I will research all known jamming technologies in use by the agency."

"Alright, not bad, a plan that Devin would be proud of. Now, let's get to something a little more…Jazz. Show me a list of the weapons in the trunk and a list of abilities that I've acquired so far."

Jazz's HUD display was flooded with information. Model numbers of weapons populated the initial list, and below that a much shorter list of the abilities that Jazz had acquired during her training.

"Damn, Amy really went all out on the weapons. One problem, I don't really know what any of the model numbers mean, can you add a description to each weapon so that I know what they do?"

The list updated to show each weapons model number, and then a list of technical specifications, many of which made no sense to Jazz, "That's not as helpful as I was hoping, any ideas here?"

"I would recommend in the future that you not go into battle until you have been fully briefed, that would alleviate the current difficulties."

"Noted," Jazz said smiling, thinking of the many times that she heard Devin say that same word to Amy, "I wish there was some way for me to see the weapons and just have you tell me what each one can do, but we don't have time to stop."

"By using the release near either window in the back seat you can fold the seat down and access the rear trunk."

"That's right, Amy mentioned that. Alright, let's give it a shot," Jazz said as she folded down the seat. She looked into the trunk and grabbed the first thing she could see, a small black box, and pulled it out, sitting it on her lap.

Flipping the two latches on the front of the box she opened the lid to reveal two sets of gloves, "What are these?" She said holding a glove in front of her, looking it over.

"Model number AL-788456. Non-lethal energy weapon. The gloves fire small, charged darts, similar to a taser. The major difference being that with a taser the dart is connected via wires and a trigger must be pulled to release the flow of energy that can incapacitate the intended target, these have no wires or trigger, the impact of the dart into the victim activates the stored electrical charge."

Jazz smiled, "Taser gloves, that what I want you to call these in the inventory. How many charges do they hold?"

"Each glove holds 15 darts, for most targets one dart is sufficient to incapacitate. For an enhanced individual, depending on enhancement, as many as four may be needed."

"Good to know, I'll definitely be putting a pair of these on before the fight. Alright, moving on," Jazz said as she reached into the trunk again and pulled out a small handgun. Looking it over she noticed that the stock of the weapon was much larger than a traditional handgun, "What is this?"

"Model number IM-4432. Improvised munitions handgun."

"What does that mean?"

"The magazine on this weapon holds up to 30 rounds of ammunition, but if the magazine is expended, materials can be placed in the stock. Once there, nano bots will break down the materials into their base components and form and feed ammunition into the weapon."

"Whoa, that's cool, but I'm not sure how helpful it will be in this current situation, let's put that one in the maybe pile."

Jazz reached back and grabbed another black box, this one slightly bigger than the last, and opened it, revealing what she thought looked like high tech pez dispensers, all black solid metal tubes, at the top a small circle that looked to be made of glass, "And these?"

"Model number SR-54431. Programmable grenades. Designed and printed by Devin's AMMI. Once activated the user can select between concussion, smoke, knock-out gas, tear gas, or frag for grenades, as well as proximity, motion sensing or timed if you would prefer to use them as improvised landmines."

"Damn, how do you activate them?"

"SR-54431 are synced to your chipset, and biometrical locked. These have been set to be used by you or Devin only. Simply slide one disk off the top of the dispensing unit, each dispenser holds fifteen disks. The entire outer casing of each disk has the ability to read your fingerprints, and a menu will appear in your HUD. With this menu you can choose how you would like the grenade to behave simply with a thought. You can also determine length of time before detention after release, as well as other attributes, such as area of impact for frag and gas. Previous settings will apply to each additional grenade until user chooses new settings."

"Man, you guys really know how to make cool shit, how has no one added something like this to Call of Duty yet? Let's call these KAG's, kick ass grenades, in the inventory, the numbers are way too much to remember. One more question, how do I carry them?"

"According to the specs that Devin's AMII uploaded in regard to your new suits, there are multiple high strength neodymium magnets all throughout, each of the weapons that have been provided were specially designed with these magnets in mind. Simply place the weapons onto a corresponding magnet. I will upload an overlay of the placement of all magnets on your suit now."

An image of Jazz popped into her HUD, spinning slowly with her arms held out. Green dots appeared all over her suit, showing all of the various attachment points for weapons.

Next she pulled out another weapon with a larger than average stock, "Another improvised munitions weapon I'm guessing?"

"Negative," Alli said, "that is model number..."

"Forget the model numbers, it doesn't matter, what is it?"

"That is an advanced grappling gun that uses super tinsel strength wire to..."

"Good enough, just call it a grapple, I'll take that for sure, gotta get on the roof somehow, I don't need to know all the specifics, but will it get me on the roof?"

"Affirmative."

"Man, Amy really outdid herself with all of this stuff. Alright, let's keep going," she said as she reached in and felt her hand settle on the familiar curve of a gun. She pulled it out and saw a weapon that looked almost identical to Cerezza, although slightly smaller and sleeker.

"I already know what this one is, update the inventory to call this one Cereza."

"Affirmative."

She reached back into the trunk, knowing that she would next find two small versions of Cereza and was pleased when she pulled out the matching weapons, "And these ones you can call James and Winona. I'm taking these for Dev, so leave their stats off of my weapons list."

"Affirmative."

"Thanks, Alli. Alright, enough planning. Get me to the drop off point. It's time to kick ass."

37

Devin sat alone in an all white room…well…almost alone. *Amy, how long have we been in here?* She asked.

We have been in this facility for three hundred and ninety-two minutes. We have been in this room for two hundred and eighty-seven minutes, Amy responded back.

Have you had any luck coming up with a way out of here?

Without access to an internet connection, I am no longer able to access additional information, but from the limited amount of information I have stored I believe that we are here.

A map of the entire facility overlayed Devin's HUD, a green dot appearing in a building at the far north of the compound. As she focused on it the map image zoomed in to show the building that she was currently being held in.

Any ideas how many guards are out there? She asked as she looked at the maze of hallways and rooms in the building.

Negative, if I could access their security feeds I would be able to give you that information, but I am still being blocked. However, this is a military complex, so there should be no shortage of guards.

Right, Devin said, *so a butt load of guards, no weapons, no Jazz, and no way out. Got it.*

For future reference can you tell me the number of guards in one butt load? Amy asked.

Devin laughed, *15…or 20, I don't know…a lot, that's what a butt load is, a lot. It means we are in deep shit.*

Deep shit from the butt load, understood.

Devin laughed even harder now, the pressure of the last few weeks boiling over until she couldn't breathe. Tears began to leak out of the corners of her eyes, but she just kept laughing.

The laughter eventually turned to real tears and Devin let go off her pent-up emotions. She allowed the tears to come, allowed herself to feel the pain.

She closed her eyes and focused on her breath, as she had done so many times when life felt overwhelming to her. *One,* she thought to herself as she inhaled deeply, *Two...,* she thought on the exhale, *Three...*inhale....*four...*exhale. She counted to ten and opened her eyes.

She was still in the same white room. Still all alone. Still had no weapons, but she felt different, more equipped. *I am the weapon,* she thought to herself and stood. "Alright," she said aloud, "come up with a plan. Amy, give me a status report."

All systems are functioning properly, with the exception of external communications which have been disabled. Your health and stamina are at one hundred percent, as well as your body armor. There is nothing in your inventory.

"Well at least I have my health, am I right?" She said with a chuckle.

Yes, as previously stated, your health is at one hundred percent.

"Ok, so no weapons, but I still have my body armor, my abilities, and my mind...and Amy. What I need is a plan..." she said to the empty room.

Planning had always been a necessity for Devin, nothing could be left to chance. Spontaneity just wasn't part of the program. It was something that she and Jazz had laughed about many times. When they were gaming Devin would stay up all night sometimes, formulating the perfect way to create a distraction, infiltrate the enemy base, and score the win, only games...like life she supposed...didn't usually play out according to plan.

Sure, there were times when they did, lots of times, but when something went wrong, went off book as they say, Devin would find herself lost and in trouble, but not Jazz. When a plan failed Jazz always ran headfirst into the action, and more times than not she scored the win for them anyway.

Maybe I don't need a plan, maybe I need to think more like Jazz, Devin thought, *what would Jazz do?*

This got her laughing again, and she decided that as soon as she was out of this mess she would order a whole bunch of those cheap plastic WWJD bracelets, except when she wore them the J wouldn't stand for Jesus.

The bracelet, she thought and looked down at her wrist to see the metal bracelet that the man had placed on her wrist in the truck stop. Amy had told her almost immediately that the bracelet was a signal jammer and responsible for her inability to communicate with Jazz or the outside world.

She had tried to pry it off, tried to push it over her wrist as she had seen countless criminals in movies do with handcuffs, but there was no budging it. It was too tight, and too strong even for her.

If I could just talk to Jazz I know I could figure this out, she thought, *I would do anything to talk to Jazz...*as this thought sunk in she pictured Jazz, her smile, her eyes twinkling whenever she said something sarcastic. That first kiss at the zoo, the many kisses that came after. Her heart rate started racing, *Alright, fine. No plan, just act,* she thought, *Amy, activate Hercules and berserker mode.*

The alert popped up in her HUD and she felt the surge of adrenaline rush through her. *Is that the most you can do, turn it up as high as it can go,* she said.

There are risks with too much adrenaline, the recommended dosage has been reached. It is not advisable to increase it anymore, Amy said.

Just do it, Devin said, *give me as much as my body can handle.*

Affirmative.

Devin felt it instantly, a surge of strength, anger and energy. She looked around the room, her eyes widening under the influence of the massive amount of adrenaline being pumped into her system. She felt like she could rip the wall in half, punch a whole straight through.

She looked over the only item in the room, a chair that stood directly in the center of the room. She didn't know what it was made of, only that it was extremely uncomfortable   and bolted to the floor, she had already tried to rip it up off the ground with no success. She moved towards it, telling herself not to think, just act.

She started to run, as she neared the chair she held her arm back, the one with the bracelet, and swung with everything she had inside of her, bringing the bracelet down onto the top of the chair. Her senses were so heightened from the adrenaline it was like everything was moving in slow motion.

She watched her arm as it soared through the air, swinging faster than she would have thought possible. She watched the arc come to a stop with the bracelet connecting directly with a corner on the top of the chair, saw stone shards fly from the chair as it began to break, but she was pretty sure that in those white shards she also saw several pieces of black metal.

The pain was more intense than anything she had ever felt. The impact shattered her wrist, alerts began popping up into her HUD.

***WARNING – BLUNT FORCE TRAUMA**
   – 65 HP
***SELF-HEALING MODE ACTIVATED**
***WARNING – STAMINA LOW**

Amy, do I have enough stamina to repair my wrist? she thought.

The gel delivery system built into the suit can provide you with additional stamina, but the nature of your injury, as well as the multiple systems activated, have pulled too much too fast. We need to shut down the other systems and focus all stamina to the self-heal ability. Your injury is bad, but not life threatening.

Devin grimaced and looked down at her wrist. Her hand was cocked at a strange angle, and she couldn't move her fingers. *Jesus,* she thought, *all this and it didn't even work.*

She brought her arm up to get a closer look at the bracelet, noticing that there was indeed a crack that ran around the entire thing from the center of impact. It was small, but it was there, and she knew that she would be able to get the bracelet off with a couple more hits like that one.

Once I heal, I can just do it again, she thought, although she wasn't entirely sure that she would be able to hit with as much force the next time knowing the pain that awaited her. *Once I heal, I'll...*but her thought was cut off as a section of one of the walls began to move.

38

Devin watched as the section of door slid back and to the left. A woman entered the room, flanked on both sides by large men in black suits. One of the men Devin saw, had a black glove on his right hand. Devin recognized him as the agent from the zoo that had lost his hand to the blast door. He smirked at her, and Devin could see the anger dancing in his eyes.

"Hello Devin," the woman said calmly, almost cheerily, "we have been looking for you for a long time."

"Who is we?" Devin said, holding her injured wrist, "Who the hell are you?"

"Oh, come on now Devin, don't pretend as though you don't recognize your own mother…" the woman said.

Devin felt all the air go out of her lungs, she opened her mouth to speak but no sound came out, she tried again but failed, *Amy, is that true, is this woman my mother?*

Unclear, and I cannot run facial recognition because I have no reliable connection to the internet. I am now able to connect for a few seconds at a time. Although it seems you were not able to disable the jamming unit, the damage you caused is allowing intermittent connection to the outside world. I will keep you updated to the situation.

Keep me updated, I need to be able to get in touch with Jazz, to tell her to go back and get my mom, I don't think she is safe where she is, none of this makes sense, Devin thought back.

"Conferring with your AMII I see," the woman said, "I don't blame you, but it will have no answers for you, you see…even if it could access the internet, to…let me guess…run facial recognition on me, I am in none of the systems. You won't find me, I have been…off the grid as they say…for going on twenty years."

"You're not my mother," Devin said and searched the woman's face, trying unsuccessfully to tell if she was lying.

"Oh, I can assure you I am. I don't really have any way to prove it to you, as you were taken from me when you were such a young child I am certain you have no memories of me, but I am indeed your mother. I've been searching for you, and now you have returned home."

Devin looked around the room, looked at the faces of the two men, and back to the woman. When she focused on the woman's face she noticed several of her own features looking back at her, "Look lady, I don't know who you are, but you are for sure not my mom. I don't know why you brought me here, or what you think you will get out of this, but I came here to get my dad."

"Your father is dead," the woman said, and Devin felt what little strength she still had leaving her. Her legs weakened and she sat down hard on the ground, tears welling up in her eyes.

"Oh, oh honey, don't cry," the woman said kindly, taking a step towards Devin, "he just held no purpose for us, other than to get you here, so once you were here it was prudent to end his life. This is a top-secret installation after all, it wouldn't do to have him running around telling people all about his daughter the super soldier."

"You're lying," Devin said, although it was barely audible.

"I was just looking out for your best interest, just like I always have. Listen, none of that is important anymore. You're back, back here where you belong…with me…with your mother…"

Devin noticed that the pain in her wrist had subsided to a dull ache, but she held on to it anyway, not wanting to let them know she was healing, "You are not my mother," Devin said, her voice tinged with anger.

The woman sighed, "Listen Devin, I know this a lot to take in, but trust me, this is where you belong. With my help you can be something so much more than you already are. You are unique Devin, I have never been able to successfully replicate the experiment, I'm not totally sure why it worked on you, but that's why you're here, so that we can find out, together."

"So you want me to help you? You killed my dad, and you want me to help you?" Devin said, her voice rising.

The agent from the zoo took a step forward, but the woman placed a hand on his chest, "Stop, we don't need to threaten her. I can make her understand, I can make her see, and to be fair I killed both of your fathers. Your adoptive father because he was unimportant and in the way, and your biological father because he betrayed me."

Devin shook her head, "What are you talking about, none of that is true. My mother and father tried to save me from this place, my father escaped with me, but it was my mother's plan."

"I understand what you have been told, but you have been misled. Devin, you were born as an experiment. After years of failed attempts at creating soldiers that could access more than one skill, Dr. Tran and I came to believe that it was because of the…limitations…of the adult brain. We requested from our superiors to implant a device into an infant, and although these men wanted nothing more than a super soldier, they balked at the idea of experimenting on a child. These men were forcing us to continue our research, forcing us to knowingly implant devices into soldiers that we knew would kill them. Hundreds had died, men and women that I knew, that were my friends, that trusted me, had died in the name of science. Our superiors demanded that we continue the experiments, so many were killed, and yet they refused to allow us to try the procedure on a child, instead forcing us to continue killing. So, we had you…and I performed the procedure on you myself, unknown to anyone else."

Connections are beginning to last longer, still only seconds but I believe that if you were to strike the device one more time it would break, Amy interjected into Devin's mind.

She looked around, the chair was too far away now, the guards would stop her before she got there, she had to come up with something, she had to talk to Jazz.

"Your father found out what I had done, he was furious, but he hid it well. I've never been good at masking my emotions, but he didn't lack that particular skill. He pretended that everything was fine, but one night, I awoke to alarms going off. Your father had taken you, stolen you from me, from all of us. Everything that I had done to prove that Project Phoenix could work, he simply took you away into the night."

"So that's all I am to you, research?" Devin asked, taking another small step forward. The large agent stiffened but remained standing where he was, eyes locked on Devin.

The woman seemed to consider for a moment and then said, "Well, yes. I know that's harsh, but it's the truth, and I am a firm believer that the truth will set you free."

Devin looked at her HUD and saw that her health and stamina had both returned to one hundred percent. "You're damn right it will..." she whispered.

Amy, activate Hercules and berserk mode, she said.

She didn't need to check the HUD to know that Amy had followed her direction, the surge of power and anger she felt was confirmation enough.

She took one look at the woman claiming to be her mother, and deep down she knew that it was true, which only fueled her anger. Tensing her muscles, she glanced at the big agent from the zoo and smiled, "Hey, don't I know from you somewhere?"

The man sneered and took a step forward, balling both of his hands into fists. With her senses heightened from the adrenaline Devin could hear the leather of his gloved hand creak as he did this.

"Ya, I think we met before, at the zoo. You gave me a hand when I was leaving the gorilla exhibit right?," she said with a crooked smile.

The big man took another step forward, he was only a couple of feet away now. The woman tried but failed to stop him.

"Well, I appreciated it...here...let me return the favor..." she said as she spun, delivering a spinning back fist that would have made Bas Rattan jealous.

She aimed for the big man's forehead, the hardest part of the human body, and connected at blinding speed, but not with her fist. She connected with the bracelet, which shattered into pieces upon contact.

The man fell, knocked out cold, small pieces of the metal buried into his skin, blood beginning to ooze from them. Devin saw the other man moving towards her and the woman claiming to be her mother turn to run for the door just as an alert popped into her HUD.

Dev, I'm here. I don't know if you'll get this. I've been trying to communicate with you, but I'm still blocked, but if you do just know…I'm coming to get you - Jazz.

39

M laid in the grass at the top of a hill looking through binoculars at The Agency compound spread out before him.

"Can you see anything?" Ronan asked, leaning in a bit to close.

M sighed, "Nothing, and back up, I don't want to tell you again."

Ronan quickly took two steps back, "Sorry, I just want to know what's going on. What's the plan here anyway?"

M shook his head, "The plan is the same as it has been the entire time, wait and watch. That was the plan when I had you place the devices, that was the plan when we left the compound, and that is the plan now. We know from the kid at the truck stop that Devin was taken and loaded into SUV's. They brought her here, I'm sure of that. Which, by the way, is where she was already headed. They knew that, the strike at the truck stop was to ensure that she came on their terms, to make her lose the element of surprise. So now she's here, probably being held in one of the detention buildings."

Ronan shook his head in agreement, "Ya but if they already have her what are we doing here?"

"We're here in case she is able to get free. If she does we will be ready to collect her."

Ronan laughed, "How the hell is she going to break free, there must be a couple of hundred trained soldiers down there, and she's alone and I'm sure the first thing they did was take her weapons and deactivate her chip. They are probably already cutting open her brain to see what makes the chip work for her..."

"Possibly," M said, squinting through the binoculars, his attention focused on the hill behind the northwest building, "but we tried to disable her chip when she got to our facility, unknown to her of course, but it didn't work, it doesn't operate like the others. Tran and Kevin believe that her AI did something to it…"

"Ya, or maybe it's just that it's a totally unknown chipset, did they ever think of that?"

"Of course, they thought of that, and that was actually their belief until they installed the chipset into Jazz."

"What does she have to do with it…"

M put the binoculars down and turned to look at Ronan, "Devin and Jazz did something to the chipset that was installed into Jazz, or more accurately, Devin's AI did something to the chipset. The AI was able to augment the operating system of Jazz's chip, and so now it ignores commands originating from the outside, it also cannot be shut down. One of the first things they learned when starting this project was that if you give someone a lot of power, you need to be able to take that power away, and fast. The last thing you want is a battalion of super soldiers that goes rogue with no system to put them in check. So, while it's possible that a kill switch was not included in the experimental software put in Devin's head eighteen years ago, you can be damn sure it was in whatever the hell they shoved into Jazz. Designed and installed by Kevin and Tran, and yet, when they tried the kill switch on Jazz it also had no effect."

Ronan thought about that for a second as M went back to his binoculars, "Ok, so she still has her abilities, but with no weapons; do you really think that she could make it out?"

"It's unlikely," M said, noticing something moving on the hill, "but I'm not sure she will be without weapons for all that long."

"Why's that?" Ronan asked.

M handed him the binoculars and pointed towards the hill. Ronan put them to his eyes and after a few seconds of scanning saw it too.

A figure in all black was crouched low, making their way down the hillside towards the building farthest away from their position. Ronan zoomed in, using his chip to control the binoculars. "Fuck me…" he whispered.

40

Jazz checked to make sure that she was still on the illuminated path in her HUD. Alli had mapped everything, cameras, guards, sight lines, and was monitoring for any changes, updating the path as she went. *This is so cool,* she thought to herself as she made her way down the hill, pausing at the bottom just long enough to check the path and make sure her weapons were still secured.

The stretch from the hill to the back of the building where Devin was being held seemed to stretch forever. Jazz hated the idea of being exposed, but Alli had assured her that if she stuck to the path she was as good as invisible.

Alli, activate Quicksilver, Jazz said in her mind.

The alert popped up and Jazz felt all the muscles in her legs tense. This was a skill she had only acquired two days prior to leaving the compound, and had only used once, with limited success. The Quicksilver skill, as one of the senior agents had explained to Jazz, used the chipset to stimulate the motor cortex of the brain, overriding the brain's natural protective structures, while also giving you a healthy dose of adrenaline, and allowing you to run at inhuman speeds.

While it didn't allow you to run so fast the rest of the world would slow down, Jazz had found that she could now most likely win gold in just about any Olympic sprinting event. Her first attempts had gone great, until she had to stop.

Running at top speeds in a straight line wasn't all that hard, your body seemed to know how to keep itself upright at any speed, but turning corners and stopping at close to fifty miles per hour was more of an acquired skill, and Jazz had yet to acquire it.

Desperate times and all that though, she thought.

The path turned red, and an alert popped into view.

***CAMERA SWEEP IN PROGRESS, HOLD POSITION FOR 5,4,3,2,1**

The path turned green again and Jazz sprinted across the field, grabbing the grapple gun from her back as she ran. She reached the corner of the building much faster than she was expecting, and when she went to turn lost her footing, hitting the ground hard and rolling for four complete revolutions before coming to a stop in a cloud of dust.

A series of alerts popped up.

***RETURN TO PATH.**

***JAMES HAS BEEN REMOVED FROM YOUR INVENTORY**

***KAG COUNT HAS BEEN UPDATED IN YOUR INVENTORY**

She watched as the count of KAG's in her inventory, which had started at sixty halved to 30.

"Fuck," she whispered as she looked at her HUD.

Her fall had taken her off the path, and to reach the weapons that had been dislodged she would need to move to an area that was covered by cameras. *Well, we'll just have to make it with what we have, and hope they aren't looking all that close at the cameras. I didn't roll into the camera coverage though, at least I don't think I did, Alli, did I cross into the coverage at all when I fell?* She thought.

Negative, the weapons have landed in an area of coverage, but you stopped with two feet to spare.

Damn that was too close, ok, fast but maybe a little bit cautious, she thought to herself as she made her way to the back of the building. She raised the grapple gun and pointed it towards the roof, hoping it would be self-explanatory how to use it. As she did an overlay of a satellite image of the roof came into her HUD as several orange grapple hook icons, the kind she had seen in countless video games, from Far Cry to Uncharted, overlayed the image. With a thought she selected one of the icons and pulled the trigger.

A soft whoop sound accompanied a bigger than expected recoil and she watched as a thin wire shot out of the barrel of the gun. An alert notified her that an attachment point was secured and with another thought the gun became a winch, pulling her fast straight up the side of the building.

She wasn't ready for the speed of the winch, and for the first several feet it dragged her up the side of the building. Damage alerts popped into view as she banged against the building. *Disable quicksilver, enable Daredevil.*

The corresponding alerts popped into view. All at once a flood of information hit her brain, registering the angle of the wall, the speed of the winch, the speed of the wind against her, the drag of her body through the air, the exact correct placement for her feet against the wall. With the added information she was able to get her feet against the wall and begin to run.

The roofline was coming fast, but the Daredevil skill provided her with so much information that she knew exactly what to do and it almost seemed as if she wasn't doing anything at all, like her body was reacting without her directing it. As her foot hit the top of the wall at the exact right place she let go of the grapple gun and pushed off, turning her body in midair and tucking, landing on the roof in a combat style roll and sliding to a stop in the gravel that covered it.

She lifted her head and laughed, picturing what she looked like. One hand down on the ground, one leg bent out behind her, the other bent in front, ready to spring into action. Her right hand up, helping her to keep her balance. "A perfect superhero landing," she said to the empty roof top, as the grapple gun slid to a stop against her left foot, "And no one even around to see it."

"Almost no one," a deep voice said from behind her.

She spun to see a man in all black, pointing a weapon at her and smiling.

"It was a good landing, although I don't think I would call you a superhero. Now…I'm going to need you to come with me."

Jazz started to reach for Cereza, attached at her back, but the man said calmly, "None of that, don't move. Lay down on the ground and I won't shoot you. Reach for any of your weapons and you're dead."

Jazz scanned the HUD, looking for anything, trying to think. *Got any ideas Alli?*

Negative.

*Thanks…*Jazz thought. *Shit, if only I had…*

JAZZZZ…Devin's voice screamed in her head, *Jazz can you hear me…I'm here Jazz…*

The voice was so unexpected that Jazz took a step back, the man tightening his finger on the trigger. Jazz looked at the man and smiled, only one thought remained in her mind.

Devin…

41

Devin...the word came into Devin's mind in Jazz's voice. A sense of relief swept through her. She watched as the woman claiming to be her mother ran through the door, pausing just long enough to glance back with what Devin thought might be sadness in her eyes, or anger, confusion, maybe disappointment. If she were being honest she had no idea what the look had meant.

The door began to slide closed as the other agent still in the room took another step towards her. Alerts and icons were updating constantly as Amy gained access to all of the information of the compound. *Amy, mute alerts until I'm out of here, please, it's too much info, I can't focus.*

The alerts and icons disappeared. *Better,* she thought, her mind racing, *now it looks like I've got about five seconds to get past this guy and through that door before its closed, I don' think I can make it, unless...*

The man was running now and reaching towards her, Devin saw her opening. She allowed the man to close the distance, his hand reaching out to grab her, apparently she was still too valuable to these assholes to just shoot on site. As his hand closed towards her shoulder she grabbed his forearm with both hands, dropped to the floor, bringing both feet into his midsection and kicked with everything she had, which due to years of training, the berserker skill and the Hercules skill, she had a lot.

Twisting on her way to the ground she used the man's weight and momentum and launched him towards the door. His body collided with the top of the door frame, and he dropped, directly into the path of the closing door. Devin watched as the door bumped against him, failing to close completely.

She ran towards the door, jumping over the man and out into the hallway. She looked down at him as she passed, a large pool of blood was oozing out from around his head, if he wasn't dead she thought he would be soon. *It's a video game,* Devin thought, *After I turn the corner he will just fade away, another NPC down.*

The thought helped her stay moving but didn't alleviate all of her guilt. She had little time to think about the man on the floor though, Jazz was here. She quickly scanned the hallway, it was empty, at least for now. She pulled the map back up, *Amy, identify Jazz on the map.*

A green icon popped into view, almost directly on top of Devin. *What the hell,* she thought.

Jazz is on the roof, searching for a security feed now. Also, there are two buttloads of guards converging on this location as we speak, may I suggest a route to keep you clear of them?

Devin laughed, *Yes, give me the route, and put the info back on, agents, cameras, whatever you think I'll need.*

Devin watched as a green line overlaid the map, and icons began popping up all over it, many of them were the red icons indicating chipped agents, some were the orange icons indicating the unchipped, or Cheeto agents, as she and Jazz had taken to calling them.

She watched as two tightly packed groups of icons moved through the hallways from different ends of the building, both moving towards where she was located now. *Damn, that is indeed a buttload of agents,* she thought to herself, and then said out loud, "Jazz, can you hear me?"

Jazz's voice came back in an instant, *Sorry Jazz is unavailable right now, she's about to kick a guy's ass and then come save her girlfriend...*

Devin smiled, a sense of relief swept over her, "Jazz, it's so good to hear your voice, I'm so glad you're safe, I can't believe you came...you shouldn't have come...I just wanted you to be safe..."

Devin, if I may interject, you need to be on the move, right now, Amy said.

Right, Devin thought back, *find us a safe place, one that we can both get to without being seen. Give Jazz and I both a map, can you do that?*

Already done, Amy said as the alerts began to pop up on Devin and Jazz's HUDs.

Oh man, Jazz said, *It's good to have you back Amy.*

42

"Hey, enough messing around over there," the man with the gun pointed at Jazz said, "I know you're talking to your AI, trying to figure out some way out of this, but let me help you out. There's no way out. It's impressive that you made it this far kid, but I got the drop on you. You're all alone and trust me…you are outmatched. So why don't you just get on the ground, hands behind your back, and I'll take you in and we can sort this mess out."

Jazz looked at the man, hands still raised in front of her. She looked around the rooftop and then down to the ground. She looked back up, "You did get the drop on me, you got that part right. I wasn't expecting anyone to be up here, in fact I'm impressed that a bunch of neanderthals like you had the foresight to put a man on the roof…I didn't think you all would be too worried about a couple of girls…"

Jazz seemed to comply with the man's orders, lowering herself to the ground, hands still raised. *Amy, got any ideas here?* She thought, and watched a string of commands fill her screen. She let one knee hit the ground and looked back up at the man, a small smile twitched at her mouth, "but you did get one thing wrong…"

"And what's that," the man said, taking a step forward, lowering the gun and pointing it directly at Jazz's head.

Jazz closed her eyes, *Activate macro, Daredevil - Hercules - Deadshot* she thought and heard the ding of affirmation from Amy, "I…am never alone…"

She dropped to the ground rolling towards the man and grabbing the discarded grappling gun, attaching it to a mag point on her side.

With Daredevil activated she saw everything, seemingly before it happened, and responded to each stimuli.

She adjusted her roll to the left, as a projectile from the weapon slammed into the roof an inch from her head, spraying gravel.

As she continued her roll she placed both hands on the ground and pushed hard, turning the roll into a forward handspring, twisting just enough at the top of the motion to avoid the second shot. Her feet landed and she saw the alert pop in to view as she launched forward with all of her strength,

***HERCULES SKILL ACTIVATED**

The man watched, dumb struck as Jazz leaped into the air, flipping over his head. At the apex of her arc, her body perpendicular to the man on the roof she looked down and smiled, grabbed both of his shoulders, and as she completed her rotation flung him from the rooftop.

The man screamed as he flew from the rooftop, sailing over the edge of the building. Jazz grabbed the grapple gun from her side, targeted the man in her HUD and fired. She jammed the gun into the gravel on the rooftop and with a thought two sets of spikes sprang from the sides, slamming down, attaching the gun to the roof.

The line pulled tight, and Jazz sprinted to the edge of the roof, taking a quick glance over she saw the man dangling upside down, the wire wrapped around his leg. His gun lay on the ground 40 feet below.

"Sorry, I gotta go," Jazz yelled down to the man, "but just hang out here, I'm sure someone will be around to get you."

She ran towards the large central ventilation shaft at the center of the roof and checked her overlay. There was now a large yellow star with a green path snaking through the building. She noticed that her objectives had been updated. Only one remained.

***NEW OBJECTIVE**

***PROCEED TO RENDEZVOUS - ALPHA**

She smiled and knowing that Amy would transmit the message to Devin said, "Get ready, I'm on my way…" as she dropped into the shaft.

43

Devin sprinted down the hallway, checking her position on the map, seeing the first group of agents closing in on her fast. The rendezvous point was not far from here, but it appeared the soldiers would reach her before she could reach it. *Jazz, how close are you?*

Pretty close I think, Amy has been updating my map as I go, but it's a little hard to tell exactly where I am, I'm in the damn air vents like I'm Tom Cruise in Mission Impossible or something, and the maps we have for the vents aren't exactly right, I have had to double back a couple of times because I don't fit through some of them, Jazz replied back.

Damn your gorgeous bubble butt, Devin thought as a smile pulled at the corners of her mouth.

*Ya, I never thought squats would be the thing that got us both killed, but here we are...*Jazz said.

Devin laughed, *Not sure what to do here Amy,* she thought, *how can I avoid these guys?*

I am not sure that you can, Amy said, *I am trying to override the door security now but the encryption they use is quite sophisticated. If I am unable to open the doors I think you will have little choice but to stand and fight.*

Stand and fight, ya right, how many of them are there?

The first group of agents contains one buttload, Amy said.

I think my chip might be broken, it sounded like Amy just said one...buttload...of agents is on the way? Jazz said, and Devin knew that her laughter was bouncing off of the metallic corridor surrounding her.

Devin laughed, *Indeed she did, I'll explain later...so twenty, is that right?*

Seventeen. You told me that a buttload is fifteen or twenty, seventeen falls within that parameter.

Devin shook her head, *Yes, yes I did. So how do you suggest I fight seventeen armed and enhanced agents?*

Very carefully, Amy said.

Devin stopped running, looking at the map trying to piece together some type of plan, *Is that a joke?*

Indeed.

Not funny, Devin thought back, trying hard to conceal a smile, *I need real help here.*

I apologize, I was intending to lighten the mood through humor. These agents have limited knowledge of your skills. You may be able to use that to your advantage.

"Maybe this could help," Jazz said, her voice coming from directly over Devin's head, "Might want to look out…"

There was a loud metallic clang and the vent above Devin's head fell to the floor. Two black booted feet swung through, and Jazz dropped lightly to the floor.

Standing up she brushed herself off and looked at Devin, grabbing the small pistol attached to her side. She tossed it to Devin, "Here you go, sorry I lost the other one on the way in, you only have Winona now but I…"

Jazz was cut off as Devin grabbed her in her arms, kissing her deeply. She pulled away after several seconds and let her hands linger on Jazz's waist, "God is it good to see you,"

Jazz smiled, and in that moment Devin knew that everything would be alright. "I couldn't agree more," she said, "I've got more stuff for you, I brought some extra weapons."

I hate to keep being that guy, Amy said in both of the girls' heads, *but you have incoming.*

Jazz and Devin both turned towards the end of the hallway, still in a half embrace as the first of the agents rounded the corner, sliding to a stop, weapons drawn.

Devin looked at her map, seeing that now the second group had corrected course and was converging on this location. *They must have alerted their buddies,* she said.

Looks like it, you ready? Jazz asked.

Devin smiled and put her hand on Jazz's face as the first of the agents began to slowly advance towards them. The agent heading up the charge looked young, almost as young as Devin and Jazz, and he looked very unsure of himself, he yelled out, "Don't move, we don't want to kill you."

They're scared of us, Jazz said, *you can tell by their faces.*

Devin thought that could be true, but in her mind their faces could be showing any number of emotions; fear, anger, confidence, having to go to the bathroom, but she trusted Jazz, she knew that she could read people.

Devin smiled and let her hand drop from Jazz's face, *They should be,* she thought as she took a step towards the men at the end of the hallway.

"So, do you guys want to do this now or should we wait for a couple minutes?" Devin asked, looking down at the gun in her hand, stroking it lightly with her left hand, appearing as though she was polishing it.

The agent in the lead looked confused, "Don't move..." he said as he lifted his weapon to his shoulder.

Devin shook her head, "Alright, we can do it now, but you really should wait for your buddies to get here. There's only seventeen of you," she said as she gave the young man a small wink, "you're gonna need more guys."

44

"M, you need to come see this," Ronan said, pulling the binoculars down from his eyes.

M walked around the corner of the SUV, pulling the slide of his handgun back and letting it snap back into place, holstering it at his side. He had access to all of the new weapons, the high tech, sci-fi based stuff that Kevin and Tran were constantly working on, but nothing made him feel better than the sound of a chamber racking into a Glock. *Let the kids have the toy ray guns,* he thought, and then walking up beside Ronan said, "We have movement?"

"You could say that…east side of the north building…" Ronan said handing him the binoculars.

M lifted the binoculars to his eyes and using his chip to control them focused in on that area of the building. He saw the man dangling there, his sudden flight off of the building is what had spurred M into action. He had watched Jazz throw the man from the roof, and then drop into the ventilation shaft. After he saw that he handed the binoculars to Ronan, letting him know to tell him if he saw anything else, and went to the truck to get his weapons ready.

These girls were turning out to be more resourceful than he thought, and he wanted to be ready if they did somehow manage to get out of the agency compound alive.

As he watched, a group of agents came running from one of the other buildings, he counted at least thirty. He looked back up to the dangling man and was surprised to see that the man had become agitated, it looked like he was shouting at someone on the roof.

M followed his eye line and saw another agent on the roof, holding something against the cable. As he watched the agent on roof cut through the cable, the line snapping back, and the man began to fall. M traced his fall, and actually grunted a little as the man hit the ground, remaining motionless.

He looked back towards the front door of the building and saw the rest of the agents rushing in and put the binoculars back down to his side, turning to Ronan, who stood, squinting and trying to make out what was going on, although the distance was too great to see much of anything.

"What's happening?" Ronan asked.

M handed him back the binoculars, "A group of agents just entered the building, at least thirty of them, maybe more. An alarm has gone up, I would imagine we will see more groups coming, although I have no idea how many agents are currently at the compound. They were not expecting the raid to happen so soon, I'm guessing that's why they changed tactics and collected Devin at the truck stop instead of letting them come to her. Maybe this is all they have…"

Ronan looked through the binoculars, "Well, thirty guys just ran in, I'm sure there are others already in there. So probably at least fifty to take on two girls, I think it should be more than enough,"

M squinted into the distance, "I'm not so sure, these girls keep surprising me."

"Ya, well, we also have our little insurance policy, so either the agency kills them, and we go home, or they escape, we go get them, and we take them back to Kevin and Tran, either way they lose, and to me that's what matters." Ronan said.

M tensed and stared at Ronan, a flash of anger in his eyes, but Ronan, still looking through the binoculars didn't see anything.

"You really hate them, don't you?" M asked.

"Nah, I don't hate them, I just hate the way everybody fawns over them. Tran acts like Devin is the second coming of Christ or something. I know they think she will unlock the great secrets of the universe and they can finally figure out soldiers with multiple skills, but it will never work, she's a freak…that's all…no real mystery."

"So maybe your judgement has been clouded by your ego being hurt?" M said, taking a step closer to Ronan.

"My ego doesn't have anything to do with it," Ronan said, still scanning with the binoculars, "Hey, what happened to the guy Jazz threw off the roof? Looks like he fell, I think he's dead. He ain't moving at least."

M pushed the binoculars down from Ronan's eyes and turned the younger man to be facing him, "Another of the agents went up to the roof and cut the cable," he said.

Ronan's eyebrows rose, "Why would they do that?"

"They did it to remind everyone what the cost of failure is," M said placing a hand harshly on Ronan's shoulder, "and it's a lesson you should pay special attention too."

45

Another group of agents has just entered the building, Amy said in both girls' heads, *they are headed to your position now.*

Devin turned and looked at Jazz, "Maybe we shouldn't wait after all," she said with a small smile.

"I couldn't agree more," Jazz said and spun towards the group of agents at the end of the hall, "check this out…"

As Jazz spun she balled her hands into fists and raised them in front of her, *Deadshot*, she thought and heard the affirmation ping. In her HUD she saw red targeting reticules frame the agents' heads, and with a thought sent discs from her taser gloves flying.

The first five men of the group dropped to the ground, their bodies seizing as the electric current ripped through them, causing loss of all muscle control. *Keep them down for ten minutes, slow bursts, don't kill them unless you have to*, she thought.

The other agents in the group quickly retreated around the corner.

Affirmative, Amy said.

"No way, I want some!" Devin said as she began walking down the hall, watching the other agents retreating down the corridor in her HUD from a video feed. The men ran halfway down the corridor and stopped, regrouping.

"Taser gloves are just the beginning," Jazz said smiling and tossed Devin one of the tubes attached to her side, "here, check these out."

Devin watched as an update appeared in her HUD

*INVENTORY UPDATED

•KAG 15/15

Next came the flood of information as Amy downloaded the specs for the KAG's into Devin's brain.

"Kick-ass grenades…" Devin said pulling one of the small disks out of the tube and turning it over in her hands, "I'm gonna guess you named these…"

"That would be correct Madam," Jazz said with a small bow, "haven't used them yet, but they sound awesome!"

"Yes they do," Devin said as she scrolled through options in her HUD, landing on proximity mine, she selected it and targeted a spot on the wall at the opposite end of the hall. She tossed the disc and watched as it sailed on target, striking the wall and adhering to it exactly where she had targeted.

She wasn't surprised that the disc adhered to the wall, she knew from the specs that had been downloaded to her that the function was achieved in some way through nanotech, what surprised her was the accuracy of her toss. She noted, with a bit of shock, that her Deadshot skill had been activated.

"Amy, did you activate Deadshot?" Devin asked.

I did not, Amy said, *it would appear that you are gaining mastery over your skills, and that some of them are now activating and, I can only assume, deactivating as needed.*

Bad ass, Devin thought, as she armed two more proximity mines, throwing them into the corridor where the second group of agents were headed. With Amy's help she placed them against support structures in hopes of bringing the ceiling down on top of the men.

Jazz and Devin walked towards the end of the corridor and glanced at one another. This was a situation they had been in many times, so there was little need for communication. They got to the corner and stopped, both leaning against the wall.

Jazz pulled Cereza from her back and rolled her shoulders as Devin closed her eyes and took a deep breath. They both checked the location of the men in their HUDs, and then looked at one another. Devin raised her eyebrows and Jazz gave a small nod.

She edged as close as she could get to the corner of the wall and held up a hand, three fingers extended. Devin dropped to a knee behind her and raised her weapon.

Jazz dropped one finger, then the other, and rounded the corner.

As she did the sound of weapons firing and bullets striking the walls rang out. Devin rolled into the hallway, Jazz taking the high side, Devin taking the low.

In her HUD Devin saw the targeting reticule turn red. With a thought she selected non-lethal tranquilizer projectiles, stopped her roll, came up on one knee and began to fire.

Winona sent the small missiles out almost silently, the gun barely moving at all in Devin's hands. She watched as men dropped, updates scrolling across the bottom of her HUD. With Deadshot active the gun seemed to move on its own, targeting the men with extreme precision.

"Mother fucker…" she heard Jazz yell and looked up in time to see Jazz staring down at Cereza, "They shot her…"

She threw the gun aside and began to run forward. Devin jumped up and ran behind her. The men weren't ready for this sudden change of tactic and momentarily stopped firing. Devin watched as Jazz reached the group of men and began to fight.

The first man reached out to grab her, Jazz easily ducked to the side, grabbed his arm and delivered an elbow to his nose. His face seemed to fold in on itself as he dropped to the ground, blood pooling around him.

Jazz wasted no energy, each movement seemed to be perfectly placed and timed for maximum destruction. She stepped over the downed man and rushed forward towards an agent as he raised his weapon and pulled the trigger.

Jazz side stepped, with her left hand she grabbed the hand that the man had on his gun and wrapped herself around him, using her momentum she spun him in a semi-circle. Devin saw what was coming and dove to the ground as the man, unable to let go of the trigger as Jazz held his hand, continued to spray automatic weapon fire through the hallway.

Devin watched as the remaining agents fell. Jazz let go of the man's hand and dropped, sweeping his legs out from under him. The man fell backwards and landed hard, his head hitting the ground with a sickening crack. Several small explosions rang out as the proximity mines that Devin had placed detonated.

Jazz stood and surveyed the hallway. The floor littered with bodies, blood and spent shell casings. Smoke filled the air, light fixtures hung broken from the ceiling. She walked over to where Devin lay on the ground and smiled, offering her a hand and said, "Well, that was fun…"

Devin smiled back as Jazz pulled her to her feet, "We have different definitions of the word fun I think…"

Jazz began to laugh but then her expression changed. Devin tried to read what it was, but as usual had little luck deciphering it.

Devin saw a warning pop into her HUD just as Jazz grabbed her and pulled her close. For a moment Devin thought Jazz was hugging her but then she spun around and tensed, and Devin felt Jazz's body shake…and then she saw it.

The two agents that had made it through the proximity mines were standing at the end of the hall, both with weapons raised. Devin reached to her side and with blinding speed pulled Winona up firing twice and watched as the two men dropped.

Her other arm was still wrapped around Jazz, and she felt her weight slump against her. She looked at the hand holding Winona and saw that it was coated in blood, Jazz's blood.

"Jazz, are you ok?" She almost screamed.

Jazz smiled weakly, "Ya, I'll be alright, I think it was just…," but she trailed off, as her body slumped further.

Devin lowered her to the floor, *Amy, what the hell is happening.*

Jazz has been shot, the bullet was a new type of armor piercing shell that penetrated her dragon skin body suit. The bullet entered in her back and has caused massive internal damage, Amy said.

Well activate her self-heal function, turn on the Wolverine skill for god sake, Devin shouted in her mind.

Jazz has not yet acquired the self-heal skill, Amy said, and then after a brief pause she said, *I am sorry Devin. There is nothing I can do.*

Devin looked around the hallway frantically. She held Jazz in her lap, the blood continued to flow out of the wound in her back, her color draining. "No, no, no, no…" Devin was saying over and over as she placed her hand on Jazz's face, "Hey, come on Jazz, wake up. I need you, you can't leave me…"

Jazz's eyes flickered, opened for a brief moment and she smiled at Devin, "It's ok Dev, it's ok…" and closed again.

"Jazz, please, I love you…I need you…please just hold on, Amy will figure something out…" she pleaded as tears streamed from her eyes.

Jazz opened her eyes again, "Dev, I love you too, I always have. I don't know if there is anything Amy can do for me…I just need you to know that….I love you…I love you so much," she said as she placed her hand on Devin's face.

Devin reached up and put her hand over the hand on her face, and wanting to feel her skin against her she pulled the taser glove off and threw it to the side, putting Jazz's hand against her face once again.

Warnings were going off in her HUD, but she didn't pay attention to any of them, she didn't care. Without Jazz none of this mattered. Without Jazz…nothing mattered. She pushed her face deeper into Jazz's hand and kissed her palm, her tears running over her skin.

"Amy….please…" she begged.

The response took considerably longer than normal, *I am sorry Devin. There is nothing I can do.*

Devin opened her eyes and pulled Jazz's hand away from her face, holding it in both of hers, staring at her skin, her beautiful skin, and with sudden realization said, "No, but I can…"

46

Maxine Hobson sat, staring at a bank of tv screens all showing various security camera footage. Her attention focused solely on one. She had just watched the two girls take out seventeen enhanced, highly trained agents in a matter of two minutes. More were on their way, but she knew that was unnecessary now.

The death of her girlfriend had broken Devin. The fight in her was gone. *And now we can begin our work, and she will see that everything I am doing is for the best*, she thought as she watched the young girl that was her daughter.

The daughter that she had never known.

The daughter that was taken from her.

The daughter that she only had to put an end to the senseless death of so many.

She knew the story that Tran had told her about her surprise pregnancy, her decision to implant the Phoenix chip into her own child to protect her, her desire to leave the agency, the group of rogue agents led by Tran to fight against the agency.

She knew the story because she had written it. The truth was, she was the agency, she would never leave it. This work was important, maybe the most important scientific endeavor ever in the history of the world.

This wasn't about super soldiers, it was about the evolution of the human race, and she wasn't going to allow the moral objections of the men with the checkbooks to prevent her from finishing her work.

When she had first approached them with the idea of experimenting on infants they had instantly turned her down, saying that it would never happen, that they would never approve it. She tried, unsuccessfully, for over a year to get them to change their minds, to get them to see the truth.

How many men had to die before they would allow her to show them the way forward, she had asked.

These men that had sanctioned the dangerous experiments, sanctioned the killing of hundreds, maybe thousands of men and women in the name of their goal of world domination, wouldn't allow her to experiment on one single baby. So, she had taken matters in to her own hands.

She got pregnant.

She pretended to be surprised when she heard the news. When the baby came, she worked with Tran in secret, and they implanted the Phoenix chip. Tran was the only one that knew how important this was, the only one that would stop at nothing to see it through.

Then Peter had found out. He pretended to understand, pretended that he agreed with what she had done, but once he got the opportunity he had taken the child. He hid her from them. It took years of searching but they had found her, and now she was here.

Max sat looking at the screen. She had been impressed with Devin's abilities…but if she were being honest she had been more impressed with the girl herself…and a little worried.

She had thought that once they had her here, once she saw that she was in a battle that she could never hope to win she would simply give up. Allow them to do the experiments that would tell them what they needed to know. Allow them to help her unlock her true potential, because even with how impressive Devin's skills had proven to be, Max believed that they were merely scratching the surface. She had thought that they would be able to control her, and for good reason.

Every chip that had ever been implanted, from the very beginning, had a secret that very few people had known about.

Mind control.

This wasn't the kind of mind control that turned people into thoughtless automatons, it was more of a…suggestibility. Once the chip was in place, the same technology that allowed information to be downloaded into the brain, or thoughts to be sent from one chip to another, also allowed the chipped person to be influenced, unknown to them.

Chipped soldiers didn't act in a way that was surprising, because they were constantly being subtly, subliminally manipulated into doing whatever the person in control wanted done. This did not seem to be the case with Devin.

From the very first interaction with Tran, she had acted against the suggestions that were being fed to her. After the first few days of her chip being active the suggestions simply failed to deliver.

Max assumed it had something to do with the AI that had somehow grown beyond its programming in the years that it sat dormant in her daughter's mind.

This had been surprising, but equally surprising had been the fact that that same AI had also figured out a way to protect Jazz's chipset from the suggestions, and this had been the most worrying part to her. She had needed to isolate the girl, and her bond with Jazz had proven stronger than they could have imagined.

But now, she thought to herself, *now we can begin our work.*

She watched the screen, watched the tears stream down Devin's face and she smiled. She smiled knowing that the fight was over.

She put her hand on the screen, placing her fingers against Devin's pixelated face. She did love her; she was after all her creation. The culmination of all of her work.

She watched and thought, *maybe one day you will understand, I didn't have a choice, this was the only way forward, this was...*but her thought was cut off as the face beneath her fingers changed.

The look of utter despair and hopelessness was gone, replaced by a look of fierce determination. Devin was looking down at Jazz, wiping the tears from her own face.

Max leaned closer to the screen, trying to somehow see through the it and into Devin's thoughts. As she leaned in close, Devin turned and looked directly at the camera. It was as though she was looking directly at Max, and all at once Max knew with certainty that she was.

She watched, confusion blooming into fear as Devin lifted her arm, a single finger raising from the middle of her balled fist.

47

Devin stared into the camera, knew that Maxine was watching her, and flipped her off. Then bringing her hand back down she whispered, "Jazz, you're going to be ok, I promise."

Amy, turn off everything, all skills, and activate self-heal, Devin thought.

There was a confirmation bing and Devin exhaled, *You are in control,* she thought to herself, *only this one skill, nothing else…*and she reached down and placed her wrist on the slightly raised patch of skin on Jazz's wrist.

Nothing happened. She didn't know what she expected would happen, she hadn't done this before, but nothing happened at all. *Amy, did it work?* She thought.

Unknown, Amy said, *Jazz's chipset is not currently online.*

Come on, Devin thought desperately, *come on Jazz, this will work, I need you…*

She heard footsteps coming down the hall but ignored them, if she couldn't save Jazz none of it mattered. She pushed their wrists together harder and leaned down putting her forehead against Jazz's. Her skin was cold, colder than it should be, and Devin feared that she was too late.

She took a deep, shuttering breath and put her lips against Jazz's lips and whispered, "I love you…and I need you…"

Shouts were coming from the end of the corridor, but she didn't move. Every thought in her mind turned to Jazz. She thought of the first time they met online, the years of friendship, the countless hours spent video calling, laughing together until three in the morning, the first time she saw her at the zoo, that first touch, the first kiss, every kiss since…she focused these thoughts and pushed them towards Jazz.

She focused every ounce of energy in her body and mind to one simple task. *Break through to her*, she thought, *make her see all of it…*

She heard a small ping and saw a notification pop up but paid no attention to it.

Her purpose was singular.

The footsteps were closer now, almost on top of her, but she ignored them still, thinking the word over and over, trying to build its power, *Jazz….Jazz…Jazz…Jazz…*

It became a chant, a mantra. She felt herself slipping into a meditative state, felt the world around her dissolve. She continued the mantra, continued to focus her energy until the only thing that existed in the entire universe was that one word. *Jazz…*

She heard the shout, they were here, she opened her eyes and mentally shouted, *JAZZ!!!!*

The response was instant. Jazz's eyes flicked and her body tensed, arching backwards, a scream coming from her lips.

The men that were running towards the two girls sitting on the floor in a pool of blood froze as Jazz continued to scream.

*Amy, what the hell is happening, what did I do…*Devin thought, fighting panic.

I believe that the skill transfer finally began, she said, *but a new skill had been unlocked and activated so Jazz's chipset is trying to acquire and activate two skills at the same time. It is causing her mind to overload.*

Devin looked at her HUD and saw the alert that she had ignored, still flashing at the bottom of the screen.

***NEW SKILL UNLOCKED - DARK PHOENIX**

What the hell does that mean, Devin thought, as she watched in terror as Jazz's body began to tremble all over.

Amy, stop it, can you stop the transfer?

I am trying to stop the second skill from transferring, I will alert you if I am able to do it…

"Don't you fucking move," a man yelled from close to Devin. She turned to see twenty guards, all with their weapons drawn, all pointed at Devin.

Her anger flared, and she turned to face the man, still holding Jazz's trembling body. She lifted her arm, not knowing why she was doing what she was doing, and screamed, pushing her hand toward the man, focusing all of her energy.

A wave of energy flew from her outstretched hand. The men in the hallway were lifted off the ground and flew backwards, slamming into each other and then into the wall.

They seemed to be held there, fighting gravity, as Devin still held her hand out. She flattened her palm and slammed her hand towards the ground, the men responding to the motion and crashing to the ground in a heap.

"That…was fucking awesome…" a voice rasped, and Devin looked down to see Jazz smiling at her.

"Jazz, Jazz you're alive!!" She yelled.

Jazz squeezed her eyes together, "Ya, I guess I am…thanks to you…how did you do this Devin. I was gone…"

Devin felt the tears coming again and swallowed, helping Jazz sit up, "I don't know…I honestly don't know…I just couldn't bear the thought of being without you…"

Devin became hyper focused, Amy said, *A skill that I believe her Asperger's has always allowed her to have. This focus allowed her to harness her energy to the exclusion of all else, and that was apparently the unlock cue for the Dark Phoenix skill, which allowed her to implant a thought into your mind without the aid of your chip, waking you up and allowing the transfer to commence, but the problem was that two skills were active, one of them being the newly acquired Dark Phoenix skill. This was overloading your brain, but I was able to stop the Phoenix skill from completing the transfer. I did not believe I would be able to do that, but because of the unique interface that we all share I was, which allowed the self-heal skill to upload.*

Jazz put her hand under her ribs and winced, "Still hurts like a bitch, how long does this self-heal crap take anyway…"

Devin smiled, "Not long, well, I suppose I haven't had to heal a bullet wound, so I don't really know…any ideas Amy…"

Yes, it will take roughly a buttload of minutes to complete the healing process for such a serious injury, Amy said.

Both girls laughed, "Fifteen to twenty minutes then, not too bad…" Devin said.

"It's itchy as hell," Jazz said, "but better than being dead I suppose. I can't believe you saved me Dev…you brought me back from the dead…you're….amazing…"

Devin smiled and felt her cheeks blush, "I just thought that without you there's no point in going on…"

Devin leaned in and kissed Jazz softly.

Might I suggest we find a safe place to wait while Jazz heals, Amy said, interrupting the moment.

"Not necessary," Jazz said, pulling away from the kiss and smiling at Devin, "I'm ok, let's finish this."

Devin stood and offered Jazz her hand, helping her to her feet, "You sure?"

"Yes, totally, I mean, you have telekinesis now, what are they going to do to us?" Jazz said smiling.

I would like to note that the Dark Phoenix skill requires massive amounts of energy to utilize, I would not make it your primary means of combat, Amy said.

"Noted," Devin said, "but I agree with Jazz, if she says she's ok we need to get moving, we don't have any time to waste."

Where would you like to go? Amy asked.

"Find that woman that claimed she was my mother," Devin said, eliciting a questioning look from Jazz, "I'll explain on the way." Devin said in response to the look.

A route popped up on the map along with a new objective.

***NEW OBJECTIVE**

    - FIND MAXINE HOBSON

Devin looked at the map and then at Jazz, "She told me they killed my dad," she said quietly, "I don't know if I believe her, but if there's any chance that he's still alive…"

Devin broke off and Jazz reached out and grabbed her hand, squeezing it and said, "Amy, I want you to update that objective."

What would you like the new objective to be, Amy said.

Devin watched as the new alert popped into her HUD, Jazz having apparently given Amy the direction privately.

***NEW OBJECTIVE**

- FIND MAXINE HOBSON
- MAKE THAT BITCH TALK.

48

"Do you think she actually is your mom?" Jazz asked, struggling to keep up with Devin as she ran through the hallway, following the course that Amy had placed into their HUDs. Devin had just finished telling Jazz everything that had happened since they had been separated at the truck stop.

"Do you mean do I think she gave birth to me…honestly…I don't care. Even if she did, it doesn't make her my mother…" Devin said, "my mother is Mary Thomas, and as soon as we find my dad we are going to get her and get away from all these psychopaths and get somewhere safe."

Devin checked the map; she saw the icons indicating the location of two additional groups of agents. They were no longer converging on Devin and Jazz's location, in fact they seemed to also be headed to Max's location. *We have to get there first,* Devin thought to Amy, *I don't want another fight if we can avoid it.*

I am monitoring for any additional routes, you are on the fastest course. You should arrive before the other agents, but it will be close. Amy said.

Devin looked at Jazz's stats in her HUD and saw that she was back to seventy percent health, her stamina however was below thirty percent, the suit's auto stamina gel delivery system struggling to keep up with the high demand for the self-heal function.

"We gotta get there faster," Devin said, "Jazz, do you think you can handle running quicksilver for a couple of minutes?"

Jazz glanced at Devin as they ran, "I think so, but I'm not sure I have the stamina for it, Amy, do I have enough stamina to keep healing and run quicksilver?"

In theory yes, but it is not advisable. The self-heal will not complete for eight additional minutes, during which time your stamina will not be able to rise above thirty percent due to the high demand. Running quicksilver will take your time to destination from seven minutes to two minutes, however the cost will be around twenty percent of your remaining stamina, leaving you with only ten percent until your self-heal function is complete.

"That sounds too risky. How far away are the other agents?" Devin asked.

The other agents will arrive at the destination in nine minutes.

"It sounds too risky to me not to use quicksilver…if we don't use it we get there two minutes before them, if we do use it we get there seven minutes before them…we need that time…thirty percent stamina in a fight isn't going to be good," Jazz said, "I'll take ten percent and we can hope to just avoid the agents altogether…"

Devin shook her head, "It's not worth it Jazz, at ten percent if you get shot again, there won't be anything I can do to help you…"

"Can't we just beat them there and force her to give us some stamina gel? If my stamina was higher self-heal would work faster…right?" Jazz asked.

That is correct. If your stamina was at one hundred percent the self-heal function would work much faster, which would also allow the suit to once again be able to compensate for most standard stamina requirements.

"Then it's settled," Jazz said, "Activate Quicksilver…"

"Jazz," Devin said in protest, but it was too late.

Jazz turned and smiled at Devin, "Gotta go fast…" she said as she began running down the hallway, "just watch out for the corners…"

Devin smiled and felt her speed begin to increase as she ran to catch up with Jazz. She looked down and saw with satisfaction that her Quicksilver skill had activated on its own. *I really am getting the hang of this,* she thought to herself as she caught up with Jazz.

They flew through the corridors, but Devin found the feeling overstimulating. The walls blurring past, the HUDs constant updates to the path on the map, the lights flashing as they ran below them…it all started to become an overwhelming barrage of information, and Devin could feel the panic starting to set in.

She fell behind several paces as she began to slow and watched as

Jazz pulled further ahead.

Devin's breathing was coming in ragged bursts now as she struggled to maintain her composure. Overstimulation had always been a problem for her. *Amy, help me out here,* she thought desperately, *get rid of any info I don't need on my HUD, Jazz can lead the way.*

Her hud cleared and Devin found this to be a slight improvement, *Better, but I'm still kind of freaking out, any suggestions...*she thought to Amy.

*Try focusing on a singular point and excluding all other stimulation...*Amy said.

Ya, easy for you to say, she thought to herself, but as she raised her gaze her eyes settled on Jazz. She watched her moving, watched her muscles tensing and relaxing under the tight skin of the armor. Watched the rise and fall of her strides.

*She's...perfect...*Devin thought as she followed behind Jazz, watching only her, everything else disappearing.

Her breathing began to normalize, the feeling of panic dissipated, and a feeling of profound calm washed over her. *We are going to be ok,* she thought, *we are going to get out of this...*

She was so focused on Jazz that she didn't realize they had begun to slow down, as they approached the door to the room where Maxine Hobson waited for them.

Destination reached, Amy said as they came to a stop.

Devin closed her eyes and shook her head, as if coming out of a dream. When she opened them Jazz was looking at her, smiling, "Enjoying the view from back there..." she said, a smile playing at the corners of her lips.

Devin flushed, "Well, it is a pretty great view..."

Jazz laughed, "Oh, I know..." she said as she took a step closer to Devin, putting a hand on her waist and leaning towards her.

*It would be quite a waste if we expended the remainder of Jazz's stamina to reach the destination only to have the agents make up that time while you two stand staring at one another...*Amy said.

Jazz sighed and let her hand fall from Devin's waist, "Fair enough, so how do we get in?"

Devin looked at the flat door in front of them, saw the biometric scanner, it appeared that it was a DNA scanner, beside the door, and said, "I have no idea, Amy can you get us in there?"

Negative, I have been unable to breach their security system.

Devin walked over and placed her hand against the scanner, she felt a small prick as something was jabbed into one of her fingers and noticed the damage alert pop into her HUD. The scanner screen came to life, cycling through what appeared to be images, and stopped on a picture of Maxine, words flashed above the image.

Partial DNA match made, Maxine Hobson, fifty percent match, access denied,

Devin swallowed, "Well, I guess that answers the question of if she was telling the truth about being my mother…"

Jazz put a hand on her arm and squeezed, "You ok…"

Devin shook her head, "Ya, fine…just need to get the damn door open…"

As if this was some magic phrase, the door dropped back and slid to the right, revealing a room filled with computer screens, and Maxine standing in the center of the room.

Devin took in the scene, wondering why the door had opened, *Did she open the door, did the door open because I was a partial match, did it malfunction, did Amy finally breach the security…*and then she noticed that Max was holding a gun, pointing it down and to her right. She followed the path of the gun and felt the wind go out of her lungs, only enough remained for one whispered word.

"Dad…"

49

Maxine watched as the girls ran through the hallways, transfixed. The security cameras could barely keep up with them. *Seventeen and completely untrained, they are impressive...*she thought.

She watched with interest as Devin began to fall back, clearly something was wrong although Max could not imagine what it was, but it seemed to take only seconds before the girl recovered, and then they were there, right outside the door.

She watched as Devin tried the DNA scanner, saw the look of disgust on her face when it showed the match in their DNA structure, and watched as the other girl placed a comforting hand on her.

She opened the door, allowing them to come in, because she knew that even though they believed that they were the ones with all the power, she was the one with all of the control.

She saw the look of confusion on Devin's face when the door opened turn to a look of horror when she saw her father, tied to a chair in the center of the room.

"Dad..." Devin whispered, the words barely audible.

"Alright, that's far enough," Maxine said, giving the gun pointed at Devin's dad a slight shake.

Devin and Jazz froze. Devin searched her father's face. He didn't appear to be hurt.

"If you hurt him..." she said, taking a small step forward.

"We haven't," Maxine said, "we're scientists, not barbarians. Look, I didn't want to do any of this, but it became clear from the first interaction at your home when you nearly killed two of my men, that you would not be coming easily. Tran told me you would fight, I wasn't so sure, but he was. He told me the only way to gain your confidence was to make you believe he was trying to save you…"

Devin turned to look at Jazz, confused, and turned back to Maxine, "What the hell are you talking about…"

"Come on now Devin, I thought you were smarter than this…think it through, see what you come up with…" Max taunted.

Devin's mind was reeling, she thought back to everything that had happened from the beginning. Tran showing up at her house, the fight with agents there, the zoo, reaching the compound, the truck stop, even the email to Tran from the agency that Amy found. Everywhere the agency had been, Tran had also been, except the truck stop…but she had found the tracker. She remembered talking to Jazz, saying something just didn't feel right. Where did all the money come from…how did Tran and Kevin pay for the compound…and it hit her, "Tran never left The Agency…"

Max smiled and shook her head, "Of course he never left, no one leaves…no one except you…but we found you. We looked for a long time…but we found you…"

Amy is this all true, how could you not tell me they were working together, Devin said.

I am sorry Devin, I did not know, they gave me the information they wanted me to have, Amy said, and Devin thought that she could hear a hint of pain in her simulated voice.

An alert popped into Devin's HUD.

***INCOMING AGENTS ARRIVING IN LESS THAN TWO MINUTES**

She's monologuing, Devin thought, *buying time for her backup to arrive.*

"You know what," Devin said, taking a step forward, "Who fucking cares. I am not here to play your games, give me my dad back, don't test me, you have no idea what I'm capable of…"

Max laughed, "No idea what you are capable of…I created you Devin. I know exactly what you are capable of. Everything that you are was built by me."

Devin shook her head and took another step forward, "You're wrong. You may have put this shit into my head, but I don't think even you knew what it was capable of…and you didn't raise me, didn't teach me right from wrong. You didn't help me learn how to walk, or pick me up when I fell. You are nothing to me. Fuck you, and fuck your experiments. I'm taking my dad and I'm leaving, and you should let Tran know that if he hurts my mom, my real mom, I will destroy all of you."

Another alert popped into her HUD.

•DARK PHOENIX ACTIVATED
•BERSERKER MODE ACTIVATED
•ECO ACTIVATED
•DAREDEVIL ACTIVATED

Devin paid no attention to the alerts, she took another step forward. Max placed the barrel of the gun against her father's head, but Devin noticed that her hands were shaking, "Put the gun down, you aren't going to shoot anyone…"

Maxine looked at Devin, her eyes darting, "You're right, I'm not…" she said, "but they are…"

Devin heard a single gunshot and spun, seeing a man standing in the doorway pointing a weapon at her. With the Daredevil skill active Devin saw everything as though it were happening in slow motion.

The flame from the barrel of the handgun, the shell ejecting, the bullet coming towards her. Her body reacted instinctually, she kicked off the ground, leaping high into the air in a perfect backflip, and grabbed Winona from her side. She sent a thought to Amy, *Transfer biometrics to Jazz*, and at the top of her flip she threw the gun to Jazz, who caught it deftly and began to fire as men burst into the room. Devin hit the ground and turned to run to her dad.

She stopped, saw the small red circle on his forehead, saw the way that he was slumped in his chair, saw the blood beginning to pour from the wound. The bullet that was meant for her had found her father.

She turned to see Jazz ducking behind a desk, her arm bleeding, a group of soldiers at the door all had their weapons trained on her, firing blindly.

She saw Maxine slip through a door at the back of the room, casting a glance at Devin over her shoulder, and for once knew exactly what she saw on her face. It was sadness. Then the door slammed shut.

Devin felt the rage building inside of her. Saw alerts popping into her HUD, knew that her heart rate was too high, knew that Jazz's stamina was too low, knew that everything was completely and totally out of her control. More men were streaming into the room.

She strode to the center of the room, bullets flying past her. Several hit her, some being absorbed by the body armor, others...the armor piercing type...blazing hot trails of agony through her, but she didn't stop.

The pain of the bullets was nothing compared to the pain of losing her father.

Her rage continued to grow.

She didn't need the berserker skill; these men had earned her wrath.

As a bullet tore through her shoulder she raised her hands and screamed, "NOOOOOO!!!"

The effect was a cacophony of destruction. Men flew from where they stood. Computer screens exploded, showering sparks and glass.

Devin stood in the center of the destruction, her hands raised, screaming. More men came into the room and were thrown back as soon as they entered. Their bodies slamming into the walls with sickening thuds.

The men stopped coming.

The scream abated.

Sparks continued to fall from the ruined screens and lights hanging from the ceiling. Devin collapsed to the ground. Sobs wracking her body, her eyes rolled back...and then...Jazz was there.

Jazz pulled her against her. She put her hands on her face, "Devin...Devin...come back...you're ok...come back to me..."

Her body trembled. She felt the pain of everything. It was all too much. She opened her eyes and saw Jazz, tried to anchor herself to her.

Jazz had been the one, every time that she was lost Jazz had found her, but she couldn't focus.

An alarm was blaring. Shouts from other soldiers as they rushed down the hallways.

Her senses were overwhelmed, she was hyper ventilating, in the grip of a full-on panic attack.

Jazz looked down at her, her eyes blurry with tears. Had it really only been a few minutes before that Devin was holding her in this same way...Jazz leaned down, whispered, "I love you," and gently kissed her lips.

Time seemed to freeze. Devin felt the softness of Jazz's lips, felt the wetness of her tears, felt the depth of her love. She lost herself to that kiss. She let everything else drift away until it was only her and Jazz.

The pain began to subside. She felt the weight of Jazz's hand on her cheek and lifted her own hand to cover it. She felt their bodies, warm against one another. She heard the words, *I love you*, repeating over and over in her head.

Her heart rate slowed. Her breathing stabilized. She opened her eyes and pulled back from the kiss just enough to whisper, "I love you too."

50

Max ran through the corridors, her heart racing. Nothing had gone the way she had planned, but the power...the power that Devin had displayed...it was beyond anything she could have imagined.

She used her chip, the original Prometheus chip, the first chip, and sent a message to all of the agents in the facility. They were no match for Devin, and she would need them in the future...their work was not done.

To all agents, she thought, *mission status has been updated. Retreat. Rendezvous instructions will be sent, but I repeat, disengage and retreat.*

She checked her HUD to see that the message was received and was relieved to see that the agents were responding. They were no longer converging on Devin's location; they were instead leaving the compound. She knew that they would follow the directive, *Have to follow the directive,* she thought to herself, as she came to a door that led her outside of the compound.

A car was waiting outside of the door, and she climbed in, sending the driver a message through his chip to let him know where their destination was.

She exhaled and looked down at herself. She noticed for the first time that her right side was covered in droplets of blood, but not her blood. She closed her eyes, wondering how things had gone so wrong, and sent another message.

Tran - Things went bad. Get her mother and get out of the compound. We will need her. This isn't over.

She watched as the car pulled out of the compound and was pleased to see other vehicles falling into a line behind her. Things had indeed gone bad, but what she had witnessed today let her know one thing for certain. She had to get Devin back, she had to know what made the Phoenix chip work in her, and she would do anything to make it happen.

She closed her eyes and brought her hands to her head, rubbing her temples. An alert popped up and she read the message.

Max - her mother isn't here...

51

Devin and Jazz stood in the vacant hallway. The alarms had been turned off. They seemed to be alone.

"Where the hell did everyone go?" Devin asked, rubbing her shoulder where one of the bullets had torn through her.

Unclear, although according to chip scans and camera feeds every person has left the facility, Amy said.

"This is nuts," Jazz said, "so they come in trying to kill us and then just leave…"

Devin looked at the ground, "They did kill one of us," she said, tears welling up in the corners of her eyes.

Jazz said nothing, she simply reached out and grabbed Devin's hand, their fingers intertwining as though they had been made to do just that.

Devin felt the reassuring squeeze from Jazz and held back the tears, there would be time to mourn, but it was not now. Now the only thing that mattered was getting back to her mother. She had tried, and failed, to send a message to Tran. Amy let her know that his chip had been blocked from them.

Maxine must have let him know that his secret was out, Devin thought.

I have located a supply of stamina gel, I am adding the location to your map. I would highly recommend refueling to allow your systems to finish healing before proceeding, Amy said.

Jazz looked at Devin, "It's your call, we have gel in the car, it's on the way."

Devin seemed to think it over as she studied the map, the gel was close by, it would only take a couple of extra minutes, "No, we should go and grab some now, who knows, this could be some kind of trick and when we walk outside we are greeted by two hundred more of these assholes."

They followed the path and walked into a room that was apparently an armory. Devin looked around at the weapons lining every inch as Jazz whistled, "Damn, they aren't underprepared are they…are these weapons all bio-locked Amy?"

It would appear from a cursory scan that all weapons in the facility have been bio locked and so would be useless, Amy said.

"Figures," Jazz muttered as Devin threw her a tube of stamina gel.

"Bottoms up…" Devin said as she tore off the top of the tube and squeezed the disgusting gel into her mouth. The taste was as she remembered, and the effect was instantaneous.

With their stamina levels refilled the self-heal skill begin to work faster, "Oh, that's more like it," Jazz said, "Hell ya!"

Devin smiled, "Take a couple extra tubes just in case," she said throwing two tubes to Jazz and grabbing a couple more for her. She ripped the top off of a second tube and squeezed the gel into her mouth, replenishing the stamina that had already depleted as her self-heal function accelerated.

A vehicle is approaching the compound, Amy said.

"Sounds like our ride is here," Jazz said grabbing Devin's hand and heading towards the door.

It is not your vehicle. The vehicle is a large SUV and appears to have three passengers, Amy said.

"I don't like the sounds of that, here Dev," Jazz said, holding out Winona, "you should take your gun back."

Devin shook her head as they walked through the hallway, "No way, Cereza got blown up, you need it Jazz, I want you to have it, you're a better shot than me anyway.

Jazz shoved the weapon harder towards Devin, "Dev, that's sweet, but dumb. I don't think there is much I am better at than you…either way, you don't have a weapon."

Devin smiled at her as she put her hand on the door that would take them outside. For the first time she wasn't worried about what would be on the other side, she knew that they could handle it, no matter what it was.

"Really Jazz, keep it, and don't forget…" she said as she pushed the door open and stepped out into dazzling sunlight, "I am the weapon."

52

M stood beside the SUV, leaning against the back passenger door. Ronan stood off to his side. They had parked far enough away from the building to be able to see all of the exits, as they had no idea which door Devin and Jazz would come from.

They had watched the scene play out from the hill. Watched as Jazz entered the building through the ventilation shaft. Watched as alarms began to go off and agents rushed into the building, and then watched with surprise as moments later those same agents poured out of the building, got into vehicles and left.

M also noted, with interest, that as the agents fled the building there were a number of men being carried out and thrown into the backs of vehicles, most likely injured or dead.

They had waited to make sure that no one was coming back and then had made their way to the compound. The gate was closed, but no match for the reinforced SUV as it plowed into it, and then they waited.

Now he watched as the door directly in front of them opened and Devin and Jazz strode out. They looked as though they had been through a war, but he also noted that even though both of their suits were stained with blood, they did not appear injured at all.

Ronan stiffened when he saw them come out and his hand fell to the weapon at his side.

"Easy," M said, "I think if these two were able to make a couple of hundred agents turn tail and run, we should be diplomatic."

The girls approached, warily, and stopped fifteen feet away. "Well, you two are just full of surprises aren't you." M called out.

Devin looked him up and down, and he could see that something had changed in her. All of her usual awkwardness was gone, replaced by confidence, and anger.

"Call your boss, tell him if he hurts my mom I will end him," Devin said.

"No need," M said back, and opened the door he was leaning against. Devin's mom stepped out, looking confused.

"Devin, what in the world is going on here honey, you look hurt, are you hurt, please god…" Mary said, her eyes welling with tears.

"Mom," Devin said taking a step forward, noticing that Jazz had pulled Winona from the magnetic attachment point, "Mom, are you ok? Did they hurt you?"

"Hurt me?" Mary said, clearly confused, "Why would agent M hurt me, no he just told me that you needed my help and I should come. I wasn't able to talk to Dr. Tran about it, Agent M said we didn't have time. Devin, answer me, are you ok?"

Devin felt her heart breaking, how could she tell her mom that her dad had been killed…that it was her fault. That a bullet meant for her had instead found the man that she had been married to for twenty-five years.

"Mom," Devin started but was interrupted by Ronan raising his gun and shouting.

"Stop moving Jazz, I see what you're trying to do. Trying to flank us, just stop. No one needs to get hurt."

"Stand down," M growled, "don't make me tell you again…"

Ronan's face went red and he turned on M, "You know what, fuck you man, whose side are you on anyway, I mean all this time they…"

A gunshot rang out, echoing off of the surrounding buildings. The movement was so fast that Devin barely registered it, but she had. M had drawn the gun from the holster at his side and shot Ronan, center mass, as the agents were fond of saying in weapons training.

Ronan dropped to the ground, blood spreading out from his side as he lay, gasping and then silent.

Devin was moving, running towards her mom, preparing to take M down, end his life before he could end hers.

She saw the alerts pop up as skills began activating on their own, saw the perfect placement of her footfalls to be able to avoid any shots from M and strike hard, driving her fist into his nose, and the bone there into his brain.

As she ran several things happened at once. Jazz began running beside her, her mother screamed, and M shouted, "Don't!" And threw his weapon to the ground in front of her.

Devin slid to a stop, inches away from delivering what would have been a fatal blow. She turned to see Jazz grabbing Mary and pulling her away from Agent M.

M simply stood with his hands raised, a look of sincerity on his face…and Devin realized that once again she knew what the look meant.

How can I tell what they are thinking…she thought.

I believe the Dark Phoenix skill is allowing you to read their intentions, Amy said, startling Devin, who had meant to keep that thought to herself, a skill that she still clearly had not mastered.

Can I read his mind? Devin asked.

I believe that with the proper training in the skill yes, but at this time that is unlikely. Amy said.

Devin turned and saw Jazz talking to her mother, her weapon still trained on M. As she looked at the big man she could definitely sense something, and it seemed she could almost hear his thoughts…but she dismissed it as wishful thinking, and said, "You have five seconds to tell me what the hell is going on here…"

M looked at Devin, still holding his hands up, "I know none of this is going to make much sense to you, but you need to believe me, I am trying to help you. That's why I brought your mother here, she wasn't safe at the compound. I know that this will come as a shock but…"

"Tran is a lying sack of shit, ya we got that part," Jazz said.

A look of shock crossed M's face, but he continued, "You have no idea, but yes, yes he is. Look, I'll try to make this fast, and if you have more questions later you can ask. Bottom line is, I found out Tran had been lying, for a long time. The chips have a…mind control…that's the best way I know how to put it, element to them. None of us signed up for that. When I figured it out I took it to Tran, he pretended not to know, pretended to want to leave The Agency. I helped him build the new facility, helped him recruit new soldiers, new agents. He told me he and Kevin would figure out a way to disable the mind control, and then he told me they had done it. They hadn't. I was still under their control. It's subtle, you never feel like they aren't your decisions, you feel like you are the one in control. When he said he had found you, was coming to you to turn on your chip, I didn't agree with him. I was certain your chip would overload you, that you would die…and I've seen more than my fair share of death," he paused and looked down at Ronan, "I've caused more than my fair share of death…so when he told me they were going to turn your chip on, kill an innocent girl, I knew that when I started to think it was the right thing there was no way the mind control was gone. I went to a person I could trust, another agent, Trinity. She helped me…she actually turned it off…freed me. She's an incredible programmer, and an incredible hacker, the best really, you know that's why she chose that name…anyway, we started digging, looking through classified files…that's when we discovered that we were still working for the agency. It had all been a ruse, a carefully orchestrated ruse. I would have seen it sooner, but the mind control…well…I just didn't see it."

Devin looked at Jazz, she raised her eyebrows and Devin heard her voice inside of her head, *I don't know what to believe anymore…*

"Look, I know this is a lot, and I know I've been…hard on you…and I'm probably the last person that you trust, but I need you to believe me. That's why I brought your mother, I knew that she wouldn't be safe, no matter what happened here…"

"Ya right," Devin said, "more like you brought her so that you would have leverage. You're the same as all of them."

M took a step forward, "Devin, if you want to leave, you can leave, you can take your mother and go, and I won't follow you…but The Agency isn't going to give up. They won't let you just walk away, and now that they know I have turned they won't let me either. I brought Ronan as insurance. I was pretty sure that Tran suspected something wasn't right with me, but they trust Ronan, they know he's a good little soldier, so I kept him close to me, to throw them off my trail…"

"Don't you see…that's the problem!" Devin shouted, "People aren't pawns in some stupid game. Ronan was a dick, but he didn't deserve to die just so you could save yourself…"

"If you knew the things that he did…why he was discharged from the military…why The Agency wanted him, I doubt that you would still believe he didn't deserve to die. I don't feel good about what I did, but there was no other way. I needed him so that I could save you, save both of you," M said, "because we need your help…"

Devin looked at Jazz, and then back at M, "Who is we?"

"Me, Trinity, and a few other agents that have joined with us. They will have left the compound now, we can meet up with them later, we have several safe houses ready…Devin, there's something I haven't told you yet…"

Devin raised her hand and motioned for M to continue.

"When Trinity and I were digging we found something, something big…" he paused, "The Agency isn't actually doing all of this to create super soldiers, sure that's a part of it, but there's more to it. They want to create a chip that can be implanted into every single human being. A chip that can be put in at birth, that people won't even realize they have, but not to give them special abilities, they will save those for their soldiers. This chip will only have one power…mind control. They've tried the procedure on other children, it's never worked, and they don't know why. That's why you are so important to them…because somehow they managed to put a chip into an infant and not kill the child…"

Devin took a step back, shaking her head, "That's crazy, you're telling me they want to chip the entire world?"

"Yes, and they have the resources to do it. This isn't just this country…The Agency reaches across borders…they want to rule everything…everyone…"

Devin looked at Jazz and thought to her, *What do you think…*

Jazz seemed to consider it for a moment and then responded, *If he's lying, I don't see how he can stop us from kicking his ass and leaving…*

Devin smiled and walked over to Jazz, taking her hand, "Alright, we'll come with you, but mostly just because we know there's nothing you can do to stop us if we want to leave…and once we get wherever we are going you're gonna need to show us some proof of all of this…"

M nodded, "Absolutely, and I give you my word, if you want to leave we won't try to stop you."

Jazz laughed, "If you saw what Devin did in there, you would know we don't need your word for that."

M squinted, "I'll be interested to hear more about it. We should leave though, get to a safe house and regroup," M said, walking towards the SUV.

"Ya we can leave," Jazz said, "but I think we'll be taking our car…"

The Tesla silently rolled to a stop, the doors opening as it did, and Amy's voice came through the car's speakers, "Destination?"

"Ask him," Devin said pointing to M, and then she walked over and placed her arm around her mother and led her to the back seat, sitting down beside her.

Jazz walked to the driver side and climbed in, calling out to Agent M, "Get in cupcake, you can ride shotgun for now. Devin and her mom have things to discuss."

M rolled his eyes and climbed in the passenger side. The doors closed and the car began to pull away.

Devin turned and grabbed her mom's hand, pulling it into her lap, tears welling at the corners of her eyes and said, "Mom, I have to tell you something…"

53

His eyes opened and he took a deep breath, it felt as though he had been drowning. He looked around but everything was blurry, out of focus. A thin green line flickered around the edges of his vision and began to solidify. He recognized it as the edge to his HUD.

He tried to sit up but didn't have the strength. He moved his left arm, feeling the wet stickiness that coated it and turned to look at it. Blood. Lots of blood. His blood.

His head began to clear, his vision came in to focus. A pair of black combat boots walked into view. He looked at the HUD and saw a single line of text appear.

***SELF-HEAL ACTIVATED**

What the hell, he thought, not expecting a response.

You have acquired a new ability, self-heal is active. Total healing time for all injuries is seven minutes. You will have twenty percent remaining stamina once healing is complete, the voice of his AI said in his head.

He could feel the strength coming back. He sat up and put a hand on his chest, searching for the wound.

"I wouldn't touch that if I were you," a male voice said from close by, "you need to let it heal more first."

Ronan spun around and felt a sharp pain stab into his gut, *Ugh, moved too fast, what the fuck is going on.* He forced himself to his feet, slowly, and looked around.

A large man in a military uniform stood nearby, looking him up and down. "I'll be damned, they told me it would work, I didn't think there was any way that it would, but I guess I was wrong. I mean, you weren't all the way dead when I got here, but pretty damn close. The only thing keeping you alive was your chip struggling to regulate your body systems."

"Who are you?" Ronan asked.

"Colonel Jim Masterson, USMC, I'm the man that gave you that self-heal skill. They told me to hold this," he held up a small black metal disk, "up to your wrist and your chip would do the rest. I don't know how it worked, I myself have a Hercules chip, always thought that was the best one, but they tell me you have that one too, and now you have self-heal to go along with it."

Ronan blinked, "What the hell are you talking about, who is they..."

"They told me you were the first person to get some fancy new chip design that can rearrange itself to use different abilities, but they never told you about it and never turned it on cause they were afraid it wouldn't work, afraid it would melt your brain, but apparently they used it on someone else and when it worked...and when they figured out you were gonna die anyway...they told me to give it a shot. Guess it worked."

*Fancy new chip...multiple abilities...what the hell...*but then it hit him, the chip they used on Jazz.

Ronan rolled his shoulders, "Ya, it's working all right, I can't believe this..."

He smiled and looked at his HUD, saw his health climbing but his stamina decreasing, "Don't suppose you got any gel on you?"

The man laughed, "Of course I do, here."

Ronan tore the top of the tube off and squeezed the gel into his mouth. He could feel the boost in stamina making the healing process even faster, "Thank you sir," he said, and paused, "so who sent you?"

"The Agency, who else would have sent me, where do you think you're at kid?" Masterson said with a laugh.

"The Agency..." Ronan said, reaching for his weapon.

"No need for that," Masterson said calmly, "I highly doubt you could get the drop on me kid. They told me you would be a bit confused, said this would clear things up, hold on, I'm gonna send you a transfer, make sure to accept it."

"Who's it from...and don't say The Agency, I want a name," Ronan said looking unsure.

Masterson smiled, "Kid, there's a lot you don't know, but this oughta clear things up," he said, and Ronan heard the ping of an alert asking him to accept the transfer, "and don't worry, you know the guy that sent it. One of The Agency's top men...Dr. Tran."

54

Devin lifted her head and opened her eyes, turning to look at Jazz who had her feet hanging out of the window that had been shattered by gunfire. She saw that Devin was awake and leaned down and kissed her forehead, "Hey sleeping beauty, how are you feeling?"

Devin smiled and wrapped her arms around Jazz's waist, snuggling her head back into her shoulder, "I've been better," she said, "but this helps…"

Jazz leaned down and kissed her. Devin breathed out a sigh, and sat up, looking into the front seat where her mom sat, hands folded in her lap, staring out the window.

When she told her what had happened to her father it had been unbearable. Her mom was inconsolable for a couple of hours, but now she seemed to have settled into a state of calm shock. Jazz saw Devin looking at her and spoke to her in her mind, *She'll be ok Dev, I know you are both going through a lot, but you have each other, and you have me.*

Devin smiled, there was no chance that she could make it through any of this without Jazz. She felt their fingers intertwine and squeezed, *I know, it will be hard, but I know we will make it through, what choice do we have?*

They sat in silence, listening to the sound of the wind coming in through the broken window, hearing her mother's quick intake of breath every time the feelings came back strong.

They drove on, she turned and looked at Jazz again. She didn't say anything, didn't need to say anything, she just smiled. She thought back to everything that had happened in the last few weeks. When they left the compound that morning Devin had been sure that everything would be over, one way or another, by the end of the day…but it turned out, it was just the beginning.

DEVIN AND JAZZ WILL RETURN IN

RESPAWN

DEVIN'S GAME BOOK TWO

Note from the Author:

I just wanted to take a moment and say thank you for taking the time to read Devin's Game. This was such a fun book to write, Devin is a character that has become very close to my heart. The idea for this book came about one day when I was thinking about my son Dylan, who, like Devin, has Asperger's.

He loves video games and one day I had the idea for a story called Dylan's game, where he pretended that his life was a Zelda style video game. So instead of having to ask a girl out on a date, he would see it as a quest update to gain renown by escorting the princess to a ball, or instead of doing chores it would be a task to gain experience points.

I thought this might be a cool way to explore what the world looks like to someone on the spectrum. This was an important idea to me, many of the people that I love are on the spectrum, and I thought this might be an interesting story. Unfortunately for Dylan, or maybe fortunately (I'm not sure he would love the idea of being a character in one of my books) as soon as I sat down to start writing this one, Devin showed up, experimental tech in her head and all, and I'm so glad she did, because I really grew to love this foul-mouthed, take no shit, Sonic the Hedgehog loving kid (that part she definitely adopted from Dylan). In fact, I loved her so much that my wife and I named our youngest daughter Devin, which based on her intelligence, ability to throw a punch (pretty intense for a three-year-old) and her affinity for foul language, was a good choice.

I hope that through Devin you can see some of the struggles that some people on the spectrum face on a daily basis, but also see the unique gifts that these amazing souls offer to the world. In the end Mary seems to be right, Asperger's is Devin's superpower, well that and all of her other superpowers. If you want to learn more about Asperger's syndrome, and yes I am aware it now called Autism Spectrum Disorder level 1, but I live in a house filled with Aspies and we refuse to bow down to the man, head over to www.autismspeaks.org/asperger-syndrome. Thank you so much for joining me on this journey, have a kick ass day.